Take Your Pleasure Where You Find It

ALSO BY J. D. MASON

And on the Eighth Day She Rested

One Day I Saw a Black King

Don't Want No Sugar

This Fire Down in My Soul

You Gotta Sin to Get Saved

That Devil's No Friend of Mine

Take Your Pleasure Where You Find It

J. D. Mason

ST. MARTIN'S PRESS
NEW YORK

This is a work of fiction. All of the characters, organizations, and events portrayed in this novel are either products of the author's imagination or are used fictitiously.

www.stmartins.com

Design by Kathryn Parise

LIBRARY OF CONGRESS CATALOGING-IN-PUBLICATION DATA

Mason, J. D.
   Take your pleasure where you find it / J. D. Mason.—1st ed.
      p. cm.
   ISBN 978-0-312-59856-3
   1. African American women—Fiction.   2. Class reunions—Fiction.   3. Female friendship—Fiction. I. Title.
   PS3613.A817T35 2010
   813'.6—dc22

                                          2009040235

First Edition: March 2010

10 9 8 7 6 5 4 3 2 1

An autograph from a best-selling author and icon to a fan
Not a Day Goes By

"JD, I thank you for the support. . . . Be blessed and be loved—"
E. Lynn Harris

We miss you!!

Acknowledgments

I want to say thank you so much for your continued support and amazing contribution to the African American literary community to TaNisha Webb and KC Girlfriends Book Club; Jessica Carter and the Waiting 2 Exhale Book Club, Yasmin Coleman and APOOO (A Place of Our Own) Book Club, Tee C. Royal and R.A.W. SISTAZ Literary Group, and Tamika Newhouse (author of *The Ultimate NO NO*), president of the AAMBC.

I also want to share my appreciation for Sigrid R. Williams, founder and organizer of the very first California Book Club Summit; Lee McDonald of The Renaissance Group (organizers of the CBC Authors Pavilion); Mocha Ochoa (organizer of the NAACP Author Pavillion); LaShaunda Hoffman, editor of *Shades of Romance Magazine*; and Ella Curry of EDC Creations.

And a special shout-out to my new author friend Carleen Brice, to my editor Monique Patterson, Holly Blanck, and my friend and agent Sara Camilli.

Take Your Pleasure Where You Find It

Tasha Darden

"I believe that one of these women could be my mother."

Tasha Darden had studied every millimeter of that grainy photo her foster mother had clipped from the newspaper thirty years ago. Avery Stallings, a detective she'd found in the Yellow Pages, studied it too.

April 20, 1979, was the date that photo was published, taken by a security camera in the emergency waiting room of the old Denver General Hospital. Authorities published it in hopes that someone would recognize one or all of the girls and get them to come forward with information about the abandoned child, but no one did, and none of those girls were ever identified.

Her heart was racing and her palms were sweating, but Tasha made a valiant effort to make sure he couldn't see how anxious she truly was. The man sitting across from her had no idea how many times she'd called his office to schedule this appointment, only to hang up after the first ring. Tasha needed a miracle and she needed it from Avery Stallings, but he wasn't a magician. He was just a man with a "satisfaction guaranteed or your money back" clause if he failed to get results that his ad had promised.

Tasha had told herself that she wasn't bitter. She'd grown into a brave, obedient, and overachieving young woman just to show everyone that the fact that she'd been abandoned as a child never impacted her in the way they all believed it should. And she'd waited thirty years to start looking for her birth mother, because for thirty years, she'd believed her own lie. The truth was that finding out that the woman who had given birth to you had left you alone in a room full of strangers after you'd barely taken your first breath was fucked up. And the fact that the bitch didn't even think enough of you to give you a name before she did it—well, that was beyond fucked up.

"See that duffel bag the one in the middle is holding?" Tasha asked, stoically. "Inside that bag is twenty-seven cents—two dimes, a nickel, and two pennies—half a stick of Doublemint gum, a receipt for a senior-year photograph package from a photography studio on Colorado Boulevard, which, by the way, went out of business fifteen years ago . . . and me."

He stared stunned at her.

"Less than a day old, six pounds, two ounces," she continued coolly.

The detective had a daughter around her age, give or take a year or two. Tasha Darden's polished and composed demeanor made her seem older than her thirty years, though. Short hair on her was very flattering, highlighting the beautiful, delicate curves of her slender face, skin the color of coffee with cream, and dark, dramatic eyes. He guessed her to be between five-five and five-seven, 130 pounds maybe. The detective in him had guessed all of that in the time she'd walked into his office, shook his hand, and sat down in the chair across from his desk.

"How did you get this clipping, Ms. Darden?"

"My foster mother clipped it and saved it for me." The young woman smiled warmly. "Miss Lucy was her name, and she was the most wonderful mother any child could ever have. She passed away last month," she said sadly. "I'm not angry, Mr. Stallings."

"Please—call me Avery."

She smiled. "Avery. I've had a very good life, and if Miss Lucy had lived forever, I probably wouldn't be here. She was all the connection I needed to anyone in this life. With her gone—" Her voice cracked. Had it been good? Had it really been that damn good? "I suppose I just need answers. I'm assuming that one of those women—girls—had her reasons for doing what she did. I have no intention of judging her, because for all I know, she's been looking for me too." She said it, but never in a million years did she actually believe it to be true. "I don't know. But whatever the case, I need to know who she is, where she is, and how she is, and I need for her to know me too."

Avery studied her for a moment. Two things made him a good detective: One was his intuition—he listened to it and trusted it; and the other was his ability to judge character, right on, usually within minutes of meeting a person. Miss Darden, here, surely had her shit together, and Miss Lucy could've very well walked on water, but no person in her right mind could truly be that cool knowing that her mother abandoned her in the lobby of a hospital emergency room.

"Tasha Darden is a name someone at social services picked out of a hat and gave to me. I need to know my real name, Mr.— Avery."

"I can't promise any miracles," he said, solemnly.

"I don't expect miracles," she said softly. "But I do expect to be able to look into my own mother's eyes at least once in my lifetime. I just want to know where I came from. I think she owes me that much. Don't you?"

Tasha stood outside of Avery Stallings's office building, took a deep breath, and held it. She slipped on her shades, rummaged through her handbag for her car keys, and headed to the parking lot across the street. In the words of Ice Cube, "Today was a good day." It was a brand-new day filled with brand-new opportunities because she'd faced her biggest fear and started her search for her birth mother. And if this Avery Stallings was worth the money she was paying him, if he found her mother, or at least the identity of those three women in that newspaper clipping, it would be like getting a second chance—and maybe she could finally put her finger on who she really was.

"Someday, you have to look for her," Miss Lucy would sometimes tell her, usually over breakfast.

"But why should I?" she'd asked, innocently. "I have you, Miss Lucy."

Miss Lucy would laugh and tenderly press her warm hand to the side of Tasha's small face. "We have each other, darling," she'd say in her thick German accent. "We will always have each other, no matter what. But I think that someday you will want to know who she is. You will want to talk to her. And you will have many questions for her."

Miss Lucy was right. Tasha had plenty of questions.

Alumni Class of '79

1

❧

In the hour since she'd first walked through the doors of her old high school gymnasium to attend her thirty-year high school reunion, Phyllis Neville had consumed two dirty martinis, six olives, and gushed (or pretended to gush) over at least half a dozen photographs of ugly children, approximately twelve reasonably attractive grandchildren, and one great-grandchild who bore a striking resemblance to Bert from *Sesame Street*. Thank God for name tags and bifocal contact lenses, because without both, she wouldn't have known who any of these people were.

Life-size photographs from the yearbook of their former, teenage selves flashed across a giant screen—er, bedsheet?— against one of the walls. Old and bloated bodies swayed from side to side on the dance floor, looking more like one giant wave of movement than individual dancers ebbing and flowing to the music of "Use ta Be My Girl" by the O'Jays blaring from the speakers, and balding heads reflected colored light under the giant disco ball twirling up above.

She'd just gotten here but had already decided that she would spend the next half hour working on the drunk-to-end-all-drunks before it was all said and done.

Why in the world had she decided to come? She wondered, frowning at the question posed in private. She had never come to any of the reunions, but for some unknown and mystical reason, she'd made the conscious effort to shop for and actually purchase a dress and shoes, get her hair done, and even get a mani-pedi, all in preparation to come to this event, which she knew she'd hate as soon as she'd walked through the doors, and dammit—she was right.

"This is stupid," she muttered under her breath, deciding right then and there that she'd had enough. Phyllis would finish this third martini she'd just ordered and these last three olives and sneak out without a word to anyone, stealthy and unnoticed, like a ninja. She chugged down her drink like it was milk and gobbled up her olives, then she happened to glance across the room. Her heart sank into the souls of her Christian Louboutin pumps, and she nearly choked to death on that damn olive when she saw him. Marcus. Her ex-husband, Marcus, and the father of her child. In fact, that child, their daughter Abby, had been the one to let it slip that Marcus would be here tonight, which was the real reason Phyllis had decided to come to this thing in the first place, despite her incessant denials.

He spotted her, too, and the expression on his face was indescribable, and not necessarily good. Phyllis made her way through the crowd toward him.

Marcus scratched his head. "I uh . . . didn't expect to see you here."

Phyllis tried not to stare, but even after three decades, he was still the finest boy in the school. He wore his hair cut so close to the scalp that if it weren't for the gray sprinkled throughout it, he'd have looked bald. The fine gray-and-black texture of his hair continued down the sides of his face to a perfectly trimmed beard, and dark, penetrating eyes complimented his smooth cocoa brown complexion, but other than that, he looked alright.

"I thought you didn't dig things like this," he continued, unknowingly breaking through her trance.

"I—well, uh . . . ," she stammered. "I don't, normally."

He nodded. She nodded. He shifted. She shifted.

Finally, he broke the awkward silence between them. "You look good, Phyllis. Nice."

She smiled. Hell. She blushed, but not a lot. "Thank you, Marcus. So do you."

He looked better than good. He looked delicious.

They had been inseparable from the time they'd met as sophomores in high school until their senior year. The world came to a screeching halt for Phyllis when they broke up. After that, she swore, in her melodramatic teenage way, that she'd never love again. If she couldn't have Marcus, then Phyllis didn't want anyone. Four months after graduation, they saw each other on the campus at Colorado State University and quickly rekindled their old flame. Phyllis had been blessed by the gods and ended up with the man of her dreams after all. At the end of their sophomore year, they got married, and it was bliss. Six months later, Phyllis was pregnant. That was where things got a little murky for her. From that point on, the life that she'd planned for herself—getting her BA, then her MBA—all sort of went south, and all of a sudden, ambitious, career-driven, future first African American female president of the world was somebody's wife and soon to be somebody's mother, and looking back, she really hadn't prepared herself for either.

The haunting lyrics of "their song" echoed through the tunnels of her memories.

You're still all I need to get by, Marcus.

The words were on the tip of her tongue, like they were every time she saw that man. Of course pride wouldn't dare let her repeat what she felt. Pride, and of course, what's-her-name.

"There you are." The new Mrs. Neville practically tackled the man, wrapped her overtoned arms in a vice grip around his waist, planted a slick, saliva-sloshing kiss on his lips, and glared at Phyllis with her evil python eyes. "Phyllis." It was a statement. "Wow. Abby said you weren't coming to the reunion."

Abby is about as clueless as her father, Phyllis wanted to say, but thought better of it.

Phyllis smiled and stuck out her ample chest. Wifey was as flat as a board. Yeah, the woman might've very well had a six-pack underneath that dress, but she knew as well as Phyllis that Marcus was a breast man. "Well, here I am. Good to see you too, Sharon."

She was younger than him—them, by ten years. In those cheap sling-backs, she stood nearly as tall as he did, and that was the only reason, Phyllis had always concluded, that the woman didn't look more like a linebacker. Phyllis sipped from her glass and sized up the homegrown weave, grimaced internally at the atrocious shade of pink that cow had spread across that gaping hole on her face that she called a mouth, and shuddered at the ill-fitting and tasteless sheath she'd thrown on for the occasion. Walmart? Target? Ross. Yes. It had to be from Ross. Not that she'd know anything about that personally. Phyllis only shopped at places like that for bedding and towels. Never in a million years would she have been caught dead actually wearing a cocktail dress from a place like that. But then again—she wasn't Sharon.

Standing there with the two of them canoodling like they were, Phyllis felt any ounce of love she still had for the man slowly starting to slip away, sort of like the bead of sweat rolling down the middle of her back and dissolving into the band of her thong. It was a nasty, nasty feeling, and the time had come for her to leave.

"Well, I hope the two of you have a lovely evening," she said, sounding smug. "I uh . . . I've gotta pee." She smiled.

With that she turned and headed straight for the ladies' room, and after that, she was getting the hell out of this joint.

It was her. Freddie Palmer had thought she'd seen Phyllis earlier, but it wasn't until she spotted her talking to Marcus Neville that she knew for certain.

"Jesus," she mouthed, watching as Phyllis made her way through the crowd toward the ladies' room.

"What?" Don, her husband, asked. The two of them had been shaking their groove things on the dance floor when Freddie suddenly stopped.

Her lips moved, but it took a moment to answer him. "Phyllis," she said, stunned, still staring in her direction.

Don leaned closer and shouted over the music. "Who?"

"I think I just saw Phyllis. Phyllis Whittaker," she managed to shout back.

"Oh! Well, come on," he tugged on her elbow. "Let's go say hey!"

Freddie's feet felt like they were planted in the wooden floor and she didn't budge. Doubt stopped her. Uncertainty stranded her right where she stood, and her thoughts began bumping into each other as she agonized over what she'd say to the woman.

"Hello, Phyllis. It's me, Freddie. Say, do you ever think about that kid we dropped off in that emergency room that night?" Or, *"Yo, girl. Whassup? So about that baby ... you know the one ..."*

Guilty tears clouded her eyes and broke her heart. Freddie had done a damn good job all these years, putting the past behind her. She'd gone on with her life, married her high school sweetheart, had kids, even had grandchildren now, without so much as skipping a beat about that night she shared with her two best friends more than three decades ago. And shame on her. Shame on all of them for what they'd done.

"What's wrong? Come on, Freddie," Don insisted.

Panic quickly set in and Freddie realized that she needed to get rid of Don before she started to look like a crazy woman. "Can you go and get me a glass of wine, honey?"

He looked confused. "You okay?"

She nodded and smiled. "I just need a glass of wine, Don."

He shrugged and disappeared into the crowd.

"Freddie?"

Freddie slowly turned around and stared straight into the eyes of the woman behind her. It took a moment to actually recognize her, but when she did, the sight of her took Freddie's breath away, because the woman hardly looked like her former self at all. It was her smile that gave her away.

"Renetta," Freddie said warmly.

Neither of them spoke for what felt like an eternity. They simply stared at each other, reached out and took hold of each other's hands, and squeezed appreciatively.

They hadn't seen or spoken to each other since before graduation, and after school ended, they'd each gone their separate ways without a word.

"How have you been?" Renetta asked with tears in her eyes.

Freddie grinned. "I've been good. Good. And what about you?"

Renetta nodded and then laughed. She hadn't realized how much she'd missed Freddie until now. Her memories skipped past the darkest moments of her life and lighted on happier times shared between two young girls laughing, playing, gossiping, and loving each other more like they were sisters than friends.

"Was that Don I saw you dropping it like it was hot with on the dance floor?" She laughed.

Freddie shook her head. "Girl, yes. I dropped it just fine, but he had to help me get it back up."

Renetta stared sincerely at her friend. "I'm sorry I missed the wedding."

"Me too," Freddie said softly. "So, what about you?" she examined Renetta's left hand. "I don't see a ring on your finger. Not married?"

"Not exactly," she smiled.

After studying her face for a moment, Freddie concluded that now was not the time to probe.

"It's complicated," Renetta went on to say.

"Sometimes, I guess it is."

Despite the fact that it had been years since they'd seen each other, Renetta could always read Freddie like a book. The light in Freddie's eyes seemed to fade, and it didn't take a rocket scientist to know why.

"I know what you're thinking," Renetta said, smiling, and blinked away her own tears. "Believe me, I know, but now is not the time, Freddie," she warned gently.

"When is the time, Renetta?"

Renetta sighed. "How about never?" She smiled sheepishly. "Too much to ask?"

"You know it is," Freddie responded.

"I know, but not tonight, Freddie, and not here. There's so much to catch up on. Good things, like . . . Did you and Don go overseas after you got married? Tell me about some of the places you've lived. How are your folks?"

Freddie didn't respond.

"We can talk about it later," Renetta said calmly.

"It's late enough already, Renetta. It's been thirty years, and we've never actually spoken about what happened."

"Talking about it's not going to change it."

"No, it won't but—"

"Call me." Renetta reached into her purse and pulled out a business card and handed it to her. "We'll get together, Freddie. And we'll talk until we lose our voices, okay?"

Renetta was about to walk away when she spotted Phyllis coming out of the ladies' room. Freddie turned in time to see her, too, and the three of them stood frozen, staring back and forth between each other. Freddie walked toward her. "Phyllis," she mouthed, smiling and as happy to see her as she'd been to see Renetta. "Phyllis," she called out again.

Phyllis turned quickly and hurried out of the building without ever saying a word.

No! No! No! She was not going to be dragged back into that mess! Phyllis drove home, clenching the steering wheel. *Screeeeeech!* "Oh!" she gasped, coming within inches of hitting another car at an intersection. Tears suddenly streamed down her cheeks. Phyllis composed herself enough to pull over to the side of the road to try to catch her breath. Tonight hadn't been her night. But that was putting it mildly. Seeing Marcus with his wife had been bad enough. Seeing Freddie Banks and Renetta Smith—

Phyllis had made up her mind a long time ago to stay away from both of them. Too much had happened . . . terrible things had happened, and she'd promised herself to leave the past where it belonged.

Phyllis took slow, deep breaths to calm herself and clear her thoughts. Thank goodness she'd seen them before they could get to her. Thank goodness she'd left before either of them had a chance to say a word to her. The three of them had gone their separate ways years ago. Thank goodness for that, too.

2

Three teenage girls, probably afraid, definitely confused, and no doubt dumb as hell—caught up in a situation bigger than all of them combined—came together and made a very grave decision that night, and they'd made it as a team. No one, not a stranger, and certainly not one of those girls had ever come forward about that infant left in the hospital waiting room—and that was a serious sisterhood, for damn sure.

The old Bob Marley tune "Three Little Birds" played over and over again in Avery's mind, as if Marley himself were sending vibes from the grave urging him to pay attention to his own three birds and check out the obvious.

"... of melodies pure and true;
Sayin', 'This is my message to you.'"

Were the words relevant? Avery smiled as he hummed out loud, knowing full well that every word Marley ever sang was relevant, and yes, the master was reaching out to Stallings.

Ahhhh . . . kids, he thought shaking his head. He'd have never forgiven himself if he'd have let those little girls get the best of him. No matter how smart kids all thought they were, old heads always had one up on them.

Those girls were good, he thought admiringly. They were

pretty damn smart, whether accidental or intentional, even in the midst of the biggest crisis of their young lives. It was obvious from the photo that perhaps they'd actually thought some things through. Hooded, unmarked clothing, faces cast downward to avoid being seen clearly on any security camera, these chicks had that shit down pat, and he couldn't help but be impressed—except for one small detail. It was minute, insignificant really, and it would've been easily overlooked, but it shouldn't have been. The thing was, it was 1979, a black child had been abandoned, and Avery couldn't help but wonder: Just how hard anybody really looked for these girls back then?

He sat back, satisfied that he'd found his clue and grateful that Brotha Marley had been so instrumental in leading him to it.

The receipt Tasha had also given him from the photography studio for senior portraits indicated that at least one of those girls was getting ready to graduate. There was no clear, fast, or easy way to do this, he'd surmised weeks ago when he'd first met with Tasha Darden. Detective work in its purest form was dull, tedious, and uninspiring. That part of his job never played out in the movies. The exciting shit, guns drawn, high-speed car chases, and rescuing people at the midnight hour—in the twenty years he'd been in this line of work, Avery had never once had a high-speed car chase through the city. What he was good at was the dull, tedious, and uninspiring part, like tracking down as many high school yearbooks from every major public school in Denver for the year 1979 and sitting for hours flipping through pages and pages of hormonal, pimply faced, braces-wearing, wide-eyed, and wild teenagers until he spotted a ring like the one he'd seen on that girl's hand, in a photograph with the caption "Tres Amigas" underneath it, followed by three names—Renetta Smith, Phyllis Whittaker, and Freddie Banks.

Avery sat with his feet up on the coffee table in his cramped living room, comparing the yearbook photo to the newspaper photo. The only solid connection between the two was a ring on the middle finger of one of the girls' hand that she rested in her lap. It could've just as easily have been a coincidence, but that one ring and those three girls was just too strong a possibility for him to dismiss. The longer he stared at those photos, the more he was convinced that those were the same girls, and the more clearer their similarities were starting to come into focus. The heavyset girl, Renetta Smith, had a lot of the same characteristics as the larger girl on the end wearing sweats. Freddie Banks wore the ring in the picture and appeared to be more petite than the other two. She was probably the girl in the middle. Phyllis Whittaker, well, she could've been the girl on the other end. Then again, she didn't have to be, but he took the liberty of assigning her to that role for no other reason than process of elimination.

"Hello, Tasha," he said over the phone when she answered. "I think I found those girls in your clipping."

"Really?" she asked, obviously fighting back her excitement. "I mean, you think you have?"

"I'm pretty certain," he said assuredly. "I'll need to follow up on a few things before I'm absolutely sure, but I'll get back to you once I have."

She let out a heavy sigh. "Thank you, Avery. Thank you so much."

"Well, don't thank me just yet. I should have more for you by the end of the week. Okay?"

"Yes. I'll wait to hear from you, then."

Avery hung up and sat back, confident that he was on the right track. He rubbed the tired from his eyes and sighed. Now it was time to get down to the nitty-gritty, and he needed to roll up his sleeves, fill up the tank, and find these three little birds once and for all.

It was hard for Tasha to know how she should feel after her conversation with Avery. She paced around her small Aurora apartment for what seemed like hours, replaying what he'd told her over and over again in her mind: *I think I found those girls. . . .*

Even though she'd hired him, deep down she'd never truly believed anyone would be able to find them, but the fact that he could say that, and almost mean it, suddenly made the situation seem all too real to her.

Those women had never been more than a grainy and faded figment of her imagination before now. Like characters from a story someone had made up, they'd never been real no matter how badly she'd wanted them to be.

"I think I found those girls."

She squeezed her eyes shut, trying to grasp what it could mean for her.

"Only a horrid woman could do something like that." The sound of Miss Lucy's voice drowned out Avery's. *"A selfish and horrid woman. She should burn in hell."*

Tasha slowly opened her eyes and almost smiled. Leave it

to Miss Lucy to put things into perspective. She'd wanted to press Avery for more information, to get names, maybe even a clearer photograph—something. But the reserve in his tone warned her not to get ahead of herself just yet. She needed to stand back and let him do his job, to be sure that these women were the same three women who'd left that bag in that hospital emergency waiting room. And then the rest would come. Her answers would come. *Which one of you is my mother? Are you proud of yourself for what you did? What have you been doing with your life for the last thirty years? And don't you want to know what I've been doing with mine?*

Tasha stood at the window of her apartment and stared out at the building across from her. *She had better have the right answers too,* she thought bitterly. She'd better say something like, *Baby, I've been looking for you for thirty years. I haven't been able to think of anything or anyone else but you, my child, for the last three decades,* because for her to say anything else would be unacceptable and unimaginable.

3

"Don't y'all be up all night, now." Freddie's mother said the same thing every time Phyllis and Renetta spent the night, but it never mattered. They'd stay up until dawn, whispering, giggling, and gossiping in the dark.

All three of them would cram into Freddie's double bed like sardines, talking about boys mostly, but they talked about other things too. Like about the time Renetta's mother left without a word to anybody.

Renetta was about ten or eleven back then, and if she ever did cry about it, no one had ever seen her do it.

"Maybe your daddy and her had a fight," Freddie whispered, squeezed in between the other girls. "Did he slap her?"

Renetta shrugged. "I don't think so. I think she just left because she wanted to."

"That's not right," Phyllis argued, whispering too. "The mother's not supposed to leave the kids. The daddy is."

Freddie rolled her eyes. "Neither one is supposed to leave, dummy."

"Who you calling dummy?" Phyllis sat up.

"Shhhh," Renetta interjected. "Shuddup, Phyllis, before Mrs. Banks comes back in here and makes you sleep on the couch again."

Freddie stood in the shower and surprised herself and laughed at the recollection. The three of them had become blood sisters when they were eight, each pricking her finger with a straight pin that they sterilized with a match, then mixing their blood with each other's and sucking it off, vowing that they'd never part as friends. She cringed thinking about it now. Dirty needles, children playing with matches, exchanging bodily fluids—God really did watch out for children and fools.

"How do you know? How do you know you're going to have a baby? Did you go to the doctor?"

"I missed my period."

"When's the last time you had it?"

She shrugged. "August? I think."

"August? Dang that was . . . that was over six months ago! How come you didn't say nothing?"

"I am saying something."

"Before now! How come you didn't say nothing before now?"

"What are you going to do? Did you tell—"

"No!"

"This is crazy! You gotta tell somebody. What are you going to do?"

"I don't know."

Don swung open the bathroom door, startling her. "Damn, Freddie. You wash down the drain, or what? I need to shave my head."

She sighed, annoyed. "Well, use the bathroom down the hall to shave, Don. You see me in here."

He muttered something incomprehensible, huffed, and shut the door behind him.

It was just the two of them in that house now. The last of their three children had moved out a little over a year ago, but for some reason, both of them often forgot that they had the run of the house.

Freddie let the warm water wash down her back. She'd been in that shower for half an hour and hadn't washed a damn thing.

Freddie, Phyllis, and Renetta might as well have been attached at the hip. Whenever one of them was in trouble, the other two came to her rescue. That's just how it had always been. When LaShaunda Lewis pushed Phyllis down on the playground in fourth grade, Renetta and Freddie helped her up and then chased LaShaunda across the open field until they finally caught her at the fence and gave her a pounding she'd never forget. After that, LaShaunda might've pushed other kids, but she never touched Phyllis again.

When Reggie Daniels called Freddie the B-word in seventh grade, Phyllis and Renetta marched right up to his front door after school and told his daddy, while Reggie stood behind him denying it the whole time. But they proved to be more convincing than Reggie, and anybody living on that block heard that ass-whipping.

"I can't keep it! I can't!"

It just seemed natural that when one of them needed help the most, the other two would come to her rescue the way they had all been there for each other in the past. Their years of friendship had taught them that, and at a time when they should've turned to someone else for help—for once—they operated on autopilot and did what they'd done from the moment they'd met. She needed them, and they were there for her.

"I don't want kids right away, Don," she remembered telling him. After what she'd been through, she didn't think she'd ever want kids, but she gave him another reason for wanting to hold off on starting a family. "I want to work on my career. You know how much acting means to me and how long I've dreamed of being on stage and in movies. I can't afford to let anything get in the way of that."

He was two years older than Freddie. Don was patient with her, kind and accommodating, so of course he agreed, as long as she agreed to come to Germany and work on her acting career from there. As sweet as he was, though, she knew he wouldn't understand what she'd done. And Freddie decided right away that she'd rather choke on the truth sting-ing the back of her throat than to ever confess it to him or anyone else. Two months after arriving in Germany, how-ever, Freddie discovered she was pregnant with Felicia, their oldest, and Don couldn't have been happier. For her, finding out that she was pregnant was bittersweet torture.

He'd fallen asleep as soon as his head hit the pillow, but Freddie couldn't keep her eyes shut, recalling vivid thirty-year-old memories. That night was a turning point for all of them, whether they realized it or not back then, and whether they could finally admit it to themselves now. It changed them forever, and there was no telling who any of them might've been had they made different choices.

They hadn't intended on abandoning that child. The three of them had come up with a lie that they'd planned on telling one of the nurses. "We found this baby in an alley," they'd all agreed. "We were walking by on our way home from the library, and we heard it crying. We don't know whose baby this is."

But when they got there and saw the room filled with so many people, they knew they couldn't go through with it. Emotions among them that night were sky-high and out of control. They could barely even talk to each other, let alone try and tell some stranger a lie like that.

"Let's just leave," one of them whispered. "Just leave it. They'll find it."

"We should say something," another argued.

"Like what?" She started to sob. "I can't . . . we need to just leave it."

"It's a her, not an it!"

"Let's go! They'll find it—her!"

Freddie lay there dismayed and utterly ashamed of herself for being able to keep memories like that at bay so well for so many years.

How could they have been so cruel? How could they have been that indifferent and uncaring?

4

"Grin and bear it, Phyllis," her coworker Ted Sample said, gritting his teeth. "Junior just stepped off the elevator."

"He looks twelve," Phyllis muttered dismally, and smiled at the sight of him.

"He's also the new boss. Hello, Mr. Lang." Ted hurried to greet the young executive, extending an overly anxious hand to shake, and lips far too eager to kiss ass. "I think I speak for all of us when I say we're so glad to have you leading the team."

"Well, I'm happy to be here," Lang said, glancing at Phyllis lagging behind Ted. "And you are?"

She extended her hand. "Phyllis. Phyllis Neville, Western Regional Senior Account Manager." *And far more deserving of your job than anyone on the whole goddamned planet*, she thought bitterly. *Especially you.*

Six-two, and obviously a slave to the gym, golden boy's golden brown complexion, full lips, and deep, penetrating, dark brown eyes came together impressively on the slate that was him. And under different conditions, Phyllis would've been brazenly indifferent to the age gap between them, slipped him her number, and dared him not to call her. Unfortunately, however, the circumstances being what they were, she instantly loathed him, resenting him more than she'd resented anyone since Marcus's current wife came into the picture, and she knew in that moment that hell would freeze or flood or something before she worked one day for this man.

My God! she thought in horror, as she stepped forward to shake his hand next. *I could've given birth to him.*

The beautiful vision of ice-cold Grey Goose came to mind and made her mouth water. Phyllis wasn't an alcoholic, but experts on the subject would probably beg to differ. It was a vice, much like craving chocolate or perhaps her vibrator, which came in handy whenever she felt the world had just flat-out done her wrong. Staring back at this handsome young man, who'd be signing off on her performance evaluations and approving her proposals and vacation time, she succumbed to the dismal realization that fate had screwed her in the ass, without the consideration or mercy of lubricant, and that she, alcohol, and her vibrator would all soon be one continuous stream of consciousness.

"Are you alright, Ms. Neville?" Baby Boss asked, staring at her, concerned.

Damned hot flashes!

She wrestled through the warm flush surging through her veins, the sweat beading on the bridge of her nose, and forced a smile. "Yes. I'm fine. If you'll excuse me." She turned quickly on her heels and headed straight for the ladies' room.

Phyllis was the poster child for the overachieving, dreadfully ambitious executive of the new millennium. Every bone in her body had convinced her that the position would be hers. She'd stayed up late at night, spending hours at her computer, designing projects and marketing plans for her innovative ideas, mapping strategies, and discerning new opportunities to grow the business. Phyllis had diagrams, for crying out loud! Fucking flowcharts, tables, spreadsheets, all ready to present to the executive staff the second she took over her new vice president of sales position, reaffirming to everyone in the room that she'd been the best, most qualified candidate for this job, even more than the Messiah was to lead the masses to salvation. She'd been with the company since the day they'd first opened their door for business, and these people had done the unforgivable, passing her over for the promotion that was rightfully and justifiably hers.

Phyllis braced herself against the wall inside one of the stalls, fighting desperately to catch her breath. A knock came at the ladies' room door. "Phyllis." Ted peeked in the door. "The new boss wants to meet with us in ten in the main conference room."

"Sure," she heaved, and huffed some more. "No problem."

"You okay?" Ted asked, sounding almost concerned.

"I'm fine, Ted. Leave, so that I can finish."

Jeff Lang sat confidently at the head of the conference table, next to Ralph Ruddy, her soon-to-be ex-boss. Phyllis half listened to the introduction from Ruddy and to Lang's buzz-word-laden speech—the team, value-add, strategically positioned—and all the crap she'd written into her own acceptance speech, which she still had saved on her hard drive and which she'd been practicing in her bathroom mirror for the last two months. Phyllis jotted notes on her pad of paper. To everyone around her, she appeared to be the interested and devoted account manager eager to begin working with her new boss. But in reality, Phyllis was busy composing the first draft of her letter of resignation.

5

"Either her ass is too short or this thong is too long or both, Boris. Whatever the case, it looks weird. Tuck it—somewhere or something. The client will be here in half an hour, and I promised him thongs. Thongs, thongs, everywhere—E-I-E-I-O!"

Renetta Jones scrutinized her girls as they dressed. She swam in a sea of tits and ass, finally stopping and looming over a full-figured brunette whose double-Ds threatened to topple her petite frame if the wind blew too hard. "No, no!" She spun the girl around and unhooked her lavender lace bra, yanked it off her, then flung it across the room. "Boris! I don't like the lavender on the brunette. I thought I told you that?"

She reached her hand over her shoulder, and in a moment, Boris had filled it with the red bra and thong set. "Thank you." She shoved it at the young woman. "Put this on, sweetie. And hurry."

There was no other business in the world like Sweet Nothings. Renetta had come up with the idea four years ago, and business took off almost too fast for her to keep up with. But that had more to do with men and lust and young, supple, beautiful bodies than it ever had to do with her.

Sweet Nothings was an online catalog featuring beautiful women clad in lingerie. The lingerie was for sale. The women weren't. But that never stopped a few disgusting fools from inquiring.

Occasionally, she held private showings for the more-discriminating customer. Today she was expecting one of those clients who'd scheduled this showing three months in advance. The truth was, she could've gotten him in sooner, but the more exclusive that rich people believed something was, the more apt they were to pay outrageous sums of money for it.

Bartholomew Stone was the CEO of a large telecommunications company in Louisville, Colorado, and worth millions. He was forty-two years old, tall, a bit too thin, and was only attractive because he was rich. Renetta sized him up while he watched her models strut slowly through the parlor, lingering long enough for him to get an eyeful of every detail of the strips of material covering privacies. He worked hard to appear composed and genuinely interested in the apparel, but Renetta had been doing this long enough to read between the lines of body language. Crossed legs meant he was fighting to conceal his stiff member. Hands clasped in his lap meant his palms were sweating profusely, and pursed lips meant he was fighting a losing battle to keep his tongue from wagging.

"It's for my wife," he explained over the phone when he set up his appointment.

"Well, tell me about your wife, then," Renetta asked.

"What do you mean?"

Renetta smiled. "How tall is she? What does she look like? What color is her hair? Is she thin or heavy? Curvy or straight? More ample up top? Down below? A bit of both?"

He rambled off imaginary qualities of his very real, scrawny wife. Renetta had done her homework, and thanks to Search.com, she'd seen pictures of Mrs. CEO, and the woman was built like a boy and might've weighed ninety-eight pounds dripping wet. What this man had described was nothing short of an XXX-rated fantasy—long legs, triple-D-cup boobs, and a booty that would make J. Lo do a double take. Renetta thought of his poor wife and frowned. The woman obviously lived on celery sticks and water, believing that her husband found her boyish, athletic frame appealing, when in fact, what he really wanted was a busty pole dancer named Brown Sugar who could make it clap on command.

Good old Bart might have been filthy rich, but in the end, he was still just a man, and after paying two grand for the privilege of watching women parade around in their underwear for a few hours, he left with a head full of fantasies to take home to the wife, and he spent another three grand on three thongs with matching bras, and a satin corset for some someone other than the tomboyish love of his life.

Ah yes! Business was booming.

Later that evening, Renetta stretched across her bed, languishing in the classical melodies of Andrés Segovia's flamenco rhythms, thankful that she finally had her home to herself now. Showings took so much out of her, and her models who, for some strange reason, never seemed to want to leave. Renetta loved each and every one of her girls, though, and their energy and enthusiasm were absolutely contagious.

Candles burned on her nightstands, a chilled glass of wine

sat nearby, and the folds of her silk kimono robe caressed her skin. Renetta read through the invitation to her high school reunion again and again, awed that for the first time since she'd graduated she had actually gone and had actually had a good time. Seeing Phyllis and Freddie had been a hopeful and yet unexpected surprise. It was as if fate had brought them together again and used the reunion as an excuse to do it.

The tears that flooded her eyes all of a sudden didn't surprise her. She'd been crying off and on these past few days since the reunion. It was the way Freddie looked at her and the way Phyllis wouldn't dare speak to either of them that brought tears to her eyes. Thirty years ago, they had all been silly, foolish, and selfish girls. And they'd all made a sacrifice in the name of friendship that cost them their relationships to each other and so much more.

The three of them were alone at the house that night.

"I'm calling 9-1-1!" one of them shouted. *Her voice cracked and fear filled her eyes.*

"No! Nooo—please!" another girl sobbed, grabbing the panicked girl's wrist. *"Don't,"* she pleaded. *"Don't call—"* Suddenly she clenched her teeth, squeezed her eyes shut, and growled low and deep. Instinct took over where ignorance left off, and she pushed without realizing why or how she even knew to do that.

"Oh, God! Oh, God!" another girl shrieked in horror. *"I see it! Oh—Oh, shit!"*

"Is that—? Fuck, no! Oh, my God!" The first girl fell backward on her behind and slid across the floor, away from the scene unfolding in front of her, until she backed into the wall across the room.

The girl lying on the bed groaned again, and she pushed, her eyes bulging, staring at the girl at her feet, helpless and pleading. But the girl just stared, shaking and watching.

And then it was over. She was exhausted and let her head fall back onto the pillow. She started to cry uncontrollably.

The girl at her feet let tears fall down her cheeks as she stood there, staring at it.

Renetta had come to terms with her role of what they'd done that night and accepted whatever fate awaited her on the other side, because deep down, she knew they'd done the right thing by that baby girl. She'd been telling herself every single day since it happened that the child was better off. More importantly, she believed it.

6

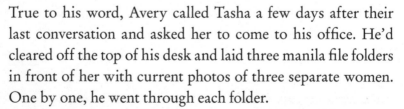

True to his word, Avery called Tasha a few days after their last conversation and asked her to come to his office. He'd cleared off the top of his desk and laid three manila file folders in front of her with current photos of three separate women. One by one, he went through each folder.

"Fredricka 'Freddie' Banks, now Freddie Palmer, married Don Palmer two months after she graduated from high school."

Tasha studied Freddie's round face, warm and open. She had medium brown skin, shoulder-length hair, glasses, and she looked like someone's mother. She looked like the type who would be wearing an apron, standing over a batch of freshly baked cookies, with children clamoring for her attention. *Nurturing*—that was the word that came to mind.

"Her husband retired from the army ten years ago, and the two of them have lived everywhere from Hawaii to Germany and a few places in between, until they finally moved back here. They have three children—a girl, Felicia, the oldest, and two boys, Don Junior and Darren. She works as a court clerk in the Denver municipal building downtown."

"Which one is she in the picture?" Tasha asked softly.

Avery pointed her out as the girl in the center of the newspaper clipping.

He then moved on to the next photo. "Phyllis Whittaker, now Neville, is the girl on the middle," he explained confidently. "She went to CSU after graduation, but only for two years, where she eventually married Marcus Neville. The two of them had gone to high school together. They were married for eight years and had one child, a daughter, Abby, before separating and finally dissolving the marriage ten years ago. She's a corporate executive at a large marketing firm called Skyland Advertising and has never remarried or had any more children."

Phyllis Neville, dressed to the nines, decked out in her tailored suit, designer shoes, and a tight-ass weave that would make Beyoncé envious. She was lighter skinned than the other two, with fine, crisp features hidden behind Dolce & Gabbana shades. She searched the polished woman's demeanor in the photo taken by Avery, looking for some hint of herself in Phyllis Neville's face.

"Finally, Renetta Jones." Avery hesitated when he

introduced this one, but it was easy to see why. Renetta had cinnamon brown skin with green eyes, and she was the most stunning of the three. She wore her hair short and smiled genially in the photo. "Smith is her maiden name. She was married to a Vincent Jones six months after graduating from high school. He was considerably older than she was, and they moved to Little Rock, Arkansas, where they lived for a number of years before returning to Denver. There are no children. A few years ago, Mr. Jones suffered a massive stroke that landed him in a nursing home south of the city. Mrs. Jones has since started her own business, an online gig called Sweet Nothings, some sort of retail business."

She stared in awe of each of the photographs, looking for something in each of them that reminded her of herself. "I can't believe you actually found them."

He could hear the awe and appreciation in her voice, and it did his heart good knowing he'd done his job. "Finding people is what I do best, Tasha."

She looked up at him with tears in her eyes. "So, now what do I do?"

"Contact information is in all the folders," he explained, seeing apprehension in her face. People were strange like that. They paid him to find the things that were lost, and when he did, almost all of them were scared to death to take the next step. She looked more fragile than he'd bargained for, and Avery surprised even himself with what he said next. "If you'd like, I could approach them with you."

She smiled nervously. "I wonder if their families know. Do you think they ever told anybody?"

"Hard to say. Husbands and wives can be as thick as

thieves, sharing and forgiving anything. But they can also be as distant as strangers. Married people can keep a secret better than anybody, especially from the person they're married to."

She took a deep breath and reached out to shake his hand. "Thank you. I appreciate your help, but I'm a big girl, and I think I'd like to handle it from here."

"Where's Dominick?" Tasha's best friend, Robin, asked over the phone.

Tasha sat cross-legged on the floor of her small living room, underneath the lamp on the end table. "Asleep," she said, taking a sip of wine. The folders Avery Stallings had given her were spread out on the floor in front of her.

"He still trying to get a key?" Robin chuckled.

Tasha rolled her eyes. "Hell will freeze over before that happens."

It was late, after midnight. She'd been seeing Dominick for less than six months, and he wanted a commitment already. She wanted it to be over already, except that the sex was good. What could she say? Tasha was a sucker for skillful men with big dicks. But he was the sensitive type too, looking for love, marriage, and kids. He was the polar opposite of Tasha but every time she told him that he smiled, kissed her forehead, and insisted on waiting for her to come around, no matter how long it took.

"Love is a mirage," she'd told him once.

Dominick laughed. "I see I'm going to have to work on that attitude of yours and change your mind," he said dreamily. Only, he was the one caught up in a dream.

"Am I wrong for wanting you all to myself, Tash? Am I wrong for wanting us to be together? Am I wrong for loving you, girl?"

Dominick had fallen too hard and too fast, and she knew that it was only a matter of time before she patted him on the ass and sent him away for good. She could never give him what he wanted. Tasha couldn't connect to another human being the way he wanted. She just wasn't wired the way most people were. Tasha had grown up feeling like she was on the outside looking into other people's lives. She had come to care for some people, like Miss Lucy, and even Robin, but never enough to confuse it for love.

"You call any of those women yet?" Robin probed.

Tasha sighed. "No. Not yet."

"Any idea what you plan on saying to them when you do?"

Robin knew the story. She and Tasha had met in their senior year of high school and had become friends. Most of the other kids had treated Tasha like she had cooties for real, once they found out that the woman coming to her parent-teacher conferences was an old German woman, with no resemblance whatsoever to her nappy-headed self. No, she told them. She wasn't Tasha's mother or grandmother or stepmother or aunt or cousin or anything. She was her foster mother. Hearing that, the expression on their faces or in their eyes would twist all kinds of crazy, and all of a sudden, she was somebody they didn't want to hang with anymore.

But not Robin. Robin had just shrugged and said, "Weird. Let's go eat, girl. I'm starving. My treat."

"I have no idea what I'm going to say to them."

Robin laughed. "You've had your whole life, Tash. I'd think by now that you'd have that speech all memorized and shit."

"I know. Right?" Tasha laughed too. "When are you coming over? I want you to see the pictures."

"I'll be over Saturday, unless Dominick is there, of course. He gets creepy when he has to share you with somebody."

"He won't be here. Maybe you can tell me if you think I look like one of these bitches, because I don't see a resemblance to any of them."

"That's because you're too close to the situation to be objective. I'll bet I can tell you, though."

"Good. Then I'll go from there."

"Any of them got loot?"

"Well, one's a public servant, so my guess is she's pretty much living paycheck to paycheck. Miss Fly Momma here in the designer duds could have money in the bank, but it kind of looks like she would just rather wear it. Now, the Badu look-alike," she said, referring to Renetta, "she runs a bomb-ass online company selling silk panties and French bras for way too much money. No kids . . . yeah. That one there might be swimming in it."

"Maybe you can take her to court and get some back child support or something."

Both of them laughed.

"You're definitely putting ideas into my head," Tasha said.

The conversation turned quiet for a few moments. "Do you think one of them is really going to admit to being your mom, Tash?"

That was the scary part—the part she couldn't fake or joke away. The whole thing was laughable over the phone with Robin, but in real life, there was nothing funny about any of it. And the very real possibility that one of these women could still look her in the eyes and reject her all over again made her sick to her stomach. She'd done it once. She could do it again. And then what would Tasha do?

"I mean, they've kept this secret your whole fucking life. Maybe it's easier to keep it than to spill it after all this time."

"Maybe," Tasha said, softly. "But I'm not leaving any of these cows alone until I get my answer. And by the time I'm finished with them, somebody's going to be singing the truth like a pre-Bobby Whitney Houston."

7

"What is it? What . . . what is . . . is it alive?"

"It's not crying!"

"Is it dead?"

"I don't know!"

"Is it dead?"

"I don't—no!"

A few weeks after seeing each other at the reunion, Freddie and Renetta agreed to meet for lunch at Strings on Seventeenth Avenue, where Freddie ordered the House-Made Penne Bagutta, with chicken, broccoli, and a spicy tomato cream sauce, with a glass of iced tea; Renetta chose the Pan-Seared Salmon with Jasmine Rice and a glass of white wine.

Small talk was easy talk, but the past hung heavy in the air between Freddie and Renetta despite their efforts to pretend it wasn't there. During the meal, they caught up with things that had happened in each other's lives since high school, discussed the weather, and finally the food, before the conversation began to shift focus back to when they were teenagers.

"Phyllis always was a walking contradiction to me," Freddie finally admitted, sipping her second glass of tea. "On the one hand, she always came across like she had herself so together, even back in school, but on the other hand . . ."

Renetta laughed. "Remember how she used to freak out over finals week? That girl wouldn't eat, wouldn't sleep—she studied those books until her eyeballs swelled up."

"And after it was over, you wouldn't hear from her for a week, and every time you called the house, Phyllis was sleeping."

"And then she'd be back to her cool, calm, and collected self again," Renetta reminisced. "Like it never happened, and like she hadn't just had a mental breakdown over those damn tests."

Freddie nodded reflectively. "Doesn't look like she's changed much in that respect," she said quietly.

Renetta sipped her wine.

"I never wanted to see either one of you again," Freddie confessed, darting her eyes at Renetta.

"Then why'd you come to the reunion, Freddie? Why'd you come when you knew one or both of us could be there?"

Freddie shrugged. "I'd gone to the twentieth, and neither one of you showed up. I figured you'd have both died of old age by the time the thirtieth rolled around," she laughed.

Renetta laughed too.

Freddie's expression darkened. "I had never seen so much blood before," she said, softly. "There was much pain."

"I was terrified," Renetta admitted.

"I can't believe how young we were, and how clueless. That baby could've actually died that night, Renetta."

"We all thought we knew so damn much," Renetta added, solemnly. "All any of us really knew was how to fuck up our lives and how to act without thinking. It was only by the grace of God that nobody died that night, Freddie."

"I'll never forget how I felt when I found out that I was pregnant with Felicia," Freddie recalled, "how I couldn't or wouldn't let myself be happy about it. Don practically turned flips when he found out, but—I was miserable. He thought I was just being hormonal."

"You never told him?"

Freddie shook her head. "He would never have forgiven me," she said, staring sadly at Renetta. "Did you ever tell anyone? Did you tell your husband?"

"I told him," she admitted quietly. "That was the second worst thing I ever did. Vincent wasn't as nice as Don." Renetta smiled. "Thankfully, we never had children. I don't think I could've handled it as well as you have."

Freddie stared coldly at her friend. "Who said I've handled it well?" she said defensively.

Renetta reached across the table and placed a comforting hand on top of Freddie's. "I didn't mean it like that, Freddie. I know you cared about that baby. I just meant that you've done well. You have a wonderful husband and three beautiful children, and that's a good thing."

"I have never stopped thinking about her, Renetta," Freddie said with tears in her eyes. "Each and every time I held one of my own children in my arms, I thought about that baby girl. If any one of us is fortunate, I'd say you were."

Renetta looked stunned.

"Not having children of your own had to have made it easier to put all this behind you, Renetta," she stressed. "You didn't have to see that child in the faces of your children and then wonder how in the hell you could've ever done what we did."

Renetta sat up straight. "Bullshit," she blurted out, startling a few other customers around them. Renetta quickly composed herself. "How can you possibly think that? Do you ever wonder why I didn't have any children, Freddie? Did it ever occur to you that maybe after what happened, I didn't want any?"

No. Yes. "Maybe," Freddie whispered.

"We all lost that night, Freddie," Renetta reasoned. "We all walked away and left a small part of ourselves behind in that hospital. Something that none of us, not one, will ever get back. But a lifetime is too long to punish yourself, Freddie. When it's all said and done, we all have to pay for our mistakes one way or another. Through the years I've learned that you've got to take your pleasure where you find it," she said and sighed. "I'm going to make the most of the blessings I have now, and I'll pay the piper when it's my time."

Freddie swallowed the lump swelling in her throat. "I've spent the last thirty years ignoring what I did, Renetta. I've gone on with my life, raised my kids, enjoyed the company of my grandchildren, and until I saw the two of you again, I had actually fooled myself into believing that I was okay."

Renetta took another sip of her wine, leaned back in her chair, and sighed. "You wanna know what I've told myself all these years?" She stared hard at Freddie. "I've told myself that we were young, and we were very, very dumb. We did something we had no business doing, and we've each kept our secret for our own selfish reasons. But I still believe to this day, just like I believed back then, that that baby was better off."

"How do you know that?" Freddie asked and frowned.

"How do you know that she wasn't?" Renetta argued. "That woman sitting in the waiting room found her. They gave her a name, and they even published in the paper that she was a healthy baby, Freddie. Somebody took care of that child. Somebody raised her and loved her in a way that was impossible for any one of us to fathom doing back then," she argued passionately.

Freddie stared blankly at her. "You really believe that?"

"If I don't believe it, then I'll lose my fuckin' mind. I'll drive myself crazy wondering what terrible things someone could've done to her. Life goes on, Freddie," she said, sincerely. "We all do things that we regret. We all keep secrets, we lie, cheat—we do whatever we need to do to get over, and we all live with regrets that we can't make right. I understand what you're feeling and I understand why, but after a time, for your sake and for the sake of your family, you're going to need to let it go, girl."

"Phyllis, this is Renetta. I got your number from Marcus. Look, Freddie and I are meeting for lunch—to talk. We'll be at Strings on Seventeenth, Tuesday at one. It would be nice to see you again. Please think about it."

Freddie had gotten fat. Way fat. And Renetta looked like she'd lost seventy, maybe eighty pounds and fifteen years off of her age since high school. Gastric bypass, Phyllis concluded, a little Botox, and a good plastic surgeon went a long way in this day and age.

Phyllis was parked less than a quarter of a block away from the restaurant. She had spent the last half hour watching the two of them sitting on that patio, talking—knowing instinctively what each of them was saying, almost verbatim. Freddie's expression gave her away. Even in high school, she'd been the conscience at the heart of the three of them. She'd been the one who made sure they all ate lunch, even when someone had forgotten their lunch money. Freddie was the one who'd packed enough food to feed the entire football team.

Renetta, on the other hand, always seemed to think the same way she moved—graceful and unhurried. She'd had it harder than Phyllis and Freddie growing up; with a father who didn't give a damn about her, and a mother who'd left them both, Renetta had mastered the art of internalizing her feelings, and now she seemed to have transformed into a woman who had learned to be at peace with them too, and even make sense of them.

Phyllis assumed that she fit somewhere in between the two of them. She saw no reason to dig up the past, because none of them could ever change it. She saw no reason to relive hard and painful memories when life had its own set of challenges that required more immediate attention. If the two of them wanted to spend their lives wallowing in shame and reliving teenage angst, let them, but Phyllis had moved on a long time ago.

8

❧

Tasha stood outside of the house she'd grown up in, marveling at how much smaller it looked to her now. When she was a little girl, that house had been a huge labyrinth of rooms, closets, and hiding places. It was home, but only to a very small degree. Miss Lucy, the only mother she'd ever known, always made it clear that Tasha, and the other foster children, were invited guests, subject for dismissal as she saw fit if they misbehaved or made Miss Lucy unhappy. Tasha went out of her way never to give her reason to send her away.

Tasha never had to be told to wash her hands before sitting down at the table to eat, or to brush her teeth before going to bed. She made sure never to get any of the pretty dresses Miss Lucy had made for her dirty, and she always remembered to say please and thank you. Miss Lucy loved manners, pretty little girls, and clean hands.

"Owwww!"

"I don't like dirty boys! How many times do I have to tell you that dirty boys make me sick?"

Raymond, a cute little redhead with freckles galore, was a few years younger than Tasha, who was eight at the time. He'd been with Miss Lucy only a few months before he made one too many mistakes. She was careful how she hit and where. The palms of his hands were streaked bloodred by the time she finished slapping that wire coat hanger across them. The next week, she put on the performance of a lifetime when the social worker arrived. Miss Lucy sat on the edge of her sofa, shaking her head, looking distraught and at her wits end, as she went on and on about Raymond.

"I try and try to be good to him but he doesn't listen," she said, dabbing her tearful eyes with a laced handkerchief. "The other children are good," she said, trying to smile, "and you know how well I take care of the children. They love it here." She sniffed. "But Raymond upsets the whole house with his antics. The other children are afraid of him, and I don't think this is the place for a boy like that. I think he needs special care."

They took Raymond that same day, and Tasha never even got a chance to say good-bye. He was a sweet kid with dirty hands, and she'd dismissed him for no other reason. Later that night over dinner, she explained why Raymond had to leave, but they already knew.

"Raymond was bad, and he didn't follow the rules of this house," she said, serving beef stew. The three children left in that house all sat quietly, hands folded in their laps, waiting patiently for Miss Lucy to tell them that it was okay to eat, and listening to her tell them about poor, unclean Raymond.

"Children like him don't belong here," she continued, casting a threatening gaze on each and every one of them. "They belong in a place that doesn't care about how dirty children are, and do you know where that kind of place is?"

The children warily shook their heads; their eyes were wide with fear.

"It's a place filled with unruly and dangerous people who live in filth with rats and roaches, eating out of the garbage, and sleeping in dark and disgusting alleys and gutters," she

said with disgust. "Nobody cares for them in those places. No one loves them, and no one wants them."

Tasha remembered feeling physically sick to her stomach when Miss Lucy told them about places like that.

Miss Lucy finished filling their bowls, and then finally sat down at the head of the table and gazed lovingly at each of them. "You are my special babies," she said, smiling. "I take care of you because I knew from the moment I saw each of you, how lovely you all were, I told the people who brought you to me to leave you and let me take care of you."

Her eyes rested on Tasha. "You have been with me the longest, Tasha," she warmly said. "And you are my best, good girl. Isn't that right?"

Tasha nodded. "Yes, Miss Lucy."

She had cared for that woman for some strange reason. Tasha had had no choice but to need Miss Lucy. Other children came and went in that house, but Tasha stayed until she graduated high school, and even then she didn't want to leave. She had nowhere to go, and Miss Lucy had made the rules Tasha's whole life.

"One day you should find your mother," the old woman reminded her again a few weeks before Tasha's graduation. "Look her in the eye and ask her why she never loved you. You should know why."

9

"I hope you don't expect me to do none of that crazy mess," Don told her once when she read a passage to him from one of her romance novels about Lance Hill, who, upon discovering the injustices and heartbreak plaguing Alisa Montgomery, swept her up into his arms and carried her into the bedroom to make slow, sweet, sanctimonious love to his woman, proving to her once and for all that not all men were cads, thereby healing her wounded heart and saving her from herself. In the end, they'd ride off into the sunset together, ready to begin their happily-ever-after and Freddie would drift off to sleep with a smile.

"I don't know nobody like that," he grunted. "You don't know anybody like that."

Freddie rolled her eyes and sucked her teeth. "So," she said irritably. "That's not the point, Don," she snapped. "It's fantasy."

He turned over to turn off the lamp on his side of the bed and muttered under his breath, "You got that right."

Reading had always been an escape for Freddie. Of course, Don wouldn't understand because Don had always been boring and sensible. They'd lived all over the world, but for her and her family, living in Berlin hadn't been any different than living in Wisconsin. They lived on military bases and followed a pattern that kept the whole household and every one in it in line, organized, and in step with routine. Freddie had fallen into step beside her husband. She hadn't regretted it or thought about it one way or another, but instead, she discovered her fantasies between the covers of her romance novels.

Freddie finished reading just after midnight and then turned off the light, pretending that she was Alisa falling asleep in Lance's strong arms.

She happened upon it rather randomly, one Saturday afternoon, while perusing her favorite bookstore. Freddie's curiosity got the best of her, and she followed a trail of readers to a book signing and reading by a local author named Bianca Hightower. Freddie found a seat in the back of the room, excitedly anticipating this rare opportunity to see a real author in person. Shortly after the room filled to capacity, the tall, polished, impeccably dressed brunette stood up behind the podium and began to read from her latest novel. Freddie had never heard of Bianca Hightower. She had no idea what type of books this woman wrote, but nothing could've prepared her for the effect this Bianca person would make on Freddie that afternoon.

"Touch me, he commanded." Bianca Hightower could've been a lawyer, a politician, or even a college professor. Her conservative and fitted slate gray pantsuit and bun was more indicative of a corporate executive than a writer. Dark, sultry eyes scanned the audience as she read. Full, red painted lips embraced words like *kisses*, and Freddie was stunned that she was as mesmerized by this stranger as anyone in the room.

"His fingertips singed her skin, robbing her of breath, when all she wanted to do was to scream his name loud and long enough to move heaven and earth. Rigid, luxurious, throbbing thrusts invaded her soul, sending shock waves and pain through her core, while his gaze held hers prisoner, and she willingly and pitifully succumbed to the prison of his undertaking."

Freddie held her breath. This was no romance novel this woman was reading from.

"This pussy . . . ," Bianca read with conviction, lowering her octaves to sound more like a man, which she did. She stared intently at the audience. ". . . belongs to me," she said huskily.

"And all she could do was to nod, feebly. He pushed as far inside her as he could, until she whimpered and convulsed, clawing talons deep into the flesh on his back. He held his place there, firmly and with all his might. Her raised knees trembled at his shoulders, violet blue orbs of her eyes rolled luxuriously back in her head, and a single tear escaped in a small stream down the side of her face. 'I came,' she mouthed to him, losing herself in the waves of the most memorable orgasm she'd ever had."

Freddie's eyes glazed over, her chin dropped, and her palms sweated so profusely that she had to dry them on her pant legs. The audience bolted to its feet and erupted in thunderous applause. That was no romance novel, she concluded one last time as she slowly stood up, too. It was something else, and she knew that she was not leaving that store without that book.

Bianca Hightower was even more stunning up close. Freddie waited patiently in line to get her book signed by this woman, more nervous than she'd ever been about meeting anyone.

Finally it was her turn, and it took every ounce of willpower not to stare at this woman and to will words out of her mouth. "Hello," Bianca smiled at Freddie. "Who am I signing this to?" she asked politely.

Freddie forgot her own name. "Um . . ."

Bianca laughed. "Is that you or your lover?"

Her presence was commanding, awe-inspiring, dignified. But something in her eyes was soothing, somehow comforting, and with a look, she willed Freddie to search her memories to find what she needed.

"Freddie," she said, clearing her throat. "That's my name."

Bianca smiled and penned her note in Freddie's book. "Well, thank you for coming, Freddie."

Freddie's thoughts whirred like a cyclone in her head. This woman had filled her with inspiration unlike any she'd ever felt before, and there was so much she wanted to ask.

How do you come up with stuff like that?

Do you write the way you do to intentionally make people squirm in their seats, or does it just come naturally?

Are those real people in your book? Is she you? Do you actually know a man like him?

Bianca held out Freddie's book to her. "Thank you, again."

Freddie nodded meekly. Her hands shook as she reached out to take the book from Bianca, and damn if she wasn't blushing. She was so giddy with excitement that she didn't even notice the person standing behind her and bumped right into the woman. "Oh," she laughed nervously, reaching out to the woman who stumbled a bit. "Excuse me. I am so sorry."

"It's alright," the woman smiled. "I guess I didn't get out of your way fast enough."

Freddie gushed, "Isn't this exciting?"

Freddie hurried from the store, anxious to get home to read her new book.

Long after Don had gone to sleep, Freddie curled up in his recliner in the den, her knees tucked beneath her, with a cup of hot tea on the table next to her. Freddie tightly wrapped her robe around her. She lightly traced the cover of Bianca Hightower's novel. The picture was simple, of a man's and a woman's lips, millimeters apart. The title of the book was vague but intriguing: *I Know You.* Just from what she'd heard earlier, she knew that this wasn't a book to be read lightly, over a lunch break or taking a quick dump on the toilet. She slowly cracked the spine, and read the customized bookmark with the covers of all of Bianca's books and the woman's picture that dropped into her lap.

Bianca Hightower, deemed the Princess of Erotica by *In the Basement* magazine, is a nationally best-selling author of three novels and writes an award-winning column for *She* magazine. She makes her home in Denver, Colorado. Look for her highly anticipated follow-up to *I Know You* in March 2010.

At the bottom of the bookmark were Bianca's Web site and a note detailing a writer's workshop hosted by her at a local library. Freddie's heart raced in anticipation of what she was about to read. She felt almost sinful for even having this book in the house. Never in a million years had she ever been remotely interested in reading erotica. But Bianca Hightower's words were pasted into her memory, and if nothing else, Freddie had to satisfy her curiosity. Maybe, when she finished, she'd think this book was junk and that Bianca Hightower was nothing more than a shameless and cheap word peddler who suckered unsuspecting women like Freddie into buying a book that wasn't worth the paper it was printed on. But after reading the first chapter, Freddie fanned herself, shifted in her chair, adjusted her gown, and knew without a doubt that Bianca Hightower was nothing short of a hidden treasure.

Tasha seldom ever got emotional, and under normal circumstances, she certainly wouldn't have let the tears fall in front of Dominick, but when she rushed out of that store she needed—someone. She needed someone in a way that she never needed people, and as if he were psychic or something, he called her cell phone right as she was searching through her contact list, frantic about finding someone she could talk to about what had just happened.

"Come on over, baby," he said soothingly. "I'll be here."

He caught her in his arms on the steps of his duplex and brought her inside. Tasha cried several minutes before she finally started to calm down. Dominick let her go long enough to go into the kitchen and bring her back a cup of hot chamomile tea with honey.

"I was as close to her as I am to you right now," she explained, struggling to regain her composure. "She bumped into me, and . . ."

He lovingly rubbed his hand up and down her back. Dominick knew she'd grown up in foster care, and he knew that she was trying to find her mother and that she'd hired a detective to help her. He'd seen the files, but whenever he asked what she'd planned to do now, she'd change the subject or tell him she was tired and didn't want to talk about it. As far as Tasha was concerned, her personal life had nothing to do with him. Yeah, she could fuck him, but no, under normal circumstances, he had no business inside her heart or her head.

"You couldn't bring yourself to say anything?"

She shook her head, and more tears fell. "I wanted to talk to her away from her house," she said, sniffing. "You know? Away from her family. So I waited outside her job and followed her, and she ended up at the bookstore. So, I think—great. It's a public place. I could confront her there, and it would just—it would be better than trying to talk with her in private."

"So what happened, love?"

Tasha shook her head. "I couldn't . . . I didn't know what to say," she admitted pitifully. "Hello, lady. I might be your long-lost daughter? I mean"—she stared desperately at him—"she'd think I'd lost my mind."

He nodded. "Maybe. But it doesn't matter what she would think," he said, reasonably. "I think she still deserves to hear it, just as much as you deserve to say it. What she does with it after that is up to her, and you. But it needs to be said, Tasha, no matter how crazy it might sound."

Dominick was right, but as easy as he made it sound, Tasha knew that it wasn't as easy to do.

"I'm afraid, Dom. What if I say it and it turns out that I'm wrong?"

He stared quizzically at her. "Honestly, Tash. I think you are more afraid of being right than wrong."

"I need to find my mother," she said sternly. "I'm not afraid that I will. I'm afraid that I won't."

He leaned forward, closer to her. "Say you find her and she's not the person you've always dreamed she'd be. Say you find her and she still doesn't want to have anything to do with you. Say you find her and you don't feel anything for her, she doesn't feel anything for you. Finding your mother is a terrifying thing, Tasha," he reasoned. "Any sane person would be afraid. So"—he smiled mischievously—"are you telling me that you're an insane person?"

Tasha tried to smile, too, but it was difficult. He made sense and she resented him for it. For a moment Dominick had almost made her forget that she really didn't give a damn about him.

10

She stared at her reflection in her bathroom mirror, and for the first time in a long time looked past the crow's-feet and laugh lines into the eyes of a woman speeding fast toward fifty. Despite her best efforts to ignore the truth, time wasn't on her side anymore, and it slapped her square in the face with her new boss, who looked young enough to be her son.

Her life felt as if it were shattering in her hands like glass. That's how it had been since she left high school. Phyllis's life had turned into a series of "almosts." She had almost been a good wife. She'd almost been a good mother. And now she'd almost been a damn good vice president. The dismal thought that she was cursed started to creep into her pity party.

She was drunk off her ass, sprawled out in the middle of her living room floor with a bottle of Grey Goose, some ginger ale, and her misery.

She'd called in sick and stayed in bed most of the day, watching every movie Lifetime had ever made, dozing in and out of sleep, until finally, halfway through the *Maury* show, she decided to get up and do something useful. She'd been drinking ever since.

She'd given her life to those people at Skyland Advertising, and they all but threw that life back in her face, after spitting on it, of course. Phyllis hated them for it.

"Every last one of y'all can kiss my ass!" she spewed out loud, mixing another drink.

And then, as if God in heaven couldn't just let that go without rubbing salt in her wounds, she'd run smack dab into Renetta and Freddie at an event she wished had never happened. Thirty fuckin' years! Goddammit! Who in the hell is still alive after graduating from high school thirty motha-fuckin' years ago? "No-goddamn-body!" she slurred, nearly falling over backward.

Nineteen-seventy-fuckin'-nine! When in the hell did she get to be that fuckin' old? Hot tears stung her eyes, as she stared at the paper lying next to her, the words blurring into squiggly lines. Where the hell were her reading glasses? "When the hell did I start wearing goddamn reading glasses?" she screamed.

Phyllis melted into a pathetic mess on the floor, deflated and exhausted. "What happened?" she yelled. The floodgates opened and she started to cry like a baby. "I'm a fuckin' loserrrr!"

"*Vote for me and I promise to make this school a better place!*"

She won senior class president of Richfield High School by a landslide.

"*Of course I'll marry you, Marcus. After we go to college and get our degrees, we can get married.*"

"And start our own family," he said, smiling.

Phyllis didn't respond.

Phyllis "Who Can Do Whatever She Sets Her Mind To" Whittaker-Neville. That's who she was. She had it all planned out, too. She'd been accepted into Colorado State University, where she majored in business administration, and Marcus chose to major in political science. Her plan was to graduate with honors, transfer to an Ivy League school to get her master's (taking him with her, of course), and ultimately get her PhD. Somewhere along the line, she'd have started her own business, and by the time her thirtieth-year high school reunion did roll around, she'd have appeared at least once on the *Today Show,* promoting her latest best-selling book, *101 Ways to Succeed in Life, Business, and Love— Just Like Me.*

The true version of her life had been vastly different from the fantasy. Phyllis ended up pregnant two years into college, and she and Marcus were married by a justice of the peace shortly after she'd found out. Marcus ended up being a melodramatic dweeb. One day she made the mistake of telling him as much, and eventually he told her that he wanted a divorce and full custody of Abby. No one was more surprised than Phyllis when she agreed that he should have it. She loved Abby, but the older she became, the closer Abby seemed to grow to Marcus. Looking back now, it was obvious how that had happened. Marcus did the kinds of things with a child that Phyllis never could—or would. Marcus hugged her, bounced her on the knee, played dolls with her, taught her to swim, and went to all of her soccer and basketball games. He enjoyed being her father, and Phyllis—Phyllis had no idea what it meant to enjoy being a mother.

She sat alone in her living room now, wallowing in booze and disappointment, with one foot in the door of corporate America and the other dangling outside in the gutter. She took a drink straight from the bottle, then remembered that she had a glass and that it was empty, and Phyllis filled it again; this time, she left out the ginger ale.

She stared at the phone on the coffee table. It was ringing, but it took a moment for it to register with Phyllis that she probably should answer it. "Hello?" she asked, gruffly.

"Mom?"

Mom. That must mean her.

"Mom? Are you there?"

Mom. If Phyllis was mom, then that meant . . .

She felt herself smiling. "Hey, baby," she said to the love of her pathetic life. Phyllis's daughter, Abby, lived in Colorado Springs, which was good, too, because it was an hour away from where Phyllis lived.

"How are you?" Abby asked.

She thought about telling her baby that she was drowning in vodka and depression and that she'd become the failure she'd always dreaded she'd become and never believed she could become, and that the job she'd worked so hard for all of these years had gone to a boy around the same age as her own child, and that she was old, but ultimately, she decided not to burden the girl.

"I'm fine, sweetie," she said lovingly. "How are you?"

"I'm good. Work's keeping me busy, but I'm doing fine, Mom."

"When are you coming home?" Of course, she missed Abby. The girl was only an hour's drive away, but in Phyllis's current state of mind, she felt like they were worlds apart.

"Soon, maybe. Hey, are you sitting down?"

Phyllis checked her surroundings. Yep. She was sitting down on the floor wearing her bra and panties, grateful for the fact that she'd had the hindsight to sit down long before she became as drunk as she was now. "I am," she confirmed proudly.

"Well . . ." Her daughter hesitated. "Mom, I've got something to tell you."

Phyllis felt warm inside, listening to the sound of her sweet child's voice and wallowing in the fact that this girl loved Phyllis despite herself. Abby's father might have been one of Satan's spawn, but he sure raised a wonderful baby girl.

"What is it, sweetheart?"

Leave it to Abby to add a little sunshine to her mother's dreary existence. Leave it to this wonderful gift from heaven to call her undeserving mother in her hour of need and lift her spirits as only a loving child who cares deeply for her mother could do. Phyllis waited with bated breath for Abby to share her good news.

"I'm pregnant." Abby paused for effect. "You're going to be a grandmother, Mom!"

Phyllis sat frozen, as the final nail of fate's ugliness was hammered into her dark and dreary coffin.

"Mom?" Abby repeated. "Did you hear me? I said . . . you're going to be a grandmother."

Grand—mother? Grandmother?

Dread filled Phyllis's entire body, as the room seemed to shrink around her, mashing all the air into one solid, condensed cube that was impossible to breathe.

"No," she whispered, pitifully. "Really?" She swallowed hard.

"Yeah, Mom. Really."

Phyllis opened her mouth to say something motherly—even grandmotherly—but her mind went completely blank, and whatever words she had inside of her had caught in her throat and blocked her airway.

"Ricky and I have decided to get married," Abby continued, unaware that her mother was on the verge of stroking. "Of course, we're going to have to do it soon," the girl said, laughing.

"Mom? Hello? Mom, are you still there?"

Suddenly, Phyllis dropped the phone. She struggled to get to her feet several times before she actually succeeded.

"Mom?" the girl's voice came from some faraway place. "Mom?"

Phyllis made it to the bathroom and frantically rummaged through the cabinets and drawers. "No," she groaned painfully. "No more—no, Abby! No!" Shock coursed through her veins. Vivid images of a bloody mess on floral bedsheets and the sounds of screams flooded her memories.

This was a nightmare! A horrible and dreadful nightmare that she couldn't wake up from! She stumbled into the bathroom and stared at her disheveled face in the mirror and slapped herself several times, and when that didn't work, when she still didn't wake up, she pinched her arm so hard, she screamed in agony. "Ow!"

Phyllis stumbled from the bathroom into the kitchen and desperately sifted through the drawers until she came across a dirty steak knife in the sink. She had other knives. Didn't she? Death was welcome in this house tonight. "Do it!" she growled, pressing the perforated knife to her wrist. "Go ahead! Do it!"

Of course, the alcohol suddenly drained from her brain, and before she could take herself out of her own misery, Phyllis heard the sound of her daughter's voice calling out to her frantically from the phone on the floor in the living room. Phyllis looked at the knife pressed against her wrist and dropped it into the sink, then made her way back to Abby calling to her.

She picked up the phone. "Yes, darling." She choked back a sob.

"Mom, are you okay?"

No, baby. She wanted desperately to confess. Mom just had a nervous breakdown. Instead, she opted to lie.

"I'm just so happy, Abby." The knot in her stomach swelled to boulder size.

11

Renetta's life centered on rituals. Years ago, she'd experienced her own private nervous breakdown, but Renetta likened it more to an awakening, a rebirth. She'd disappeared inside the chaos of herself and come out enlightened and refreshed on the other side, with a new perspective and understanding that saved her from the depths of her depression.

Her scars were her badges, symbols of her transition from despair to tranquility and empowerment.

She lit six unscented white pillar candles one by one, and then poured a few drops of champac oil into her bath. Her bathroom was her sanctuary, her haven. Renetta's antique claw-foot porcelain tub anchored the room, enveloped in a sea of crimson and gold chiffon sheer curtains that wrapped around her spirit like a luxurious blanket of opulence. Renetta untied her silk sarong and let it cascade down her back and land on the floor at her feet. She stared at her reflection in the full-length mirror and smiled. Women half her age envied her body. Long, lithe, and perfectly toned, there wasn't an ounce of fat on her.

Renetta's ample breasts were firm, the nipples centered, dark, looking back at her like a set of eyes. She turned slightly and gently grazed her fingers across her narrow hips and firm, round ass. The muscles in her thighs and calves flexed with the slightest move. Yoga. Years and years of yoga were to thank for her physique and her relaxed and appreciative state of mind.

Renetta had been sixty pounds heavier in high school. Shy and insecure, she was not the pretty or popular girl. Going to school was torture. Girls laughed at her, boys avoided her, and except for Phyllis and Freddie, she had no other friends.

Growing up, she'd lived alone with her father. The man walked around like the living dead, hardly noticing that Renetta even lived in the same house. She was invisible to him, and she'd been invisible to her mother. She'd have blended into the walls if it hadn't been for her two best friends.

"Don't let it bother you, Renetta," Phyllis said, shrugging. "You got stuck with some shitty parents, but that don't make you shitty."

"Phyllis is right," Freddie chimed in. "Know what I'd do? I'd grow up and get famous. They'd see me all over television and on talk shows, and when they came around acting like they remembered who I was, I'd be nice and all, but . . ."

"But nothing!" Phyllis interrupted. "When they came around acting like they missed their long-lost daughter, I'd roll my eyes, get into my Rolls-Royce, and drive off like I'd never seen them people."

Renetta smiled at the memory and at the fact that those two girls actually believed that overweight, pitiful, and sad Renetta was even capable of getting famous.

She dipped her toe into her bath to test it before finally easing herself down into the warm, welcoming, scented water. Renetta savored the aroma for a moment before reaching across to a small table next to her, finding a perfectly rolled joint, and then lighting it. She inhaled deeply, closed her eyes, and held the intoxicating smoke in her lungs for as long as she could hold it, before slowly letting it escape from her lips.

The most important lesson she'd learned through the years was the importance of cherishing herself. Renetta had learned to be patient with herself and never to hurry or rush, no matter how urgent the matter was. She learned that she was worthy of proper care, nourishment, replenishment, and as time went on, she tended to her own needs in ways no one else ever could. Every moment of every day was her precious gift to do with as she pleased, to savor and to explore.

Without realizing it, Renetta had slipped her fingers into the folds between her thighs and slowly massaged herself.

Making love slowly, deliberately, was the only way to truly appreciate all that lovemaking had to offer. Fucking slow enough, she could last for hours, and a man could, too, if he just let her take the lead and show him what she needed. Renetta took another puff on her joint, closed her eyes, and moaned out loud.

After her bath she crawled in between Egyptian cotton sheets, appreciating just how far she'd come in life in spite of the setbacks that had threatened to ruin her, and there had been plenty.

"No?"

Renetta nearly fell over from the force of his blow, but fought this time to stay on her feet. Vincent rushed her, grabbed a handful of the front of her gown, and pushed her back into the wall behind her.

"You don't tell me no!" he spat in her face. "You don't ever tell me no!"

She didn't know where she found the courage, but Renetta was so sick of his ass, and she raised her hands to his face and dug her nails deep into the skin until he screamed and let her go.

"Shit! Renetta! Renetta, I'm gonna . . ."

She tried to crawl away from him, but Vincent grabbed her by the hair and the back of her gown, lifted her off of the floor, and shoved her head-first into the wall. She was dazed; warm blood began to pool at her scalp and then slowly trailed down the side of her face.

He turned his back to her, more concerned about the scars she'd left on his face than the hole he'd put in the wall with her head, and when he did, Renetta managed to get to her feet, and she pushed him. She pushed him with every ounce of strength she had in her, hard enough to send him torpedoing on top of the coffee table.

Vincent was a sonofabitch, mean, sadistic, and hateful. It wasn't the fact that he'd beat her that nearly destroyed her, it was the loathing, and even worse, it was her belief that she had deserved it. It really wasn't even his fault. Vincent was an extension of the miserable life she'd suffered for as long as she could remember. He did to her what she couldn't very well do to herself, and she let him get away with it for years.

A light tap on her bedroom door announced his arrival. "Tom, Tom, the piper's son," she called out in rhyme. "Is that you?"

A dashing young man, twenty years her junior, slowly opened the door and peeked inside. "Am I too late?"

Renetta winked. "Almost," she cooed. "I warmed it up nicely for you, sweetheart. You can finish the rest."

Thomas was six-two, two hundred pounds of delicious man-flesh. He was paid for, but he was worth every penny. Not that Renetta had to buy her dick. She just preferred it that way—her money, her terms. It was as simple as that. Besides, she'd done the relationship thing once or twice and realized long ago that she just didn't have the interest for commitment anymore.

"Shall I start with your toes?" he asked, kneeling at the foot of the bed, bare-assed naked, muscular, and eager to please.

She pulled her feet out from under the bedding, placed them in front of him, and wiggled her pedicured toes. "Absolutely, Thomas dear. And take your time."

12

"I've been calling you all week," Robin said, coming into Tasha's apartment. The place was a mess, and so was Tasha, looking as if she hadn't slept in days. Her bloodshot eyes sank into dark, half-moon circles, and she looked as if she'd even lost a few pounds. "What's going on, Tasha?"

"Check it out." She tugged on Robin's arm.

Robin stared at her like she was crazy.

"Come on, Robin," she insisted, leading Robin to the spare bedroom. "I want you to see something."

The room was even more of a mess than the rest of the house. Paper was strewn all across the floor; half-empty coffee cups, Chinese food containers, and a pizza box littered the twin-size bed. But when Robin saw what that fool had done to the wall, it took her breath away.

Glassy-eyed and anxious, Tasha pulled Robin over to the wall. "I've been working on this nonstop for days."

"What is this?" Robin asked, stunned. Tasha had lost it. She had truly lost it.

Tasha suddenly glared at Robin, frustrated, almost as if she expected that Robin should've been able to decipher that mess. "It's everything, Robin. It's them and everything I've been able to find out about them."

She started pointing at photographs of these women. "This one, Freddie . . . Look, Robin." Tasha pointed between Freddie's picture and the one of herself she'd glued to the wall. "We have the same skin tone and maybe lips or mouth." Her hand shook. "See? Can you see it?"

Robin tilted her head. "Sort of."

Tasha rolled her eyes. "Okay, so this is Phyllis. Sterile, career woman, designer every-damn-thing. Our eyes"—she fluttered her fingers first at Phyllis's picture and then to hers—"see the eyes. Same eyes, girl. Same damn eyes!"

Robin looked at her. "When's the last time you had any sleep, Tash?"

Tasha ignored the question. "And Renetta." She pointed to the next picture. "I think our faces are shaped the same. And the nose." She ran her finger down the bridge of her own nose. "See. I mean, it looks a lot alike."

"So, what? All three of these women are your mother?" Robin asked, frustrated.

Tasha rolled her eyes. "No, Robin! Damn!"

Robin shrugged. "You've been picking apart facial features trying to match them with your own—I mean, Tasha— you're tripping."

"One of these women is my mother, Robin," she argued. "Look, I took these pictures. . . ."

Robin was shocked, staring at pictures on the wall of houses, cars, and these women having lunch together, shopping. "You've been following them?"

Tasha stared blankly at her. "No. Sort of. I mean I had to. How else am I going to get to know who they are?"

"Tasha, that's crazy. Tell me you're joking."

"I need to get to know these women. I need to know what I'm dealing with and what I'm getting into."

"Why don't you just ask them, Tash, or get a damn DNA test, but you're driving yourself crazy with all this."

"I am going to ask," she said, defensively. "I just thought I could tell—find a resemblance or something about them that—"

"Ever think that maybe you look like your father, Tash?" Robin reasoned. "I look just like my daddy and nothing like my momma."

Tasha looked at Robin like she'd just thrown her a curveball to end all curveballs. She cleared her throat. "I hadn't thought about that."

Robin was worried about Tasha. The woman was becoming obsessed with this and making it too damn hard. She turned to her friend and took hold of her hands. "You need to get some sleep, sweetie," she said, tenderly. "And you need to take a step back and be more reasonable about all of this. It really is as simple as making a few phone calls, Tash. Really, girl. Call them, tell them who you are, and go from there. That's all you can do."

Half an hour later, Robin was gone. Tasha had showered and had finally crawled into her bed for the first time in what felt like days. Robin meant well, and she made sense, but she was wrong about one thing. There was nothing simple about this. In less than a month, Tasha's whole world had turned upside down, and the mystery that had plagued her whole life was on the verge of being revealed. How could she dismiss this concept as easily as Robin seemed to believe she should? Robin was her girl and all, but she had no idea what finding the truth meant to Tasha, or how it would change her entire life.

When Miss Lucy died, the only surviving relative she had was a son, Michael, who was the beneficiary to her hundred-thousand-dollar insurance policy. He also inherited the house. But Miss Lucy also had managed to save more than forty-seven thousand dollars, and she'd left all of that money to Tasha, her best little girl, with instructions to "use this money to help find your momma."

Tasha was still Miss Lucy's good girl, and she was doing exactly as she had been told. She'd quit her job as an administrative assistant at the real estate office where she'd worked for three years, paid off her car, and dedicated all of her free time to finding her momma, as the old woman had put it so eloquently.

She had actually run into Freddie Banks not long ago at the bookstore. Tasha had made up her mind to start with Freddie and to step up to her that day and say, "My name is Tasha Darden, and I could be your daughter." But when she actually came face-to-face with the woman, the truth caught somewhere in her gut and stayed there. Freddie Banks was a real person, all of a sudden. She wasn't an obscure girl in an obscure photograph, or a smiling, happy woman from Avery's picture. She was quite possibly the woman Tasha had wanted to know her whole life, and she was three-dimensional. The stage for an admission like the fact that Freddie might be her mother had to be just right, and a bookstore wasn't cutting it.

Tasha was looking for something that wasn't in pictures. She was looking for a connection that transcended the physical and cut deep down to the spiritual, where mother and child were bonded beyond an umbilical cord.

13

The small meeting room in the library where Bianca Hightower held her writing class was the size of a high school classroom, able to hold no more than thirty people. Freddie found a spot in the back corner of the room with easy access to the door, in case her second thoughts got the best of her. She'd wrestled with herself all day about whether or not she should really come to this seminar, and at the last minute, on her way home from work, she turned left instead of right and found herself here after all.

She just needed—something, a break from the routine that her life had become, and a distraction from the guilt that just wouldn't go away.

"Worrying about it now won't change what happened, Freddie. We live with it the way we always have and we go on."

"Ever thought about trying to find her?" Freddie asked, sheepishly.

"Have you?"

"Sometimes," she confessed.

"What would you say to her if you did find her?"

Freddie shrugged. *"I'm sorry."*

Tears filled Renetta's eyes. *"I don't believe that just being sorry is enough, Freddie."*

Renetta had been the one to encourage her to pursue this. She'd invited Freddie over one afternoon for wine, and after

Freddie told her what she'd been thinking of doing, Renetta took it and ran with it.

"Writing?" Renetta clasped her hands together and laughed. "Freddie, that sounds like a wonderful idea. I didn't know you liked to write."

"Well," Freddie said, smiling. "I journal, and I dabble in writing a little poetry here and there, but . . ." It would be a new adventure, a new challenge, one that could be just what she needed right now. The more Freddie thought about it, the more excited she was beginning to get. "It does sound fun, doesn't it?" She grinned.

"Girl, yes! To actually write a book—to get one published! Freddie, you should do this," she said earnestly. "You really should go for it." Renetta's expression suddenly changed, and she stared intently at Freddie. "I know you can do this if you set your mind to it, Freddie. I've learned firsthand, that a woman can do just about anything she sets her mind to. My husband taught me that," she said bitterly.

Renetta was always careful not to say too much about her marriage, but she'd implied plenty. Maybe it was pride that kept her from telling the whole story, or maybe it was the fact that reliving it would keep it fresh and close to the surface. Renetta went out of her way to try and live beyond the pain of her past, but as hard as she tried, it was obvious to Freddie that she wasn't nearly as free and clear of it as she pretended to be sometimes.

"How did you finally find the courage to leave him?" Freddie softly asked.

Renetta surprised Freddie and laughed. "Whoever said I left him?" Freddie didn't know what to make of the expression in Renatta's eyes, but the woman quickly changed the subject. "I think you need this. I think it's exactly what you need."

Maybe this was all divine intervention and Freddie had been led here by a higher power, and perhaps, if nothing else, she could express her aspirations in a journal or even in a book that no one else would have to read but her.

There were no more than fifteen or twenty people in the room with Bianca, looking more relaxed and approachable in her maxi dress and sandals, with her hair hanging loose and past her shoulders. She asked everyone in the group to introduce themselves and to tell why they wanted to become writers. While the others took turns speaking, Freddie wrestled with herself, trying to come up with something witty to say, but when it was her turn, her mind went totally blank. She tentatively stood up and hoped that nobody else could hear her heart beating as loudly as it sounded to her.

"M-my name is Freddie . . . Palmer," she said hesitantly.

Languid and sultry Bianca Hightower stared intensely at Freddie, waiting patiently for her to finish what she had to say. She looked like a long piece of red licorice in the floor-length red dress she had on. Her dark tresses cascaded down her shoulders. All eyes were on Freddie as she frantically searched for something to say, until finally she had no choice but to surrender to the truth and confess it out loud.

"I don't know if I can do this," Freddie said quietly. "Write—a book." Her voice quivered, and Freddie suddenly began to feel very sorry for herself. She'd spent her whole life taking care of everybody else—Don, her children, sometimes her grandchildren. And unlike the people in this room, she couldn't call up one interesting fact about herself worth mentioning, and it broke her heart. "I want to do something wonderful in my life," she continued. "Something that has nothing to do with my husband or my children, or anybody else—just me." Freddie stared back at Bianca and shrank under the weight of that woman's talent. "I'm tired of being ordinary," she finally admitted, and with that, Freddie sat down in her seat and resisted the urge to run out of that room screaming.

Bianca smiled warmly. "I know exactly what you mean, Freddie Palmer."

The other students politely but warmly applauded.

"Sorry," a young woman rushed into the room and took her seat in the back corner of the room. "I'm sorry I'm late."

Bianca smiled. "That's quite alright. We've just finished our introductions, so why don't you tell us your name and a little bit about yourself before we get started."

The woman glanced nervously around the room. No one noticed, but her gaze faltered on Freddie before turning her attention to the moderator. "I'm Tasha Darden," she said.

"Are you a writer, Tasha?" Bianca asked.

Tasha smiled. "Not yet. Not officially, but I've got some great stories in my head that I desperately need to share."

Bianca's eyes twinkled. "Thank you, Tasha. And welcome."

14

Yes, Lord! Phyllis was beginning to feel like her old self again. She leaned back in her new leather chair, behind her new mahogany desk, in her new corner office with the picturesque mountain views, curtailing the urge to growl like the queen of the corporate jungle that she was.

Phyllis closed her eyes and imagined that the conversation must've gone something like this:

VP Jeff Lang: "Phyllis Neville has single-handedly managed to keep the western regional division afloat and thriving in the midst of this goddamned recession. She has consistently earned more revenue than any three senior account managers combined, and I don't care what you have to do, Ruddy. Promise her the moon and stars if you have to, but I want that woman back on board here at Skyland Advertising, and I want her on board now!"

Muddy Ruddy (turning a frightening shade of red): "Y-y-yes, Jeff. Right away, Jeff. Whatever you say, Jeff."

As it turned out, Phyllis agreed to withdraw her resignation for something less costly than moons and stars, but not much: prime real estate in the corner office that had been promised to Ruddy; a 20 percent pay increase, and a brand-new title to boot—Director of Strategic Planning, Sales Division. Whoever came up with that shit was a fuckin' genius, and she decided the moment she heard it that she would wear it like a badge of honor.

"Looks good on you."

Phyllis spun around so quickly at the sound of his voice that she nearly fell out of her chair.

Jeff Lang chuckled. "Sorry." He leaned against the door frame, smiling. Or was that a smirk? "I didn't mean to startle you. Deep in thought? Strategy planning, I suppose." Did he just wink?

"Uh . . . yes."

He sauntered into her office and stopped in front of her desk. "This was supposed to be Ruddy's office," he said, leaning slightly toward her. "Did he tell you that?"

Phyllis pretended to shuffle papers on her desk. "He might've mentioned it."

"Some sacrifice on his part." He stared intently at her. "Wouldn't you say?"

Phyllis hadn't become the savvy businesswoman that she was by not knowing how to read between the lines. What he was really trying to say was "So if I gave you this, what are you going to do for me?" But he hadn't been alive long enough to play this game as well as she could. Now was not the time to tell him that, though.

"Well"—she smiled confidently—"we all must make sacrifices sometimes for the greater good, of course."

He gave a slight nod of affirmation. "So we must."

Jeff Lang had played his hand, and now he was looking for Phyllis to play hers. He'd wanted her back and had made her an offer she couldn't refuse. So now what? The question lurked behind that crooked and sly grin of his.

She stood up, smoothed down her skirt, and stared him square in the eyes. "I have always given this company a hundred and fifty percent of my attention, Mr. Lang."

"How many times do I have to remind you to call me Jeff?" He smiled.

Phyllis ignored his juvenile attempt at being The Man. "And I will continue to do so in whatever capacity is needed to see to it that Skyland continues to thrive. I think that my performance this many years should be proof that I am perfectly capable of talking the talk and walking the walk better than anyone in this division. Or are you not quite convinced?"

She dared that fool to argue. *Back down, Junior!* She thought privately. *You don't want none of this.*

The expression on his face darkened, and he suddenly looked older, wiser, and certainly like he knew he'd just been owned—or could be.

"You are appreciated, Ms. Neville."

She smiled. "Call me Phyllis."

As she watched him turn and disappear from her office, Phyllis breathed a deep sigh of relief and shuddered. "Goodness gracious!" she muttered to herself. She reached behind her to find her seat and sat down before her knees gave way. Was she turned on? Yes, she had to admit that she was. That whole puma to puma, animalistic, covert corporate-power-play thing with her new young, handsome boss had made her moist, and Phyllis discovered herself throbbing in places she hadn't throbbed in ages.

"Madam Director." Gail, her administrative assistant, came into her office and held out an express package to her. "This just came for you."

Phyllis snapped out of it, whatever it was. "Thank you, Gail."

"I'm going to go get some coffee. Do you want a cup?"

"Um . . . yeah. Sure. Thanks."

Phyllis used that envelope as a fan after Gail left, until she finally regained her composure. She didn't recognize the return address on the label, but Phyllis shrugged it off and opened it, only to find a smaller, legal-size letter envelope inside. Inside of that was a piece of copy paper folded in thirds. Phyllis unfolded it.

INFANT ABANDONED IN HOSPITAL EMERGENCY ROOM

Phyllis stared numbly at the document she held in her hands. The image on the paper was a photocopy of the actual article and photograph that had run in the *Rocky Mountain News* more than three decades ago. If she didn't know the girls in the photo, she wouldn't have been able to identify any of them, but Phyllis knew each of them because she remembered that night, that moment, as clearly as if it were yesterday.

"Phyllis?" Gail had called out to her several times before Phyllis finally looked at her. "Are you alright?"

No. She was far from alright. She hurried to fold the paper back the way she'd found it and stuffed it in the envelope. Gail had set a cup of hot coffee down in front of her. "Thanks."

The woman stood there looking concerned. "What's wrong?"

Phyllis shook her head. "Nothing. Nothing—thanks for the coffee, Gail."

"Phyllis, you look—"

"I'm fine," she snapped. "Close the door on your way out, please." Phyllis made a feeble attempt to sound apologetic.

After Gail closed the door, a small cry escaped from the back of Phyllis's throat. Her hands shook, and she felt as if someone had kicked her in the gut.

After Gail left, Phyllis hesitantly took the picture from the envelope again and stared at it. The copy was horrible, but she still managed to study each figure in the image until her eyes finally rested on the duffel bag.

"Why can't one of us just hold it?"

"No! Just put it in here!"

"It's a baby! Not sneakers!"

"It'll be easier if we just put it in here."

"I don't like this."

"I know. I know."

She remembered Freddie and Renetta crying buckets. Phyllis had watched them like she watched a scene unfold in a movie. But she didn't recall crying at all. That's not to say that she didn't. She just didn't remember. They'd all been afraid and confused, but for Phyllis, it had been an out-of-body experience that to this day still didn't seem real. Maybe that's why it had been so easy for her to put it behind her. Had it been real, or had it all been just a terrible dream? Obviously, the picture she held in her hands was proof that Phyllis's bad dream was very real.

Who would send her that nonsense? Two faces immediately came to mind—Renetta's and Freddie's. Ever since the reunion they'd been trying to get her to meet with them, to talk, to relive the past, to remember that terrible night and what the three of them had done. Why the hell couldn't they just leave her alone?

It took awhile, but she finally composed herself in time to make her two o'clock meeting. They had another thing coming if they thought they could bully her into seeing either of them. Phyllis had made up her mind that night that she was through with both of those bitches, and she meant it. Now was not the time to turn back the clock and try to get a do-over. They had made their fuckin' bed, and there wasn't anything left to do now and going forward but to lie in it. Phyllis was not going to let either of them be constant reminders to her of a situation gone terribly wrong.

"Hello everyone," she said, smiling as she walked into the conference room and took her seat at the head of the table. "Let's get started, shall we?"

15

❧

Riding Dominick was therapeutic. He had the stamina of a long-distance runner and the patience to match. Tasha closed her eyes and allowed the wave of motion from her hips to carry her away from her worries. She could feel him watching her, but making eye contact with Dominick while she was fucking him was as potent as a marriage proposal to him.

"That's it, baby," he whispered. "Take your time."

A man like Dominick would make some woman a good husband someday. He'd make some kid a great dad. The problem was, he wanted her to be that woman, and he wanted her to have that kid. He wanted her to love the way he loved. But Tasha wasn't the one.

"It's not you, baby," she'd tell him. "It's me."

Dominick placed his hands around her waist and lifted

Tasha off of him, then pushed her facedown on the bed. Instinctively, she raised her ass and spread her thighs, moaning as he entered her from behind. Any other man with a dick as big as his could've hurt her in this position, but Dominick was skilled and careful, and half a dozen strokes into the position, Tasha was on the verge of exploding, and as long as he could lay down the pipe this good, she concluded, as her eyes rolled back in her head, he wasn't about to be dismissed anytime soon.

"Damn, Domin . . . Damn!"

Unlike Tasha, Dominick had a job to get to, and he crawled out of bed just before dawn, careful not to wake her, got dressed, and quietly headed to the bathroom down the hall. Dominick stood over the toilet pissing and thinking about the evening he'd spent with his girl. Yeah, she was going through some things right now, but once she got all this shit straightened out, he was confident that the two of them could work on being together and building a solid foundation that would last until they were both old and gray.

Tasha had commitment issues. She'd told him that when they first met, and now he understood why. She'd been abandoned by her mother, which was some toxic shit. For real. He had to be patient with her, though. Since she never learned how to accept and love someone unconditionally, he needed to be the one to teach her that nothing or no one could make him change how he felt for her. Dominick loved hard—he would never deny that—and he loved deep. He loved her more than she could know what to do with, but he'd be the exception to her rule, show her that love wasn't something to turn your back on. He was there for the duration, for as long as she needed him. He was there.

"Tasha. Tasha, wake up."

"Mmmmm," she moaned, stretching luxuriously and smiling at Dominick standing in the doorway of her room. "I thought you left. What's up?"

He walked over to the bed and dropped photos and printed copy paper on top of her. "What the fuck have you been doing?" he asked, staring at her like she was crazy.

Tasha sat up in bed, turned on the lamp next to the bed, and stared in horror at the mess he'd made of her things.

"What is all this?" He stood over her like the police over some goddamned body. "Pictures . . ." He flipped through the papers he'd strewn across her. "Fuckin' driving records, birth records, addresses—you got a damn shrine in that room, Tasha! That shit don't make no motha-fuckin' sense! Are you following those women? You stalking them?"

Hot, angry tears swelled in her eyes. Tasha's hands began to shake uncontrollably as she stared at all of her hard work that had been ripped down from her walls and tossed carelessly into this pile on her lap. "What did you do?" she found the voice to ask.

"No!" he said, defiantly. "What did *you* do? This is crazy, girl!" He made the mistake of sitting down on the bed next to her. "Tasha," he said, trying to sound calm, "baby, you can't do this to yourself. Have you even spoken to any of these women? Have you tried calling to even ask which one of them is your mother?"

The veins on the sides of her neck pulsed. She had put it all together. She had spent days, weeks painstakingly piecing together the puzzles of these women's lives. Tasha was beginning to know them, intimately, without so much as ever saying a word to any of them. And she'd done it so that she would know, maybe without ever even having to ask, which of them had been the woman who'd given her life. She'd done it so that when the day came that she walked up to any one of those women, she wouldn't have to ask the question, "Are you my real mother?" She wanted to be the one to walk up to that bitch, whoever she was, look her dead in the eyes, and say, "You are my mother." And this motha-fucka right here, had the nerve to put his hands on her shit? To fuck with her life? She slowly raised her eyes to meet his.

"I know this isn't easy for you, baby," he said tenderly. She heard the sound of his voice, watched his lips move, saw something in his eyes akin to sympathy. But none of it mattered. None of it registered. "You're torturing yourself for no reason, Tash. You're making this harder than it has to be."

Harder than it had to be. Dominick's dumb ass had no idea how hard this shit was. He couldn't possibly understand what she was going through.

"Just ask them," he said, softly. "Which one of you is the woman who had me? Just ask, Tasha."

They were all her mothers. Since the day Miss Lucy first showed her that picture, Tasha had envisioned that all of them, any of them, at one time or another had been the woman who'd had her. And when she ran out of fantasies for one, she moved on to the next one, until in time, she realized that it didn't even matter, because they had all been there that day, they had all left her there and walked away without giving a damn about her.

Dominick made the mistake of touching her. "If you need me to be there with you when you confront them, Tash . . ."

Rage!

She leaped through space and time and landed naked on top of Dominick, stunned and on his back on the floor. "How dare you put your hands on my things!" she screamed and growled, slapping and scratching at his face, pulling viciously on the collar of his shirt. "It's my shit! Mine, Dominick! Don't ever . . . touch my shit! Motha-fucka! Don't ever . . ."

"Tasha!" He called her name several times, but she only heard it once.

Tasha was livid and Dominick had overstayed his welcome.

16

⤡

"What do you mean, you don't have my reservation?"

The young woman behind the counter turned a frightening crimson color as Phyllis glared at her. "I-I'm sorry, ma'am," she said, sheepishly and visibly shaking in her shoes. "I can't seem to find your name in our—"

Phyllis had been anticipating this appointment all day and had rushed straight over from work. Clad in an ivory

Armani pantsuit and Manolo Blahnik sling-back snakeskin pumps, she looked as expensive as any diva would who could afford to spend a small fortune at a spa. Phyllis folded her arms and drilled a steely gaze into the girl. "I made this appointment seven months ago," she insisted, angrily.

The woman looked confused. "But we've only been open for four months."

"Seven months, four months! What's the difference and where the hell is my masseuse?"

Pastel Petals Spa was the hottest ticket in town right now. It was expensive and exclusive and hard as hell to get into, and this heffa had the nerve to lose her reservation!

She was about to raise holy hell in this place when the manager finally showed up. "Is there a problem?" The woman stared at Phyllis like she was a slug that had just crawled out from underneath a rock.

"I can't seem to find—" the receptionist started to say.

Phyllis interrupted. "I made a reservation months ago," she said, after taking a deep breath and putting her sistah-girl vibe on check. If this cow wanted to go toe-to-toe with Phyllis, then she would come at her in a way she understood: Calmly, professionally, and as cool as a frozen daiquiri. "Your assistant here says it's not in the system."

The woman took over the computer to look for Phyllis's reservation herself. "Your name?"

"Phyllis Neville."

After a few minutes, the woman looked at Phyllis and smiled apologetically. "I'm sorry, but you're not in the system. Perhaps you'd like to reschedule?"

Fuck rescheduling! "Reschedule?" Phyllis responded too calmly, clenching her jaws.

The manager checked the computer again. "We could get you in as early as November."

It was July.

"And we can put you on our waiting list," she said smugly. "We would contact you in the event of a cancellation."

Phyllis was just about to jump over that counter and get all Armageddon on that woman, when the gods stepped in and intervened.

"Phyllis?"

She recognized the voice but she didn't dare break the steely gaze she had going on with that platinum-haired, overpaid pit bull.

"Is that you?" Renetta stood next to her all of a sudden, and Phyllis couldn't help but turn to her.

"Renetta," she said simply. Could this day possibly get any worse?

Renetta suddenly made the whole situation awkward, stretched out her arms and wrapped them around Phyllis. "I can't believe it!" she said, elated. "How are you?"

Phyllis tensed up and took a deep breath. "Fine, Renetta." She glanced at the woman. "I'm fine."

"I called a few times." Renetta's expression turned serious. "Did you get my messages?"

"I've been busy." The undeniable twinge of a migraine was coming on. Now was not the time for rescheduling seaweed wraps or shooting the shit with Renetta. She'd had a very trying day and a very long week, and it took every ounce of self-control she could muster not to lay into Renetta and this other broad right here in this reception area.

"Have you been here before?" Renetta asked, sensing that dark force that was Phyllis Neville rising like the phoenix.

"As a matter of fact," Phyllis said coolly, "this was supposed to be my first time." She glared at the manager glaring back at her. "But somehow, they seemed to have lost my reservation and are trying to convince me to reschedule." She smiled wickedly.

"Just until November," the woman corrected her.

"Whatever!" Phyllis winced. She took a deep breath and turned her attention back to Renetta. "It was good seeing you again," she lied as she started to leave.

Without thinking, Renetta reached out and gently took hold of her arm. Phyllis turned to stone. "Laura," Renetta said to the manager, quickly letting go of Phyllis's arm. Renetta smiled apologetically. "I'm sure you can make an exception this one time. Phyllis is a very dear friend of mine, and I'd really appreciate it if you could accommodate her today."

Phyllis looked at Renetta, and then she looked at good old Laura, who seemed to shrink about five inches right before Phyllis's eyes. Her smile faded, and the vivid and tumultuous blue in her eyes faded quietly to a dull, lifeless gray.

"Of course, Renetta," she agreed quietly. The woman cleared her throat, and then addressed Phyllis. "What services had you reserved for today, Ms. Neville?" she asked politely.

Phyllis almost couldn't speak; she was so stunned at the transformation. "A facial, manicure, pedicure, and deep-tissue massage."

A part of her wanted to get the hell out of that place and as far away from Renetta as she could, but Phyllis didn't budge. The thought of that massage made her mouth water.

"And please have them use the geranium bourbon essential oil for her massage," Renetta added. She looked at Phyllis.

"You'll love it, girl. It smells great and has a wonderful balancing affect on your skin and emotions." She winked. "Relieves stress and anxiety—oh, and wards off mosquitoes too."

"Yes, Renetta," the manager responded meekly. "Shawna," she said, addressing the receptionist, "will you escort Ms. Neville to room three?"

Shawna nodded and smiled weakly at Phyllis. "Please follow me, Ms. Neville."

Phyllis turned to Renetta, who was smiling broadly back at her. "Thank you, Renetta," she said, mustering up all the sincerity she could manage, which wasn't much.

"Anytime, Phyllis." Renetta smiled again. "Enjoy."

Phyllis's massage had been heaven-sent. Every muscle in her body had been transformed from concrete to a soft gelatin, renewed and relaxed. She leaned back against the wall in the small room, closed her eyes, and savored the half-hour visit in the steam room, waiting until someone came and got her for her pedicure. She'd almost drifted off to sleep when the door opened and in walked a tall and willowy apparition, as graceful as a swan. The long, beautiful bird slowly dropped her towel, sat across from Phyllis, inhaled deeply, and let out a melodious sigh. Moments later, Phyllis let her heavy eyelids close, and willed herself to drift away again on the sea of tranquility.

"Hello, Phyllis," the beautiful bird screeched.

Phyllis opened one eye and then the other, gradually emerging from her coma-induced Swedish massage and intoxicating and mind-erasing mentholated steam. She stared until the lovely swan materialized into Renetta.

She had spent the last hour and a half trying to forget that Renetta was even in the building, and until that moment, she'd done a pretty good job. *Whatever happened to fat Renetta?* she wondered, willing the woman to vanish in the fog of mist in the room. *Whatever happened to dumpy, frumpy, humpty Renetta?* Phyllis decided on the spot that she liked that Renetta so much better than this one.

Renetta smiled and then leaned back against the wall and sighed. "Girl, isn't this just heavenly? I tell you, this place is worth every single penny I spend here, and it is such a coincidence, us meeting here like this."

Phyllis's gelatin-soft muscles swelled rigid again, as she resisted the temptation to reach out and slap the skin off of Renetta. "Is it?" she asked, sharply.

Renetta turned her innocent gaze to Phyllis.

"Is it a coincidence, Renetta?"

"What are you trying to say, Phyllis?"

"I'm not *trying* to say anything," she said, sitting up slowly. "I *am* saying that I really don't appreciate the little bullshit games you and Freddie have decided to play."

"Games? What—games?"

Phyllis rubbed her temples hard enough to drill holes into the sides of her head. "You know what I'm talking about," she muttered, agitated.

"I don't."

"This!" she snapped. "This with you who just happens to be here when I'm here. The reunion? I haven't been to a reunion since ever, and the one time I decide to go, you and Freddie both show up?"

Renetta couldn't help but laugh. "It was our high school reunion, too, Phyllis. And we did get invitations."

Phyllis ignored reason. "And then here you are today, just in time to save the day for poor old Phyllis." She twisted her lips and said in a mocking voice, "I'm sure you can make an exception, Laura. And use the geranium oil for her massage."

"I was trying to help."

"Ever since that damn reunion you've been blowing up my damn phone, trying to get me to join in some fuckin' lovefest with you and Freddie so that the three of us can relive the good old days!"

"To talk to you, Phyllis. To catch up on—"

"To talk about shit I'd just as soon forget and that the two of you should leave the hell alone," Phyllis argued.

"See, that's always been your MO," Renetta reasoned. "You never could handle pressure, Phyllis. You never could deal with anything that wasn't perfect and pleasant and didn't revolve around you!"

"Yeah, well I certainly don't want to deal with you and Freddie, Renetta! Damn! It was thirty years ago!"

"And we never talked about it then, Phyllis. We never said a word to each other about it after it happened."

"And?"

"And we should've!"

"For what?" Phyllis asked, exasperated. "It happened. We did it! We did that, Renetta, and then we got the fuck on with our lives like we were supposed to. So now, you and Freddie want to get together and play Let's-See-Who-Can-Be-the-Biggest-Martyr? Let it go, Renetta! Let it go!"

Renetta sat back and shook her head. "You haven't changed one bit. You were always so fuckin' selfish, Phyllis, and—"

Phyllis put her hand up between her and Renetta, warning her to stop. "Don't go there."

"You never cared about anybody but yourself," Renetta continued, ignoring Phyllis's warning. "You never gave a damn about me or Freddie, unless somehow, some way helping us helped you."

Phyllis was irate. "Oh, I'm the selfish one!" She glared back at Renetta, fuming that Renetta would say something like that. She gathered her towel around her and marched over to the door, stopping just short of leaving. "If you and Freddie want to spend the rest of your lives buddying up and dwelling on what happened that night, that's up to you. But leave me out of it, Renetta. It's not my kind of party."

"It bothers you like it still bothers us, Phyllis," Renetta said softly, knowing that getting through to Phyllis wasn't going to happen now or later. The woman had her mind made up, and Phyllis was as stubborn as they came.

"Stop following me," Phyllis said. "Stop calling me. And stop sending shit to my office."

Renetta looked at her, confused.

"What are you talking about?"

Phyllis rolled her eyes. "Like you don't know."

"I don't. I haven't sent anything to your office, Renetta. I don't even know where you work."

"You know you've never been good at lying," Phyllis said smartly.

"Then you should know I'm not lying. Why would I send you anything?"

"Look, I'm just saying stop it. Alright? Keep your paraphernalia to yourself, because seeing that picture isn't going to change my mind about getting together with you and Freddie over mojitos for a group pity party."

"What picture, Phyllis? I don't know what you're talking about."

Phyllis studied Renetta for a few moments. Looking at her now, Phyllis was starting to see that some things never did change. Renetta wasn't lying.

"The picture they published of us in the newspaper. The one of us . . . after they found . . . You didn't send it?"

Renetta shook her head. "No. I swear I didn't. That would've been cruel."

"Well, if it wasn't you, then it had to have been Freddie," Phyllis quickly concluded.

"I don't think she'd do something like that."

"You tell your friend that I said to leave me alone."

"But Freddie wouldn't do that."

"Tell that cow to stop harassing me before she regrets that she ever even knew my name."

Phyllis left abruptly before Renetta could say another word.

Renetta hadn't seen the photo taken of the three of them since it was published in the paper. She would never had sent something like that to Phyllis and she doubted seriously that Freddie had sent it either, but someone had. And if it wasn't either of them, then . . . *Where would a person even find that old clipping?* she wondered uneasily. *And why?*

17

❧

Boris tapped lightly on her bedroom door before entering. "Renetta," he whispered. He sat on the side of her bed and touched her lightly on the shoulder. "Time to wake up, sweetie. The girls are arriving and getting into hair and makeup, and the photographers are on their way."

It was four-thirty in the morning, and she so appreciated the gentle way he had of waking her. She pressed her hand to his cheek and smiled. "Thank you, dear Boris."

Renetta hadn't slept a wink all night, tossing and turning and repeating the conversation she'd had with Phyllis over and over again in her head.

"*. . . And stop sending shit to my office . . . the one published in the paper of the three of us. . . .*"

The *Rocky Mountain News* had published the article about the baby abandoned at Denver General Hospital three days after they'd left her there. Renetta had seen the article one afternoon after she'd gotten home from school when she'd glanced at the newspaper left on the kitchen table by her father. He'd read that paper, and he'd seen that picture, and the thought that he'd seen it and probably recognized her in it made her physically sick to her stomach. She spent the rest of the night waiting anxiously for him to come home and confront her about what she'd done, but he didn't come home that night. And when she saw him the next day, he never said a word.

"I haven't sent anything to Phyllis," Freddie said earnestly over the phone when Renetta called her after seeing Phyllis at the spa. "I don't even know where she works."

"Me, either," Renetta said, despondently.

"Who would've done something like that, Renetta?"

"I don't have a clue."

The house was buzzing with activity by the time Renetta slipped into her red velour sweatsuit. Ten girls had been brought in to model for the fall catalog, along with two hairstylists and two makeup artists, including Boris.

"Good morning, Renetta," Tiffany, a young redhead, said, hurrying past her on her way to the wardrobe room.

"Slow down, sweetie," Renetta chimed back. "We've got all day." Renetta made her way into the kitchen, following the scent of freshly brewed coffee. "Thank you, Boris," she said, sending him her spiritual appreciation for knowing that she wasn't worth a damn without her java in the morning.

"Renetta." Stacy, a twenty-two-year-old mocha-complexioned, beautiful wonder, found Renetta in the kitchen.

"Yes, dear."

"I have to leave by eleven," she said, anxiously. "I have a biology test to make up, and—"

Stacy had a way of letting the stresses of life get to her much too easily for someone so young. Renetta patted her shoulder. "That's fine, Stacy," Renetta reassured her. "We'll just make sure to shoot you first so that you can get out of here in time."

"Thank you," she said, sincerely. "You're the best, Renetta."

"Morning, Renetta!" Tawny, a curvaceous biracial girl-child, flew into the kitchen, grabbed a chocolate-glazed do-nut off the serving tray, poured herself a glass of milk, and disappeared as quickly as she'd come in. "See ya, Renetta!"

God was good. These girls might not have come from her body, but they were her children, even if just for a little while. Her home was their home. When she shopped for groceries, she bought enough food with them in mind. They stopped by to do their laundry, to eat, sometimes to sleep. She was their friend, and in a way even she couldn't explain, their surrogate mother, especially to those who had mothers in some other part of the world.

Renetta's forty-five-hundred-square-foot home was sepa-rated into her workspace and her living space, which was her upstairs bedroom with a sitting room and a master bath. Downstairs were her kitchen, of course, and her beloved lanai, out back. Her expansive living room, with its large picturesque windows and high ceilings, had been purposely left open and was used as the main shooting stage for her online catalog. Filled with luxurious chaise lounges, white silk curtains, faux fur, a sexy fireplace, and a crystal antique chandelier, the room was a blank canvas that could easily be transformed to suit any season, any clothing line, any theme, at any given time. Visitors who were unfamiliar to Renetta's business found it odd, but her girls loved it.

"Where do you want us to set up, Ren?" Marco, the photographer, asked in his thick Italian accent.

"We'll start in the southwest corner of the room, Marco," she said, authoritatively. Renetta was wide awake now, and it was time to get down to the business of shooting her cata-log's new season.

They started shooting at six in the morning, right on schedule. She believed in promptness, because time was money and Marco was expensive. They were well into shooting when a knock came at the door. Renetta was positioning Stacy on the leopard-print chaise when two policemen followed a scantily clad Tawny into the room.

"Um, Renetta," Tawny said, oblivious to the fact that the two men behind her couldn't take their eyes off of her, "cops are here again."

"I'll be right with you, officers," she said, fidgeting with Stacy's hair.

She stepped back and admired her work. "Perfect," she said, admiringly. "Shoot it, Marco."

The two policemen were so busy admiring the girls that they didn't even noticed Renetta coming up to them. "Yes, gentlemen."

She'd been through this drill enough times to know what this was about. These two fellows were new, though. She hadn't seen them before. But Renetta wasn't worried. She had her paperwork in order, and she wasn't breaking any laws.

"We've uh . . . ," the taller one started to say, but then got sidetracked when Amy, a petite blonde, strutted passed them both, wearing a white lace push-up bra, thong, and red stiletto heels.

"Yes?" Renetta asked again.

The other officer cleared his throat and tried to compose himself. "We've got a complaint from someone in the neighborhood about suspicious activities going on here, Ms.—"

"Jones. Renetta Jones."

"This is your place of residence?" the taller one finally composed himself enough to ask.

"Yes, it is," she responded. "And my place of business."

"What uh . . . ," his eyes wandered off again. "What kind of business?"

"I run an online retail business, officer," she explained. "And we're shooting our fall catalog this morning. I hope we weren't being too loud. We did start rather early."

"Well, uh . . . one of your neighbors seems to think you're running some kind of . . . I don't know . . . brothel, for lack of a better term." He blushed.

Renetta shook her head. "No. No brothel here, officer." Renetta chuckled. "Look, I have a business license and permits posted on the wall behind you, as required by the city. I live in a district zoned for businesses like mine, and if you'd like, I'll even give you a tour of the place and my Web site address, if it'll set your mind at ease."

After they made a quick inspection of her permits and business license, Renetta offered the policemen a cup of coffee, donuts, and front-row seats to the photo shoot, which they greatly appreciated, even though they didn't come out and say it. The looks on their faces spoke volumes. The young women working for her got a kick out of the whole thing and really put on a show for them, which Renetta appreciated because she managed to get some phenomenal shots from their enthusiasm.

An hour later, the two gentlemen thanked her for her hospitality, apologized for any inconvenience they might have caused, and headed back to their squad car.

Ian and Claudia Johansson, Renetta's neighbors, stood on their front porch in their robes and slippers as one of the officers walked over to their house.

"You're not arresting any of them?" Claudia blurted out, agitated.

"No laws were broken, ma'am," he said professionally.

"She's got women running around in bras and panties and men showing up at all hours of the night, and you stand there and tell me that something illegal isn't going on over in that house?"

"I assure you, ma'am," he sighed, "there is nothing illegal going on in Ms. Jones's residence. Now"—the officer smiled condescendingly—"you folks have a nice day."

Renetta quietly materialized as the officer was leaving.

"Sorry again for the inconvenience, ma'am," he said, smiling.

Renetta nodded. "You're just doing your job, officer," she said, smiling back. "Have a nice day."

Ian shook his head and disappeared inside the house. Claudia started to follow him, but the smug expression on that woman's face refused to let her. She marched toward Renetta with her arms folded defensively across her.

She stood toe-to-toe with Renetta, her head no higher than Renetta's shoulder. Claudia snarled. "I don't know what kind of power you have over the police," Claudia said, clenching her teeth. "But if they won't do anything about you and what you're doing, I'm sure the homeowners' association will."

"It's just business," Renetta responded softly. "I assure you, dear, there's nothing illegal—or immoral—going on in my house."

"I will not have my children grow up around that filth!"

"Filth?" Renetta asked, offended. "What filth?"

"I know prostitutes when I see them!"

"My girls are not prostitutes, Mrs. Johansson," she responded calmly.

"Oh, stop it with that condescending tone!" Claudia loathed this woman. "I'm not an idiot! I know you're selling sex or making porn or—"

Renetta laughed and stared down her nose at the near-hysterical woman. "So, I'm a pimp? Me? I've been called many things in my life, but never a pimp."

Claudia studied this woman. She was lovely but much older than Claudia. She could've been a model when she was younger. This woman was probably someone's mother, maybe even someone's grandmother. And gradually Claudia was beginning to feel a tiny hint of embarrassment.

"Well if it walks like a duck and talks like a duck . . ."

"I must be pimping ducks then," Renetta chided. "Is that what you're trying to say?"

Claudia clenched her teeth and glared at Renetta. "You can play your silly little games all you want, Ms. Jones. But you mark my words: I will not allow that disgusting business of yours to thrive in my neighborhood, where I raise my children. One way or another, I will see you hauled off by the police."

Renetta watched as the woman disappeared inside her house, and then she turned and headed back inside her own. She hadn't broken any laws with her business, and her neighbor's threat, as far as that was concerned, fell on deaf ears.

The woman was close to fifty. The sun had just barely settled in the morning sky. She wore no makeup, had a house filled with people, had been harassed by the cops and her neighbors, and Renetta still looked like she'd just stepped out of the pages of a fashion magazine.

Tasha watched her come outside her house and charm the badges off of those cops and put her neighbor lady in check with the grace of a queen. Renetta was an anomaly. She looked absolutely too good to be true, too flawless to be real, and everyone around her, with the exception of her neighbor, seemed as drawn to her, as mesmerized by her, as Tasha, like a bee to honey.

Tasha sat parked outside Renetta's house for several minutes, waiting and watching, before finally turning the key in the ignition and pulling away from the curb.

Avery watched her drive off. He'd been sitting on that bench in the park across the street from Ms. Jones's place of residence for the last hour, curious to see what Tasha Darden was up to and a bit anxious to satisfy some questions of his own. Renetta Jones was an interesting woman, to say the least, gorgeous and Tasha had seemed to be entranced by the woman, but then, wasn't he? Ms. Jones was breathtaking.

18

❧

Freddie was busy in her office reviewing the court's docket when her husband, Don, called. "How's my favorite wife doing?" he asked jovially.

Freddie rolled her eyes. "Better than the rest of all your other wives, I suppose."

"I'm glad to hear it, baby," he joked. "If I have to keep

one of them happy, it might as well be you. You know it's hard being a playa."

She sighed. "You have my sympathies, honey. You know I'm busy, Don."

"To everybody else, you're busy. But not to daddy."

She laughed. "Why are you calling me?"

"I forgot to kiss your cheek this morning before I left."

"*Hmpf!* You did, and I had planned on talking to you about that when I got home, too."

"No need." He made a wet, kissing sound over the phone. "There. Did you get it?"

"Now that hit the spot," she said, fondly.

After all these years, they still had their moments. From the second she first laid eyes on him, Freddie always knew that he'd be the one she'd grow old with. They'd been together off and on since she was in middle school, and except for an occasional fantasy of Denzel Washington or Billy Dee Williams, the thought of being with any other man never crossed her mind.

"I got about twenty dollars on me," he continued over the phone. "Why don't you let me take you out tonight after we get off work?"

"Twenty dollars?" Freddie grimaced. "Man! Where you going to take me for twenty lousy dollars?"

"Since when did this relationship start being about money?" he asked, pretending to be offended. "I thought you loved me for my doggy style."

She laughed. "Yeah, it ain't bad. But twenty dollars ain't buying more than a couple of Happy Meals, Don. You know how I've never been a cheap date."

He sighed. "Steak and lobster?"

"Yes."

"Okay. Then lemme go over here to this club, do a few pole dances to pick up a few more bills."

"Call me when you get through," she teased.

"You'd better be ready to put out when it's all said and done, girl," he commanded playfully. "I mean it. I'm going to be taking my pill before we leave, so I'll be good and ready for a nice long night, Freddie."

She sighed. "I told you that you don't need that Viagra, sweetie." Yes, he did.

"Yes, I do," he retorted. "Sometimes, a man's gotta do what a man's gotta do, darling. And believe me, Viagra has saved the dignity and sanity of a whole lotta men, so don't be trying to steal my glory."

"Never, baby."

Her old man read her like a book, and he knew the way to her heart was through slow-smoked jerk chicken, fried plantains, and rice and peas from 8 Rivers Restaurant. Don had his usual stewed oxtails with butter beans. Every now and then, in between filling his mouth with food, he'd glance knowingly across the table at her, nod his head, and wink as if to say, "I know it ain't Saturday night, but—what the hell?"

She chuckled. "You take your pill?"

He shook his head. "Decided I didn't need it."

Freddie couldn't help but laugh.

Don studied her for a moment before finally deciding to ask, "So, you wanna tell me what's been going on with you lately?"

Freddie looked surprised. "What?"

"I'm asking you. You been acting funny, moodier than usual. Is it the change?"

She stared at him, trying to figure out if he was joking or if he was actually being serious. It was hard to tell. Freddie rolled her eyes and shook her head.

Don heroically continued. "Cause from what I hear, female hormonal problems can wreak all kinds of havoc on women. Make you crazy and irrational." He used his hands to emphasize crazy and irrational.

"No, but you're about to make me crazy and irrational if you don't shut up and eat."

"I'm just saying, baby," he put down his utensils, which meant he was serious. "I'm worried about you, that's all. You seem like you got something on your mind, and, well, you know I'm here if you need to talk about it. We ain't never had nothing between us that we couldn't talk about, Freddie."

This was it. Freddie felt it down to the core that this was that moment in time, that perfect opportunity that she'd avoided so many times in the past—or ignored—to tell her husband the truth. She'd come close to telling him before, but then something would happen to stop her, like the phone would ring or the kids would start fighting or crying about one thing or another. Don was her best friend. She'd trusted him with her life, and looking at him now, she couldn't help but wonder why she hadn't told him about that night when she and her two high school friends had done the unthinkable. She almost melted in her seat, awed by the love for her and concern for whatever was bothering her coming from his eyes.

"Spit it out, baby," he said, tenderly reaching across the

table to take her hand in his. "Just say it, Freddie. Whatever it is, we'll work through it like we've always done."

Freddie realized then and there that there was no easy way to tell him about what had happened, and she realized that even though he might judge her harshly at first, Don would eventually try to understand. And she knew without a doubt that he'd never stop loving her no matter how angry or disappointed hearing the truth would make him.

"Well, isn't this romantic?" Don Jr., DJ, suddenly appeared out of nowhere as if by magic and stood next to their table with the flavor of the week trying her best to look as happy to see Freddie and Don as their son was.

"Hey, boy!" Don bolted to his feet and hugged the kid like he hadn't seen him in years.

"You getting your mack on, old man?" The boy laughed and teased.

Don laughed too. "Sit down, son. Let me teach you a few things about macking."

DJ leaned down and kissed Freddie on the cheek. "Hey, beautiful."

Her children always did have perfect timing, she concluded, relieved and disappointed at the same time. It was almost as if they knew when she was in dire straits and needed rescuing.

"Sit down, baby," she said, patting the seat beside her. "You two join us for dinner. Your father's treat," she winked at Don, who suddenly looked blindsided.

The girl looked pissed but pretended not to be. On the other side, DJ's face lit up at the invitation, and all of a sudden, that boy looked ten years old again to Freddie.

The night went on without a hitch or a confession. Freddie conveniently forgot to remind Don of their conversation before DJ and his girlfriend showed up at the restaurant, and Don forgot all about it. But later, after they got home, he did remember his original intentions for that romantic dinner and followed through like a champ.

"Mmmmmm, baby girl," he moaned in her ear.

Don made his best love when he was close and not in a hurry to turn over and go to sleep. He lay on top of her, his hands underneath her behind, cupping her booty, pushing rhythmically in and out of her with movements as controlled and fluid as a well-oiled machine, talking dirty in her ear: "Is this mine, girl? Say my name, baby. Call it out. Tell me who it belongs to."

"It's yours, daddy."

"Give it to me, then. Give it to me good."

She smiled, knowing that giving it to him good was the only way she could give it to him.

19

"Abby," Phyllis said cheerfully into her cell phone, as she hurried toward the elevators down the hall from her office. "Yes, I'm on my way down. Just meet me in the lobby, dear. Two minutes."

"Phyllis." Jeff Lang almost bumped into Phyllis as he stepped out of the elevators.

"Jeff," she replied cordially. Since her promotion, the two of them hadn't seen much of each other, which was fine by Phyllis. Sure, the man was her boss, but she was still in charge of running her own show, and the new job title he'd bestowed upon her only solidified that fact. "How was New York?"

"Bustling," he said, impatiently. "I need to meet with you this afternoon," he said, brushing passed her.

Shit! "After lunch?" she said, smiling.

"I'm free for half an hour at three. Have Alice put you down on my schedule."

He wasn't watching where he was going and accidently bumped into a woman behind him. "Excuse me! I'm sorry."

"No, I'm sorry," she said and smiled. "It was my fault."

He'd never seen her before, and if he had, surely he'd have remembered. This woman was gorgeous, soft brown eyes, a heart-shaped mouth, and stunning figure, long and curved, that was reminiscent of the Halle Berry figure he coveted so much.

The woman hurried past him and managed to step into the elevator just before the doors closed.

Phyllis was behind her, less than a foot away and close enough for Tasha to smell her perfume. It took everything inside her not to turn and stare. She'd never been this close to the woman before. Tasha had seen her from a distance, carrying herself like royalty, head held high, shoulders back, impeccably dressed, Phyllis Whittaker or Neville looked every bit the top-level executive that she was.

Tasha got off the elevator first and stepped aside, lingering and pretending to search through her purse long enough to let Phyllis pass. She made sure to stay a few steps behind the woman, until Phyllis stopped in the middle of the lobby and spread her arms wide and waited, smiling, as a young woman walked into them and the two embraced.

"Hey, baby!" Phyllis said elatedly.

"Hi, Mom," the girl responded, embarrassed but happy.

"I've missed you so much."

"I've missed you too, but can we go eat? I'm feeling a bit queasy."

Phyllis wore a different kind of smug these days along with her Prada business suits. The new phrase coined for her and printed with the likeness of her image—"valuable asset"—had taken on new meaning, and as Ruddy came to learn too quickly, once he realized she was no longer a member of his team, he had very little to say to her anymore, which was as it should be, as far as she was concerned. Ruddy had never been more to Phyllis than a cockroach, standing between her and corporate superstardom.

Sitting next to her daughter at a small bistro around the corner from where she worked, Phyllis dove with reckless abandon into her spinach, strawberry, and walnut salad with raspberry vinaigrette dressing. "They figured it out." She stuffed a forkful of salad into her mouth. "They knew that if I left, my accounts would leave with me, and that's the last thing they wanted. I've made them millions, literally millions, baby girl." She stopped long enough to take a sip of her iced tea. "The Vista Cable account—I won that account, and landing that one helped put the whole western regional division on the map for this company, raising the bar and setting the standards for every other division in Skyland, which no one else has even come close to meeting," she explained passionately.

She'd been going on and on like that ever since she and Abby sat down to eat in the restaurant, and not once had she mentioned the baby. But then, that's how her mother was. For as long as Abby could remember, Phyllis had always been about the business of Phyllis. Abby's father had experienced it firsthand, and Abby had watched her parents' marriage fall apart because of it. As a kid, the only time she could seem to get her mother's attention was if she was sick or had done something wrong. But this time she hadn't done anything wrong and wasn't sick. She was just pregnant, that's all, and it sure would've been nice to have her mother's support at a time like this.

"Ruddy can't stand knowing that he's not my boss anymore," Phyllis continued. "I wouldn't be surprised if he decided to leave, girl." She laughed bitterly. "He lived to ride me like a pony and take credit for my achievements, and now that he can't, he spends all day long walking around in circles, trying to find new ways to prove that they need him."

"Mom," Abby finally interrupted, "you haven't even mentioned the baby."

Phyllis paused slightly for a moment and then continued eating, almost as if the girl hadn't said the B-word.

"I'm three months pregnant, Mom, in case you were wondering." Abby didn't bother trying to hide her disappointment. "I go in for an ultrasound next week, and I was hoping you'd come with me."

Finally Phyllis put down her fork, wiped her mouth, and sat back and stared at her daughter. "And where's Ricky, Abigail?" She asked, knowing the answer before she'd even asked it. Ricky was Abby's so-called man. She'd dropped out of college for Ricky so that she could work and help him get his music business off the ground. Ricky was a wannabe producer with big ideas, big expenses, and no money. But he had what he needed in Abby. He had a fool too in love with him to see straight and capable of twisting herself into a figure eight if it meant making him happy.

Abby's eyes averted her mother's gaze. "This isn't about Ricky," she said dismally.

"I thought the two of you were planning on getting married?"

Abby shrugged and sank deeper into her seat. "Maybe not. Ricky's not—" Abby shifted uncomfortably. "We broke up."

"Before or after you told him you were pregnant?" Phyllis asked matter-of-factly.

"Does it matter?" Abby stared at her mother. Tears filled her eyes. "I'm a grown woman, Mom. I don't need Ricky. I never did."

Phyllis looked at the girl like she was crazy. "This is a fine time to see the light, Abby." She wanted to take it back as soon as she said it, but it was too late. The damage was done, and once again, her Mother of the Year card was probably going to be revoked. "Is he going to help you with this child?" she asked, more sympathetically this time.

"He couldn't even help himself," Abby said sadly. "Let's face it, Mom: This is something I'm going to have to do on my own."

"Does your father know?"

Abby sighed. "Yeah. I told him and he's about as excited about this as you are."

"It's not that we aren't excited, Abby—" Phyllis started to say.

"But you think I'm making a mistake," Abby angrily interrupted. "You think I'm being impulsive and stupid and that the best thing I could've done, besides getting pregnant in the first place, is to have an abortion. Is that it, Mother?" Tears streamed down the girl's face, and Phyllis suddenly felt horrible.

"Keep your voice down, sweetheart," she said, ashamed. Pregnant women and emotions and unsympathetic mothers didn't mesh well. "Fuck you, Mother!" Abby burst into tears and threw her napkin across the table. Then after a minute: "I didn't mean that," Abby said sheepishly.

Phyllis stared blankly at her daughter. It took a few moments for the "Fuck you, Mother" part to register, but eventually it did, and Phyllis wrestled internally with how she should handle the situation. Should she, one: Bend her over her knee and whip her ass the way she'd done when the kid was six? Two: Slap her hard across the face the same way she would any grown woman who'd spoken to her like that? Or three: Dare to empathize with the girl, apologize profusely, promise to be more understanding, and tell her that the kid could call her Nana in lieu of Grandma?

The feeble part of her that did know how to mother surfaced in the knick of time, as Phyllis reached across the table to rest a comforting hand on top of Abby's. "If you ever talk to me like that again, I'll kill you," she said, calmly.

"I know," Abby said, smirking.

"Let me know when and where, and I'll be there for the ultrasound."

Abby pulled away and tried to smile. "You mean it?"

Phyllis thought for a moment. "You sure Ricky can't go?"

Her daughter rolled her eyes.

"Yes," Phyllis added reluctantly. "I'll be there."

She didn't want to be a grandmother! *I don't want to be a grandmother! I don't want to be a . . .*

"Can I get you anything else?"

Tasha stared at Phyllis Neville and her daughter from across the room, a few tables over, as if she were watching a movie.

"Miss," the waitress asked again, "do you need anything else?"

Tasha finally sighed. "No. Just the check please."

20

❦

Timing is everything. A trip to the grocery store, and a befuddled expression on a man's face in a quandary over produce was all that was needed for an excuse to strike up a conversation.

"Bok choy or cabbage?" he asked, standing there holding one of each in each hand. Avery looked at Renetta Jones. "Bok choy is cabbage. Right?"

Renetta Jones nearly gave him an erection when she smiled. "A type of cabbage. Yes."

He looked even more confused. "Good for coleslaw?"

"I think it's better in stir-fry."

"Can I buy you a drink?" he said, without hesitating.

She tilted her head to the side and stared at him thoughtfully. "Did you just set me up?"

"Only if you say yes," he said confidently.

Twenty minutes later, Avery found himself sitting in a little bar a few blocks away, across from one of the most stunning women he'd ever laid eyes on.

"Cheers," she said, raising her glass of Riesling for a toast. Avery raised his beer. "To one of the smoothest pickup lines I've heard in a very long time."

He laughed. "Oh, I'm sure you get them all the time."

She shrugged. "But seldom are they that innovative. That

bok choy cabbage dilemma really reeled me in. I fell for it like a sucker."

"My motives may have been ulterior, but my ass is as dumb as they come as far as produce is concerned."

Renetta laughed. She usually paid for the intimate company of men. It was easier that way, for her and for the man in question. Paying for romance kept things in perspective for Renetta. She'd been unlucky in love her whole life, guilty of falling too quickly and too easily, and in the end, she always ended up regretful. But the older she'd become, the better she was at being in control of her heart and of the men she let in her life. Every now and then, however, it was nice to go with the flow and to give in to temptation that didn't involve cash. Being fucked by a man simply because he was attracted to her, and not because he was being paid to do it, was flattering and a necessary stroke to her ego. Of course, she still hadn't decided if she would fuck this one—yet.

She looked at his hands. "No ring."

Avery smiled. He dug this woman already. "I'm not married."

She held up her fingers and wiggled ten long, beautiful digits. "No rings here either."

Of all three of those women in that photo, he'd developed a particular interest in this one. She was gorgeous. That much was true and undeniable. But in the research he'd done on each of them, Renetta's past had a few dark patches in it that were as clear as mud, and that intrigued him. Some things didn't add up, and he couldn't put his finger on a reason why. He concluded that it was just gut instinct, but gut instinct was what made him so good at what he did.

"So, what do you do for a living, Avery?" Renetta leaned

back in her chair, crossed one long, shapely leg over the other, and stared at his ass like he was lunch.

That's all it took for that boner to swell in his pants again. And damn!—If the good Lord blessed him with just a taste of what was sitting across from him, he'd take his ass to church every Sunday from now until Judgment Day. Avery was many things, not all of them good, but he believed wholeheartedly in being truthful—to a degree.

"I'm a private investigator."

Renetta didn't flinch. She didn't blink or stir uncomfortably like someone who had anything to hide. When he told people what his job title was, most of them had a reaction, because most of them believed, even if only briefly, that he'd been set loose on them.

"Sounds interesting," she said coolly. "Do you enjoy it?"

The sound of her voice was intoxicating, and he wondered if some kind of drug had been slipped into his drink. Whatever she said was lost in translation. For real. His gaze fixed on her lips and lingered there for a few moments before slipping down to the delicate curve of her chin, the long sweeping slope of her neck, and continued its journey to the swell of her cleavage.

Renetta laughed. "Well?"

Avery snapped back to his senses. "Yes. I do, as a matter of fact. It's interesting work." He shrugged. "Most of the time."

"And the other times?" she asked, without missing a beat.

He felt himself grinning. "It's boring as hell. I spend a lot of time sitting in cars and waiting."

"Waiting for what?"

"To take the perfect picture of a cheating spouse, usually."

"Sounds tedious."

"To say the least. So, what about you? What do you do?"

"I sell lingerie online," she said easily.

He raised an eyebrow.

"Just lingerie," she clarified.

"People buy that online?"

"People buy anything online."

"How's business?"

She smiled. "Lucrative."

Avery leaned back and sighed. "Need a partner?"

Renetta laughed. "No, but thank you for offering, Mr. Detective."

She had been married. Vincent Jones, her husband, had been almost twenty years older than Renetta when the two of them tied the knot. He'd have been nearly seventy now. Ten years ago, a disability claim had been filed for early Social Security for Vincent, who'd officially been declared disabled. Avery had dug a little deeper and discovered records that the man had been placed in full-time nursing care in a home in Pueblo, Colorado. It seemed cut-and-dry enough, but that nagging gut of his sent up too many flags for Avery to be comfortable with. Why would she put him in a home in fucking Pueblo, for starters? Pueblo was a two-hour drive and over a hundred miles away. The thought made him uneasy, probably because he'd hate to think that any wife of his would stash him away in the sticks if he had a debilitating condition. Especially a wife as fine as Renetta.

"You're a beautiful woman, Renetta." Avery's eyes locked with hers.

"Thank you, Avery," she said, almost in a whisper. "I like you too."

"Enough to give me your number?" Avery already had

her number in his files at the office, but she didn't need to know that.

Renetta studied him a few moments before responding. "Maybe a little more than that."

Grown folks know how to interpret a vibe when they feel one—unlike young people who beat around the bush, play fucking guessing games, and try to make something out of nothing or turn nothing into something, forcing the issue and making a fucking mess of things. Avery and Renetta were grown.

He followed her to her place and trailed behind her through the house, up the stairs to her bedroom, his mouth watering, his dick throbbing, and his mind racing about all the things he wanted to do to this woman.

She insisted that he undress first, and Avery didn't have a problem with that. Renetta smiled at the rigid piece between his thighs pulsating and pointing up at the ceiling. She reached into the drawer in the nightstand by her bed, pulled out a handful of condoms, handed him one and placed the others on the table.

"I don't want to end up pregnant," she whispered, teasing. Renetta stepped close to Avery, stared wide-eyed at him, and then tugged on his bottom lip with her teeth. When she let it go, she slipped her delicious tongue into his mouth, wrapped it in his, then pulled away and licked her lips.

"Good," he said.

"Yeah."

She took the lead, but eventually he had to conclude that maybe she'd had it all along, even before the bok choy incident, and Avery was more than content to let her drive. Renetta took her time, mounting Avery with her back to him and rolling that beautiful ass of hers, spread like a feast in front of him, until he was just about to come. And then she stopped. She lay on her back, put both legs up on his shoulders, and met him thrust for thrust as he pounded inside her, and just when he was about to release—she stopped. Next, she bent over the side of the bed to let Avery enter her from behind. He pushed and pulled while she swayed and rolled, and when he was on the verge of release—she stopped. Avery's nut filled his balls to capacity, and if she didn't let him have it soon, they were going to bust wide open like water balloons.

She sat him down on the edge of the bed and straddled him. Renetta force-fed him ripe and luscious nipples until his jaws ached, and then she stared into his eyes and finally announced, "It's time. Let's say we wrap this up now."

21

Robin hadn't seen Tasha in weeks. She'd run into Dominick out one night, though.

"Your girl is tripping," he said. "She needs the kind of help I can't give her. I don't think anybody can."

Dominick looked like he was over Tasha, which was surprising considering the fact that he'd have drunk Tasha's dirty bathwater the last time Robin saw him.

The last time Robin called, Tasha answered, which was also surprising, and Robin managed to talk her into meeting at Dazzles for drinks.

Tasha's mind was reeling, but she resisted the urge to talk about the situation that had turned her into the obsessive beast that she'd become. "How's the shop?"

Robin owned her own barbershop in Aurora, a Denver suburb.

"Busy. I've added another chair and gotten a few new dudes in cutting hair now."

"You always have new dudes in cutting hair," Tasha said, disinterested.

"You asked how the shop was, and that's how it is."

She felt out of place here with Robin. Nowadays, Tasha felt out of place almost anywhere. No one understood what she was going through. Dominick had crossed the line, thinking he knew every goddamned thing, and Robin had her own way of trying to rationalize what, to Tasha, was anything but rational.

The two sat across from each other for several minutes without saying a word. The air between them was thick and tense. Tasha shuffled puzzle pieces of those women's lives around in her head. She did it when she was awake and even when she was asleep.

Phyllis Neville was a corporate piranha who lived for the job, had no real friends, and no man in sight. No wonder she was so uptight. Everything had a place in Phyllis's life. It was perfect, from the car she drove and had detailed once a week, to the tailored designer suits she dropped off at the cleaners every Saturday morning at ten. That messy daughter of hers had to have given that woman gray hairs. She was the ruffle in Phyllis's feathers, the crack in her sidewalk, that hair that was uncharacteristically out of place. Adding Tasha to the mix would probably send that old woman teetering over the perfect edge of her perfect world faster than you could say "stock options."

"Phyllis Neville. My name is Tasha. Tasha Darden. Thirty years ago, you and two of your closest friends abandoned a baby girl in a hospital emergency room. Well, surprise! That was me!"

The thought made her shudder.

"You alright?" Robin asked, concerned.

Tasha nodded and sipped her martini. "I'm fine."

Freddie Banks, Freddie Palmer, was as different from Phyllis as night was from day. By all indications, she was happy, as happy goes. Freddie was looking for something, though. Tasha had sensed it watching her in that writers' group the woman had been showing up at once a week. She seemed so anxious to be good at something, to excel, and desperate to be special. If Freddie found out about Tasha, she'd be the kind to break down crying one minute and then wrap her arms around her and squeeze the life out of her the next. Then she'd talk Don into adopting her, and they'd tuck her away safely in a pink bedroom with the princess canopy over the bed. She'd be the kind to believe that she could make it all better with a few "I love you"s, some cookies, and a glass of milk.

Renetta Jones was some sort of freak. Tasha was convinced that the neighbor lady had been right, and that the woman was either shooting porn or running hos—or both. If it were true, then actually Tasha found it kind of sexy. An old hot broad, pimping young hot broads—that was a Lifetime television series in the making. Renetta was the cool one. She seemed more calm then the other two put together, and Tasha concluded that if she were to go up to Renetta and tell her that she was possibly her daughter, the woman would look her up and down, invite her inside the house, and split a blunt and some homemade nachos with her.

"What are you thinking, Tash?" Robin finally asked, staring quizzically at Tasha.

"Nothing."

"Don't lie."

Since she'd asked: "I'm wondering which of them I should talk to first."

Robin shrugged. "Why not talk to all of them at once? It would be easier. That way you could find out right then and there which one of them is your mother."

Too easy. Too easy for the three of them.

"I suppose I could," Tasha responded to appease Robin.

"I don't know why it's taken you this long, Tash. I mean, why are you dragging your feet on this?"

Robin was like Dominick. Her ass just didn't get it.

"I thought I could figure it out on my own. I thought I wouldn't have to ask."

It wasn't a complete lie. It wasn't a lie at all, but Robin wouldn't understand the truth. The truth was darker and deeper and crazy.

"Save yourself the trouble," Robin continued. "Just get them all together and ask them. They'll give in to the pressure, and somebody will come forward and say something."

And that would be that. It would be over just like that. Tasha would have the truth out there in the open, and the three of them could begin to come to terms with their guilt, work on building bridges with Tasha, beg for forgiveness from her and God, and live happily ever after.

No. They didn't deserve to be let off the hook that easily.

"Yeah, you're right," she told Robin. "I just need to do what I've got to do."

"You'll feel much better in the end when you do."

"I will, Robin. I'll feel much better."

22

Freddie had been filled with nervous energy all day, leading up to her one-on-one meeting with Bianca that evening after work. This class had been a huge blessing, helping take her mind off of things and giving her an outlet to release some of the stress she'd been under since the reunion. Renetta had been careful not to sound panicked the last time the two of them had spoken, casually telling Freddie about running into Phyllis at the spa and about being accused of sending that article to her job.

"I'm sure it's nothing, Freddie," Renetta had said, reassuringly. "Forget I mentioned it."

Freddie had been trying to forget ever since, and working on her writing seemed to be the only thing that helped.

She'd spent four weeks in the workshop, and tonight was her "final," so to speak. Everyone had been tasked to write

three chapters of their first novel. Bianca was so encourag-
ing, speaking to all of them as if they were real authors like
her. The more Freddie went to those seminars and worked
on her chapters—her novel—the more she began to feel like
an author and the more she found herself wanting to see her
work published.

Like everyone else, Freddie waited patiently outside the
small room until finally her name was called and it was her
turn to sit and chat with Bianca. She approached Bianca apprehensively. Bianca smiled and motioned for Freddie to
take the seat across from her.

"How are you tonight, Freddie?" Bianca asked sincerely.

Freddie took a deep breath and clasped her hands in her
lap to keep them from shaking. "I feel pretty good tonight,
Bianca."

"Good," she responded earnestly. "Teaching this class has
given me more joy and satisfaction than I could've ever imagined, and I'm so happy that I've been given the opportunity
to get to know you and the rest of my students."

Freddie grinned so hard her face hurt. "It's been a wonderful class, Bianca. I've learned so much, and it's been incredible getting to know a best-selling writer," she gushed.
Freddie had to slow down and take another deep breath.
"And thank you. I'm sure I speak for all of us when I say that
we appreciate what you've done for us."

"You're welcome, Freddie. Now," Bianca opened a manila
folder with Freddie's name on the cover. "Let's get down to
the business of your critique," she said enthusiastically.

Freddie's heart thumped like someone was banging on a
wall. She'd worked hard on her chapters, staying up in the

evenings long after Don had turned in for the night, writing and rewriting every weekend for the last month, polishing her project until she believed it was as perfect as it could possibly be. Writing had been liberating for her. It had opened the floodgates of the kind of creativity she hadn't had since, well, ever. Writing, she knew in her soul, was her true calling, and after this meeting, Freddie would complete her manuscript and see it through until it was finally published and sitting on the shelves of the Tattered Cover Bookstore.

"Reading through your submission, Freddie, I can certainly tell that you put a great deal of time and effort into it," Bianca explained warmly.

Freddie chuckled nervously. "Lots of late nights and weekends."

"Welcome to the world of writing," Bianca smiled.

"So, what'd you think?"

"Well, Freddie. I can certainly see that you have a passion for writing, and your attention to detail in this project is incredible."

Freddie blushed.

"Your work is very clean . . . very . . . sanitized."

Not exactly the descriptions Freddie expected, but Bianca was the expert, after all.

"Your writing is very considerate."

Freddie stared confused at Bianca. "Considerate?"

"It's charming, Freddie," she hurried to add. "Charming and, well, a little flat."

Freddie felt her ego break in three places. "Flat?"

Bianca gathered her thoughts for a few moments before elaborating. "The mechanics are there. I can tell you've been paying attention to my curriculum, and you've done a great job at dotting your Is and crossing your Ts, it's just—Freddie, can I be blunt?"

She hadn't been being blunt already? Freddie nodded meekly.

"The potential is there for great writing, interesting and compelling writing, but . . . there's no juice, Freddie. When I read through this piece, it looked pretty on paper—all the words are spelled correctly, your punctuation is perfect—but I didn't feel anything. I didn't feel for the story line, I didn't feel the passion that this man had for this woman or the reluctant angst that this woman felt toward this man. It left me feeling uninterested, Freddie, and despite my best efforts, I truly did not want to know any more about either of these two people than I knew when I finished that last chapter."

Freddie had stopped breathing after the part about her punctuation being perfect. She was devastated and crushed, and that woman might as well have put her fist through Freddie's chest, because that's how she felt sitting there, wondering how in the world she was ever going to be able to stand up and walk across that room and out the door to get to her car.

"I'm sorry, Freddie," Bianca said, softly. "But I would be doing you a disservice if I didn't tell you the truth."

Freddie forced a pitiful smile. "That's fine, Bianca." Her voice cracked. "I understand."

"No, Freddie," Bianca insisted. "I don't think you do."

Hot, devastating tears stung her eyes as Freddie choked back a sob. "I suck as a writer," she blurted out. "That pretty much sums it up."

Bianca reached across to Freddie and took hold of her

hand. "You don't suck as a writer, Freddie. You suck at story-telling."

Freddie let the tears flow down her cheeks. "Isn't that what I just said?"

"But that's not what I said, Freddie." Bianca tried desperately to console her. "You're a good writer, but I think you need to dig a little deeper to reach your full potential to become a really great storyteller, which I believe you are more than capable of becoming."

"But I did my best, Bianca!" Freddie sobbed.

"No, you didn't," Bianca sighed. "Great writers aren't created overnight, Freddie Palmer, and I truly believe that you have it in you to become a great writer."

"How?"

"By stepping outside your comfort zone and allowing your mind, your thoughts, to take you on the kind of journey that is outside of anything you have ever known in the day-to-day trappings of your own life."

Freddie looked perplexed. "Like what?"

"I don't know. You tell me."

Freddie thought and thought, but for the life of her, she couldn't imagine any special journeys capable of taking her out of the trappings of being Freddie Palmer.

"Freddie," Bianca said, passionately. "Haven't you ever wanted to do something dangerous, or take a risk that could cost you something important to you if you failed? Haven't you ever wanted to climb a mountain or solve a crime? Have you ever loved someone so passionately that it cost you your own soul?"

Freddie shook her head and shrugged.

Bianca looked disappointed. "When you were a little girl,

what did you want to be when you grew up, Freddie? A court clerk?"

"An actress," she whispered meekly.

Bianca's eyes lit up. "Really?"

Freddie nodded. "I wanted to go to college and major in acting, but, well, Don and I got married—"

"Actors pretend, Freddie. Actors step outside of who they are, what they're comfortable with, to become other people. Throughout the pages of your manuscript, all I see is you: a very disciplined and orderly woman, with a succinct way of doing things, following life's regimented rules like she has no choice."

"That's not true," Freddie argued, wondering if she should tell Bianca about the role she'd played in leaving that baby in that hospital and then having to keep it a secret for all these years. If that wasn't acting, then she didn't know what was. That was a daring and nonorderly thing to do, and it was a risky thing to do, too. Wasn't it? And she'd have been willing to bet a million dollars that the high and mighty Bianca Hightower had never done anything as sinister or self-serving as that in her entire life.

"I write the way I do because I have wonderful experiences that I draw from my own life," Bianca patiently explained. "And I draw from experiences I want to have. And for those experiences I don't want, or will never have, I draw from knowing that someone somewhere in the world has had them or will have them, and I put myself in their shoes. I become an actor, Freddie, and I pretend to be them, and I forget myself altogether. When you can do that, then I have no doubt that you will write a wonderful novel. One that I can hardly wait to read," Bianca said, smiling.

Freddie composed herself and took a deep breath. "I'm not sure I'll ever be able to do that," she confessed. "I'm not sure I can step outside myself like that."

Bianca stared intently at Freddie for several minutes before finally offering a suggestion. "Will you do something for me? Will you wait for me after class and come with me? I want to show you something."

"What I am about to share with you is sacred to me, Freddie," Bianca said mysteriously.

She had invited Freddie to her home, a restored turn-of-the-century Victorian in West Denver. The house was massive and impressive looking from the outside, but inside, it was something out of a historic novel: filled with rich, dark woods, ancient columns, and floor-to-ceiling windows. The decor was a mixture of Eastern and Moroccan influences, gothic and overdone at times, to the extreme, as far as Freddie was concerned.

Bianca had led Freddie through the expansive living room, past the only modern room in the house, which was the kitchen.

Nothing could've prepared Freddie for what Bianca wanted to show her.

"I love basements," Bianca said, leading Freddie down a flight of stairs. "Don't you?"

"I suppose."

"This is a very private and cherished part of my life, one that I hold sacred. It plays a huge role in defining who I am and what I value. I escape here to the woman I am at the core, and this is where I'm at my happiest."

Freddie didn't know what to make of this place. At first glance, the room looked like something out of medieval times and even dangerous to someone like Freddie Palmer. But then, after listening to Bianca explain it, it really didn't seem so scary anymore.

"I have a friend," Bianca told her. "A very good friend. And the next time you come here, we'll all play a little game."

"Oh, I don't know, Bianca," Freddie said fearfully.

"Trust me, Freddie. You have it in you. I knew from the moment you walked into my class that you were someone very, very special. We just need to bring her out, that's all."

"I don't think I could, ever—"

Bianca shushed her. "Yes, Freddie. Believe me. You can. I can be whoever I choose to be down here, Freddie," Bianca explained.

Freddie stood in the middle of the room, turning slowly, shocked by some of the things she saw and confused and intrigued by others.

"These are my toys," Bianca's voice sounded faraway and haunting. Freddie had gotten so caught up in her curiosity that she'd almost forgotten that the woman was still in the room. "I act out my darkest fantasies in this room, Freddie. I forego the woman everyone else believes me to be, and immerse myself in the world I've created. This is where my inspiration comes from. Now it's time to help you find yours."

It was nearly midnight when Freddie finally crawled into bed. Naturally, Don was sleeping like a corpse and didn't even stir when she climbed in next to him. She'd had an emotional day, and Freddie was exhausted. Bianca's candid feedback had taken its toll on her, but the longer the two of them talked, the better Freddie was starting to feel about herself.

Bianca encouraged her not to give up and to continue studying her craft. That's what she called it—"her craft."

23

Chemistry is a funny thing. For the last two weeks Phyllis had been working closely with her new boss, getting him up to speed on the highly sought-after Philben Power Tools account. She'd gone to the first meeting with Jeff, defensive as hell and ready to unleash some serious senior and seasoned account-manager rhetoric on his young ass, expecting resistance from him on her strategy, but the man practically gave her a chest bump, he was so excited.

What surprised her the most and pissed her off a little was discovering that professionally, she and Jeff were two peas in a pod. They shared the same ideals and attitudes when it came to business. Their processes and systems mirrored each other's, exactly. So, why the hell did he get the VP job and she didn't? It was a nagging question that tickled the back of her throat every time she saw him, but Phyllis had decided to swallow it and to savor her newly established position. Even she had to admit she'd fared pretty well in the end. One more threat to quit and temper tantrum, however, and she would probably end up being promoted to CEO. But all in good time, she concluded. That's one playing card she'd hold in her hand and play at a later time, after winning over a few more major accounts, and one of these days Jeff Lang could very well be calling her "sir." It was just a matter of time.

On her way back to her office from a run-through of her new presentation, she didn't have to turn around to sense that he was behind her; she felt his eyes burning a hole in the back of her head. Phyllis stopped and turned abruptly, causing Jeff Lang to nearly bump into her.

He looked startled and then quickly composed himself. "I uh . . . wanted to say nice job on the Philben presentation."

Good cologne, she thought taking a deep breath, but not so that he'd notice. *Expensive.*

"Well, I know how important it is to land this account," she spoke professionally. She always went out of her way to speak like a news anchor whenever she was in his company. It was a no-nonsense tone, one that matched her new powerful persona. They'd paid her good money to stay with the company, and Phyllis made sure she proved that she was worth every penny. "Philben Power Tools is one big fish, and we have been working to catch it for two years now." She used the word *we* selectively, showing that she was a team player and all about the company. But really, it was all Phyllis putting in every waking hour of the day and night to put together an ad campaign for Philben, one that truly did leave them awed when they left that conference room.

"Well"—He almost smiled. Was that a dimple?—"if they

don't sign on with us after the show you put on, they're idiots." He brushed past her and headed into his office right next to hers.

She had great legs, but Jeff wasn't stupid. No matter how well the two of them worked together, the woman still didn't like him. She'd made that clear from day one. Hell, she was willing to quit when she found out she'd be working for him.

"Phyllis Neville was in the running for the position also," Xavier Billings, the CEO, told him shortly after he arrived. "She's good, and she was certainly a consideration," he explained, sitting in the golf cart at the twelfth hole. "But I can't give a position of this magnitude to someone with anything short of an MBA. Call me old-fashioned, but, credentials are credentials. Know what I mean?"

No. Jeff didn't know what the man had meant, but for the ridiculous salary he'd offered, Jeff pretended that he did. She was the top performer in the division. Phyllis had won contracts with some of the biggest corporations out there, and she'd done it the old-fashioned way, working her way up from the bottom.

He caught a glimpse of her leaving her office and heading down the hall to the ladies' room. She must've known he'd be watching, because she casually turned and glanced back.

She was older, but how much older he couldn't tell. She looked good, though. Her age showed more in her mannerisms and how she carried herself.

"Down, Fido," he muttered to himself. So, he had an odd fixation for the woman. The bottom line was, he was her boss, and his fixation needed to be nipped and tucked before it ended up embarrassing him and her too.

"Hello?" he answered his phone on the second ring.

"Hi, Jeff," Tasha answered.

He leaned back, and smiled. "Hey, lady." Shapely and lovely Tasha. He'd seen her once since bumping into her in the office hallway, and he was entirely too anxious to see her again.

Fate had been good to him lately. One evening after work, Jeff was at the little pub a block away from the office having a beer when he looked up and saw the body of his dreams come through the door and sit down at the bar. She happened to glance over her shoulder and smiled in his direction, and that was all he needed.

"Can I buy you a drink?" He slid onto the stool next to her and signaled the bartender.

"This round," she said, confidently. "Whoever wins the first game of pool can get the next one."

She whipped him good in pool, winning two of their three games with ease.

"Be honest. You let me win that last one. Right?"

She laughed. "No. Not really. Sort of. Yes." He'd asked for her number but she'd insisted on him giving her his, which he did without hesitation.

"Are we still on for drinks?"

"I'm game if you are," she responded seductively.

"I could be there at seven," he assured her.

"Seven works for me. I'll see you then."

Brothas were easy. Tasha stretched her legs in front of her on the sofa and smiled. *When opportunity knocks...*, she thought, smiling. That little incident in the office was fate, pure and simple. A sign that maybe God was finally on her side. The way Jeff Lang looked at her made it clear to Tasha at that moment that she had the upper hand. Getting next to him meant getting a step closer to Phyllis Whittaker-Neville and to that perfect world of hers that she cherished so deeply. Phyllis relished her career more than just about anything, Tasha had concluded. She paid more attention to that job than she did to the relationship she had with her own daughter. Ambition was her drug of choice. Phyllis got high on the shit, strutting around with that Bluetooth glued to her ear, and her designer laptop bag. Tasha found the woman absolutely nauseating, to be honest. Outside, she had her shit looking tight, but from where Tasha was standing, all she could see was a woman who made up for all the things lacking in her life by looking like she had it all. Phyllis lacked substance, and if Tasha could shake up Phyllis's life, she'd probably be doing the woman a favor.

"Hi, Mom. Remember me?"

24

Renetta had started planning her forty-ninth birthday party six months ago. It was to have been the party to end all parties, with Renetta celebrating the end of one era—her forties— and looking forward to a new one. But she couldn't bring herself to have that party. She smiled easily enough, and her business was thriving. She hadn't missed a beat in her life on the outside, but inside her mood had grown dark, heavy, and burdensome.

The house was uncharacteristically quiet for a change. Renetta walked through the kitchen sipping a glass of merlot, stopping at the half-eaten sheet cake on the island in the center of her kitchen. Her girls had insisted on cake and ice cream. She smiled at their thoughtfulness. "We love you, Mom!" they'd shouted after singing a horrible rendition of the birthday song, and each one of them had bought her a candle. It was no secret that Renetta loved candles.

The kitchen was a mess, but she was in no mood to clean it. She turned off the light and headed back upstairs to her bedroom, which was illuminated by every candle those girls had bought her. This birthday had changed from something to celebrate into a day of reflection. Renetta's life had been bittersweet since she moved on from her marriage. On the surface, it was beautiful, but underneath it was the same ugly mess it had always been. Renetta had just grown accustomed to skating on the thin ice skimming the top of that mess.

She'd spent a lot of energy trying to convince Freddie that the three of them couldn't have made any other choice than the one that they'd made that night, but it was a lie and an excuse. They were young, but not that young, and they were dumb, but not that dumb, either. They were old enough to know right from wrong and collectively, they'd all chosen to do the wrong thing, and that's what tore their friendship apart back then. It was the guilt each of them suffered in silence and the blame they'd all put on each other that destroyed their friendship.

Renetta stretched out on her bed and then finally picked up her cell phone on the nightstand to check her messages.

"Mrs. Smith," a woman said. "Your husband wanted me to call you and wish you a happy birthday. He'd like to see you when you get some time. And he misses you."

Renetta deleted the message. Vincent had said no such thing, but the hospital staff assumed that if he could have said something, then he'd make a statement as out of character as that.

"The stroke left him debilitated, but he can communicate," one of the nurses had told her. "He can answer simple yes or no questions by blinking his eyes. One means yes, two means no."

What did she care that he could blink a response? Since when had she sat with him long enough to consider any means of communication with Vincent, except to tell him how well she had been doing without him? They thought she and her husband should care about each other, because they were good people and that's the sort of thing good people wanted to think. But they didn't know Renetta and Vincent, and the fact that neither of them were good people.

She hadn't thought of calling him, but the next thing Renetta heard was the sound of Avery Stallings's voice. She glanced at the clock next to her bed. It was after ten, and any call after ten placed to another grown person could only mean one thing.

"Hello?" he answered, sounding half asleep.

"I didn't mean to wake you," she lied. She could've cared less about waking him. "I'd like to see you."

He didn't respond right away. Renetta imagined him sitting up in bed, rubbing sleep from his eyes. Avery had called her several times since the first time they were together, but Renetta had never returned any of his calls. She had never planned on seeing the man again, because she truly wasn't interested. But tonight she was interested. Tonight, she needed someone to help celebrate her birthday, and he seemed to be as good a choice as any.

"I can be there in twenty minutes," he finally said.

She smiled. "I can hardly wait."

Full-blown menopause was right around the corner, but Renetta's libido was operating better than ever. There was an art to lovemaking that most people overlooked in search of the often overrated orgasm. Orgasms were great, to be sure, but there was so much more to be appreciated between the kiss and the orgasm, and that was where she concentrated her efforts. A woman's mouth was as erotic as her pussy, and Renetta loved using her mouth. She was selective about who she gave head to, but she could make a man squirm and purr like a kitten suckling and teasing his nipples. Avery purred. She could torture him into a frenzy, nibbling on the insides of his thighs, and nobody could revive a limp dick using her feet and hands the way she could.

The two of them never got around to having actual intercourse, but by the time she'd finished with him, Avery had been launched into outer space somewhere near Jupiter.

"Damn, girl!" he finally said, out of breath. "That was some freaky shit."

She chuckled. "You complaining?"

He vehemently shook his head. "No. Hell no!"

"You're a good sport, Avery. I didn't expect for you to be so willing."

"Well . . . you know," he said, gloating. "But, uh . . . let's just keep that finger in the back door thing between us. You know?"

Renetta nodded. "Yeah. No problem." Renetta slid out of bed and went into the bathroom to wash up. Minutes later she emerged and went over to the bedroom door. "I'm going downstairs. You want some cake?"

Avery stared at her buck-naked ass and smiled. "No thanks, sweet. I just had some."

She expected him to be asleep by the time she came back upstairs, but Avery was sitting up in bed, looking smug. Renetta crawled into bed next to him.

"Where'd you learn how to do all that?" he finally asked.

She shrugged. "I do what feels good. Don't need lessons for that."

Renetta looked gorgeous even without makeup, and like a woman half her age. He hadn't been truly awed by too many women in his life, but this one took his breath away. He'd sworn off women after that last one had come through and broken his heart years ago, but if he wasn't careful, he could fall for this one.

"How come you're not married?" he asked, pretending that he didn't know about her husband, Vincent. Avery felt like a two-faced friend, walking on eggshells, trying to keep from spilling the beans about everything he'd learned about her for his client, Tasha.

She smiled, mischievously. "Who says I'm not married?"

He feigned surprise. "You got a man?" Avery leaned over the side of the bed and pretended to look under it.

Renetta laughed. "Don't worry. He's not there."

He sat back up and stared at her. "You serious? I mean, you're married?"

"I have a husband," she said, indifferently.

A part of him expected her to lie about being married,

because she could've easily have gotten away with it. But another part of him realized that Renetta Jones-Smith was the kind of woman who shot straight from the hip. Lying just wasn't worth the effort for a woman like her.

"Separated?" he asked.

"Physically."

"So, he lives in another state?" he probed, knowing the answer already.

Suddenly, she seemed to tire of his questions, and Avery could sense that he needed to be careful. "I am married, Avery," she said, exasperated. "My husband and I live separate lives in separate cities. That's all."

"Why be married, then?" he continued. "Why not just get a divorce if you two want to do your own thing?" He was amazed at how she'd described her relationship with her husband. Renetta didn't lie, but she was careful in how she told the truth. He made a mental note of that.

Renetta turned reflective, staring off into space across the room. "Divorce, like marriage, is a state of mind," she explained quietly. "There are other ways to get out of a bad situation. There are a thousand reasons for wanting to get out. And sometimes, it's just easier to take matters into your own hands and mold your own future than to wait around for something as silly as a divorce."

He looked confused. "What the hell does that mean?"

"It means that my husband and I are both better off the way we are. We've both gotten exactly what we deserve and you need to mind your own business."

25

❧

The shorter, full-figured woman coming out of the house looking as if she were in a hurry to leave hugged the taller, younger woman quickly and kissed the little boy on his cheek before climbing into her car and pulling out of the driveway. Freddie's house was a small brick bungalow in Denver's Park Hill neighborhood. The large front yard with its lush, green lawn looked like something out of a landscaping magazine, perfectly edged and mowed, with roses and snapdragons growing in the flower bed around the exterior of the home. The only thing missing was the picket fence. In her mind's eye, Tasha saw the spirits of children playing in that front yard, laughing and rolling around on the grass, and the ghostlike image of a round-faced young woman standing in the doorway, smiling as she watched them play.

"Excuse me. Hi." Tasha walked up the sidewalk in time to greet the young woman before she could disappear inside. "Um, my name is Tasha," she smiled nervously.

The woman looked at her. "Felicia."

Felicia was Freddie's oldest child. She had the same warm, brown complexion as her mother, and she had the woman's eyes.

"I was in the neighborhood checking out some houses for sale. I like the area and was thinking about buying here," she explained. Tasha had been planning this visit for days, racking her brain to come up with a convincing story.

"Oh, really?" Felicia smiled, and when she did, she looked even more like her mother.

Felicia was about Tasha's height, and both of them were taller than Freddie. She searched silently for more similarities, but they were hard to see from Tasha's perspective. A picture of Felicia would've helped. Then Tasha could study it next to one of her own and find hints of any resemblance between them.

"Yeah, I really dig that one at the end of the block, on the corner. Anyway, I'm new to town and was wondering if you could maybe tell me a little about the neighborhood . . . if you have time," she glanced at the child holding Felicia's hand.

"Where are you from?" Felicia asked.

"L.A.," Tasha lied.

"Oh, I've been there a few times. I pretty much grew up around here and—Oh, hi, Daddy." Felicia smiled and hugged her father. "This is Tasha. She's looking to buy a house around here."

Don Palmer was taller up close than she'd realized. His face was long like Felicia's . . . like Tasha's, and being this close to him made her heart race. From what she could tell, Freddie and Don had been together for their whole lives. What if?

"You from around here?" he asked.

Tasha felt flushed and overwhelmed, and all of a sudden she wanted to turn and run back to her car. Felicia unknowingly came to her rescue, though, and answered for her. "She's from California."

That was all she needed to get herself together. Tasha couldn't afford to panic. Everything that ever mattered to her depended on her seeing this thing through. "I was wondering about the house down the street on the corner." She nervously cleared her throat. "And the neighborhood."

Don stared at her blankly. "What about it?"

"Um . . . is it a good neighborhood to live in?"

He nodded. "Yeah, it's pretty good. We ain't never had no problems," he said thoughtfully. She detected a slight southern drawl in his speech. "They just put a new roof on that house," he explained. "Tore up that old carpet too."

Felicia rolled her eyes and shook her head. "This here is the president of your neighborhood watch committee."

Don either chose to ignore her sarcasm or missed it altogether.

"That fence in the back is new, too," he continued. "Come on in," he held the door open for the women to enter, a gesture Tasha hadn't expected. "This house is laid out pretty much the same as that one."

She took a deep breath walking into Freddie's house, inhaling the scent of the woman's essence, half believing that she could know even more about her just by breathing her. Other people might've lived here, but Freddie's personality was in this home.

"This is the formal living room," Felicia explained. She leaned in close and whispered to Tasha, "Absolutely no one is allowed to sit or stand for longer than ten seconds in this room. We call it the temple."

Tasha couldn't help but laugh. The room did look like some sort of shrine to the eighties, with its white leather furniture, glass coffee table with wrought-iron legs, and an oversized fake bird-of-paradise plant in a gaudy teal vase, which seemed to overpower the whole room. And on the walls were scenic pictures of meadows, lone houses, and one that held Tasha's attention longer than it should've. It was a family photo with Don and Freddie and their three children.

Don continued talking as he led her through to other parts of the house, including a formal dining room with a huge china cabinet taking up an entire wall, filled with the kinds of impractical things that were probably never used— fancy plates, crystal glasses, figurines.

She followed Don into the kitchen, which shared space with the den. The little boy who'd come in with Felicia was sitting in front of the television.

"Boy, don't leave no crumbs on that table," Felicia fussed. "Granny'll kill you."

The boy didn't even blink at the threat of Granny, almost as if he knew that Granny would do no such thing. An ebony shelving unit in the corner of the den held more family photos. On the center shelf was a photo of a very young Don and Freddie Palmer on their wedding day. The two of them had married shortly after she'd graduated from high school. Tasha would've been about three or four months old when they took that picture—when Don and Freddie were married. *Did he know?* she wondered, staring at the back of him as he led her through that house. Did he know, and did he forgive Freddie?

Don stopped at the top of a stairwell just beyond the kitchen. "Now there's a full and finished basement with an-other bedroom, bathroom, and den. Upstairs are three more bedrooms and two bathrooms. But I can't say for sure if that place is going to have three bathrooms, because I put that one in downstairs myself."

"Maybe they put one in and just forgot to tell you, Dad," Felicia teased.

Again, he either missed the humor or chose to ignore it.

"You wanna see the backyard? It's a good size yard. I put in a new deck a few years ago, and it looks real nice."

The walls of this place felt as if they were starting to close in around Tasha. Hints of this man and this woman were starting to saturate her skin. Tasha felt the threat of tears welling up in the back of her throat. And Don Palmer was standing entirely too close.

"Thank you," she said anxiously, hurrying back through the house toward the front door. "I'll uh . . . thanks."

She gripped the steering wheel with both hands as she pulled away from the curb and slowed her breathing to help lasso in her emotions. Tasha had been in complete control when she parked in front of Freddie Palmer's house this morning. She knew what she was doing when she waited for Freddie to leave and when she walked up to Felicia and introduced herself. But she hadn't expected him, not like that. She hadn't expected him to invite her into his home and want to show her the new deck he'd built in the backyard. She had been looking for a mother, not a father. Someone like Don Palmer had been a sidebar, a distant thought, but he hadn't been real—until now.

The longer she drove, the more angry she became. What if he knew what Freddie had done? What if he knew and he forgave her and still decided to marry her knowing what she'd done? Tears streamed down her cheeks, thinking about it. Then he was a sonofabitch! If he knew and he still married that broad, loved her and made babies with her, then fuck him too! *But what if he doesn't know, Tasha?* A gentler voice filled her head and begged the question. *What if she never told him about that night and denied him the truth just like she'd denied you yours?*

Being in that house had done something to her, and she couldn't wait to get home and wash the vibe of it off of her. Don was home in that house. Felicia and that boy, her son, were at home in that house. Freddie's house. Freddie's home. She had built that home for her family, as corny and as outdated as it was, even the so-called temple was home for those people, filled with love so strong and so unconditional that even cookie crumbs on the table couldn't shake it.

"Be a good girl, Tasha, or I'll have to send you away. Be a good girl, Tasha, or I'll have that social worker take you with him the next time he comes. Be a good girl, Tasha, or you'll have to go live with people who aren't as kind as I am."

26

≈≈≈

"You have to promise me something," she told Freddie, staring intently into her eyes.

Every bone in Freddie's body warned her to leave, but her curiosity won out over warning. Freddie felt as if she were part of a secret ritual, being inducted into a mysterious cult. She stood face-to-face with Bianca in the basement, her heart racing, her stomach fluttering with anticipation and apprehension.

"Yes, Bianca?" she responded quietly.

Bianca took a deep breath and let it out slowly. "Trust me."

Freddie nodded.

"And know that I am not ashamed of who I am, but I do respect my privacy and the privacy of the man you are about to meet tonight."

Don had bought Freddie a mini-taser some months back for safety reasons, and she had it tucked securely in the side pocket of her purse. So she was cool.

"This is my private life, Freddie," Bianca continued. "And I only share my most private life with people I trust and people that I respect."

Freddie felt so honored she choked up. "Thank you, Bianca," she whispered. "I won't betray your trust."

Bianca smiled and flipped a switch on the wall that illuminated the entire room in her basement, which looked like a torture chamber out of an old horror movie.

"You wait here." She led Freddie over to a red velvet chair in one dark corner of the room. "I'll be back shortly," she told her.

She didn't know how long Bianca was gone, but Freddie stared mortified at the things in that room, tilting her head to try and change her perspective a bit and make them look like something familiar.

In the middle of the room was a black metal chair with a thin leather seat cushion and what looked like metal cuffs on the front legs of the chair and at the end of the armrests, and then there was a larger cuff at the top of the chair where the neck would be. Behind the chair was a tall metal cage. It looked kind of like a jail cell, only it was too narrow for a person to sit down in. All anybody could do in that thing would be to stand straight up. Across from that was what looked like a dog kennel. But Freddie hadn't seen or even heard a dog, and Bianca had never mentioned having one. Back against one wall of the room was a table draped in a purple crushed-velvet tablecloth, and neatly laid out on that cloth was an array of what appeared to be something you'd see in an operating room. Above that was a display of various kinds of whips and what looked like paddles, the kind teachers used to use to discipline kids back when she was in grade school.

"Stay!"

Freddie jumped, startled, when she heard Bianca's voice at the top of the stairs. She clutched her purse tighter in her lap, and all of a sudden she thought being here really was a bad idea. Freddie held her breath and waited anxiously at the sound of Bianca's footsteps slowly descending down the stairway. When she finally came into view, Freddie gasped.

Tall, willowy, sophisticated but conservative, Bianca Hightower stood half a foot taller and looked downright menacing. Her stature seemed to reach the ceiling. Her calm, easygoing aura had been transformed into something far more powerful than Freddie's writing mentor.

"I am Bella," she said, her voice deeper than it normally was, and more pronounced. "Mistress Bella Donna."

She wore a form-fitting black latex mid-calf-length skirt, a painfully tight black leather strapless corset, and matching leather pumps with six-inch metal spiked heels. Her hair had been pulled severely back away from her face and clipped in a ponytail in the back. Red latex hand gloves and a short leather riding crop completed her outfit.

Freddie couldn't speak. She couldn't move. She stared fixated on this woman, wondering what the hell had happened to her friend.

"Come!" Mistress Bella Donna shouted, snapping that riding crop in the air.

Freddie jumped, and in less than a second, a half-naked man flew down the stairs, clad only in a pair of boxer shorts, brown dress socks, and a wide leather collar around his neck. His arms were painfully bound behind him in some horrific device that looked like a straitjacket.

The man fell at Mistress Bella Donna's feet. "Yes, Mistress!" he said, out of breath.

She looked at Freddie and smiled wickedly. "This is my submissive."

The man started to raise his head, but the mistress snapped her riding crop against his back before he could.

Freddie cried out, but the man didn't.

"I never said that you could look at my friend," she told him.

"Yes, Mistress," he said, anxiously. "I have been bad, Mistress," the man said pitifully.

Somehow, someway, that woman managed to raise her leg high enough in that skirt to press her shoe against this man's naked back and push him farther down onto the floor.

"Bad boys have to suffer," she said sensuously.

"Oh, yes!" The man sounded like he wanted her to make him suffer. "I should be punished."

Bianca finally raised her gaze to Freddie, whose eyes were about ready to pop out of her head.

"Would you like to stay—friend?"

Oh, no! No! No! No! There was no way she was going to

stick around and watch Bella Donna whip up on Bad Boy here! Freddie had no business being here, and she needed to find her keys and hurry up and get the hell out of here.

But she nodded. "Yes," she whispered.

Bianca's—er—Bella Donna's eyes twinkled. "I thought you might."

An hour and a half after Freddie arrived, she found herself sitting at Bella Donna's—Bianca's—kitchen table, sipping on a cup of Moroccan tea with honey. Bianca's friend had been dismissed, after he'd endured an hour of lashes, cages, and licking the feet of Bianca's alter ego.

Freddie's hands shook as she picked up her cup off the table.

Bianca laughed. "That really shook you up, didn't it?"

Freddie took a sip of her tea, and it took every muscle she had in her neck to swallow it. "I've—uh—I've never seen anything like that before. I mean, I'd heard of people who . . . but I just never knew anybody—"

"I took it easy on you—and him—tonight, Freddie," Bianca said indifferently. "Much to his disappointment."

Freddie looked stunned. "You tortured that man!"

Bianca smiled. "Not the way he wanted me to, believe me."

"But I saw you hit him, Bianca! I saw you make him do things that—"

"That he wanted me to make him do," she said assuredly. "Freddie, this is what we do, he and I. We've been together for four years, and this is what we do, because we both love it."

"He liked that?"

"He loved it, and if you hadn't been here, he'd have gone to orgasmic heaven and back again—several times—had I felt you could handle it. We're like an old married couple, he and I, and believe me, this was nothing compared to our usual romp."

"What else was there for you to do to the man?" Freddie screeched.

Bianca rolled her eyes. "Plenty."

The two sat in silence for several moments while Freddie composed herself and tried to gather her thoughts. "So, this— what you did tonight—is what inspires you to write the way you do?"

After all, wasn't that why she'd invited Freddie over in the first place? To show her that sacred part of her life that inspired passion in her work?

"The energy of this inspires me, Freddie," Bianca explained passionately. "The raw, carnal, creative aspect of all of this inspires me to release all my inhibitions and let my thoughts and my mind flow to heights that I couldn't otherwise imagine."

"Well." Freddie cleared her throat. "That's all well and good, Bianca, but I doubt seriously that my husband is going to let me beat him with a riding crop and strap him to a chair for being bad."

"Have you asked him?"

Freddie was shocked. "No! Of course not."

"Then how do you know?"

"Thirty years of marriage is how I know," Freddie responded, appalled.

"Okay, then. What about you, Freddie?"

Freddie swallowed. "What about me?"

Bianca studied her. "I saw the look on your face down there."

"I must've looked mortified," Freddie admitted.

"But only for a moment," Bianca smirked. "You looked . . . interested."

"Oh, I did not!" she huffed.

"Then why didn't you leave? I expected you to. I expected you to get up and storm up those stairs and out my front door, never to see or talk to me again. But you didn't!"

"I didn't because—"

"Because what? And be honest with me! Be completely and totally honest with me and yourself."

Freddie was speechless.

"You didn't leave because you were fascinated. You didn't leave because you became immersed in the fantasy, in the possibility. You didn't leave, and perhaps for a moment, maybe even two, you put aside everything you know as you and you let yourself become someone else."

Freddie shuddered at what she'd just heard. "Who?"

"Me, Freddie. Mistress Bella Donna."

Freddie replayed her evening in her mind as she drove home. What she'd witnessed tonight had been one of the most ridiculous acts she'd ever seen between two consenting adults, and she couldn't help but feel ashamed for those people. She felt ashamed for what they'd let themselves become, all in the name of kinkiness. And all of the respect and admiration she'd once had for Bianca Hightower had been left in that woman's basement the moment she raised that crop to that man's back.

After she got home and took her shower, Freddie decided to write a little bit, to help clear her mind. By midnight, she'd finished a new chapter, and for some strange reason, she e-mailed it to Bianca. The next evening after she'd come home from work, she checked her e-mail and saw Bianca's response: "Much, much better!"

27

It was nine o'clock in the evening on a Friday night, and everyone in the office had left hours ago. Even the cleaning crew had come and gone, and all that was left was Phyllis, sitting in her office with her feet propped up on her desk, still basking in the afterglow of her stellar performance earlier that afternoon. Once again, she'd done it. Phyllis had put together the proposal of a lifetime and presented it as only she could to the execs of Philben Power Tools, so magnificently that she'd left them speechless with their eyeballs popping out of their heads. If Skyland Advertising landed this account, it could be worth upward of 10 million dollars. That account had come down to Phyllis's advertising savvy, her slick slide presentations and storyboards, and her stunning abilities of persuasion. If anyone could get it done, everyone in the office knew that Phyllis could. And in her heart of hearts she knew, even before the Monday morning phone call from the Philben execs, which they promised would undoubtedly come, she'd nailed it.

She needed to celebrate. Phyllis needed to toast this victory tonight over a delicious martini with . . . who? She thought for a moment, searching through her mental Rolodex of friends, and came up short. Phyllis worked too hard to have friends. A person doesn't work eighty or a hundred hours a week and still manage to nurture and maintaining something as irrelevant as friendships. Phyllis searched through the contact list on her cell phone; other than Abby, all the other names and numbers belonged to business associates, her hairdresser, ob/gyn, her tailor, dentist, and Marcus's old cell phone, which she was certain he'd changed years ago. She paused, realizing that she hadn't thought about Marcus since the reunion. Men had come and gone in her life since her divorce, but no man had ever left a residue behind like Marcus. Phyllis hadn't loved another man, and she was beginning to wonder if she ever would again. Abby was in school the last time Phyllis had had any reason to call Marcus. But with every cell phone upgrade, she made sure she put his number in her contacts list, just in case something happened. Nothing ever did, but just in case . . .

"Hello?"

Oh shit! Phyllis gasped, realizing that she'd accidentally auto-dialed his number.

"Hello?"

She panicked and hung up on him without saying a word, squeezing her eyes shut and cussing herself out for that Freudian slip of her thumb. "Please don't let him call back," she mouthed in prayer to God. "Please don't let him call back."

Moments later, her phone rang. She started not to answer it but then remembered that even if she didn't, his call would roll over to voice mail and he'd know she'd been the one who'd called anyway.

"Hello?" she asked, innocently, searching the recesses of her mind for some viable excuse as to why she'd called that man.

"Phyllis?" he sounded surprised. "Did you just call me?"

Sweet Jesus! She loved hearing him say her name. She loved the butterfly effect he still gave her whenever she remembered the two of them together. And she missed him. After all these years, and after everything that had happened, she still missed him.

"Um . . . who is this?" Dumb Phyllis. As brilliant as she was, sometimes, like now, she was absolutely and unequivocally dumb.

"Marcus," he said, as if she should already know.

"Oh . . . hi." All she had to say was that she was sorry and that she'd hit the wrong button and that it was a terrible mistake and good-bye.

"Is everything alright?"

Is everything alright, *baby*? That's what he should've said. It's what she wished he'd have said. Is everything alright, *sugar*? Her heart skipped a beat remembering being called *sugar* by Marcus. The sound always seemed to linger on his lips like sweet nectar, and she licked her own lips, thinking about his.

"Everything's fine," she swallowed. "I just . . ." She wanted to say, I had a great day, Marcus. I landed the biggest account of my life and everybody around here thinks that I am the shit and I wanted to share my victory with someone special like you.

"Phyllis?"

"Yeah, I . . . was cleaning out my contact list on my new phone and, well, I had an old number . . . I would've thought you'd changed that number by now."

"No. No, I haven't."

She sensed that he was about to hang up, and Phyllis didn't want him to hang up. Not yet. "Have you spoken to Abby?" she hurried to ask.

"Of course."

"She's pregnant," she blurted out. Phyllis slapped the heel of her hand hard to her forehead.

He sighed. "I know, Phyllis."

Of course he knew. He was the girl's father, for crying out loud. But Phyllis sensed an opportunity forming between the two of them to finally have a reason to talk to each other. She was an idiot, desperate and as love-struck as a schoolgirl who had been left in the dust by this man many years ago. And she was a demon woman, for even thinking to use the opportunity of their daughter's situation as a means to weasel her way back into Marcus's life, but Phyllis decided right then and there to go ahead and give it a shot.

"I'm worried about her." She'd said that to keep him on the phone and then suddenly realized that it was true. She *was* worried about Abby. Until this moment the situation with her daughter had been about what she was putting Grandma Phyllis through. As selfish a thought as it was, it was true. Now, in saying that to Marcus, she started to wonder about what her daughter was really going through. Abby put on a good face, like her mother. She was good at looking calm in the storm, but deep down Phyllis knew better. Being a mother wasn't easy, even for one who'd been as bad a mother as Phyllis. But being a single mother ... had to be frightening.

"That makes two of us," Marcus responded quietly. "But you can't tell Abby anything. I told her that Ricky was no good and that she could do better, but she didn't want to hear what I had to say. Now she's having to deal with this on her own. All I've got to say is that he'd better hope he doesn't run into me on the street, because he's got an ass whooping coming."

Phyllis swooned. Absolutely nothing was sexier than the thought of Marcus giving some deserving fool the beat down. "Does he now?"

"I'm serious, Phyllis. He hurt my kid, and I can't let him get away with that."

Marcus was the man like that. Old-fashioned in a lot of ways, too many, which was what tore the two of them apart, he believed in taking care of what was his, in every way. Marcus had been cool with Phyllis having a career, until he found out she was pregnant with Abby. And then he came up with some half-witted notion that she should stay at home and raise babies and come back to her career after they were old enough to fend for themselves. It sounded good in theory, but in reality, it was more than she could handle, so she opted to divorce him and take her chances with the corporate piranhas of the world. They weren't nearly as frightening as staying home with a house full of kids.

"We'll just have to be there for her, Marcus," she said quietly.

"I know. She's scared, but won't admit it. She's stubborn. I wonder where she got that from?"

Phyllis smiled. "I wonder."

"She'll be alright, Phyllis. She's got us."

Us. Now there was a pretty word she hadn't felt a part of in quite some time.

"Look, uh . . . I've got to go," Marcus said, "but we'll talk again—about Abby."

That "we'll talk again" part caught her pleasantly off guard. "Sure, Marcus. Take care, and tell Sharon I said hello."

Marcus hesitated. "Not a good idea, and you know it, but let's pretend I did."

Why, oh, why couldn't I have been a different kind of woman? she wondered agonizingly. Why couldn't she have fallen in line with his ideals, been satisfied and fulfilled being that man's wife and the mother of his children? How come Marcus couldn't have been enough? She wouldn't be sitting here feeling sorry for herself, even after landing the largest account of her life, if she could've just made him enough.

Phyllis had been working another half an hour when Jeff Lang tapped on her door. "Figured you'd still be here," he said, smiling, holding a package in his hand.

He'd been out of town the last few days, visiting the corporate offices in Atlanta.

"What are you doing here?" she asked, surprised.

He shrugged. "I got off the plane and I hurried back here hoping to catch you to congratulate you on the spectacular job you did on the Philben presentation."

Pride oozed out from every one of her pores and seeped out onto her desk. "Well, you know," she said, gloating.

He came in and sat in the chair across from her desk,

opened up the bag he carried in, and pulled out two plastic cups, a bottle of champagne, and a cheap corkscrew. "Well, in case you didn't know," he explained, opening the bottle. "I got a voice mail on my cell somewhere over Tennessee, I think, from Lilly Watts at Philben."

If he wanted her attention, he had it. "And?"

Jeff popped the cork and slowly filled both glasses with champagne. "And—you nailed it, Neville," he finally said. "You won it for us, and they are excited to start working— particularly with you—on this project as soon as possible."

She couldn't help herself. Phyllis raised both arms in the air. "Whoo!" she screamed. She spun around in her chair several times before finally stopping long enough to pick up her drink and tap glasses with Jeff. "Yeah, baby!"

Jeff laughed. "That's what I'm talking about!"

"And to think you and old Ruddy there wanted to fire me," she said menacingly.

Jeff looked shocked. "What? Where in the world did you ever get that from?"

"Okay, so maybe I'm remembering it differently," she said dismissively.

"Most definitely," he said emphatically. "If I remember correctly, I recall that you'd quit, and old Ruddy and I had to jump through some serious hoops to get you to stay on."

She laughed. "Your version of the truth is more compelling than mine."

"Damn right it is. But you know what?" The two of them quickly finished off their champagne, and Jeff filled their glasses again. "You definitely proved your worth today, and I have no doubt that you'll prove it again in the future. It's hard to get good people, especially in this business, Neville," he continued. "It's damn near impossible to find people as good at their jobs as you are in yours. So whatever it takes to keep you on—you best believe—I'm on it."

Jeff understood. Man! He really got it, and her too, it seemed. She studied the masculine square of his chin as he spoke, admired the broad flare of his shoulders, and melted inside at the seductive base in his voice. How long had it been since she'd made love to a man? She wondered. How long had it been since she'd been kissed and caressed, since someone had found her desirable? And when had Jeff Lang stopped being her enemy? "You know I wanted your job, right?" she asked all of a sudden.

He sighed. "You'd have been good at it."

"I deserved it."

He smiled and winked. "And so did I."

Phyllis surprised herself and laughed. "Oooh! Look at you. Alright. All's fair in the corporate world."

"Right or wrong. Good or bad. It is what it is."

Lord have mercy. She smiled admiringly at him. "It certainly is," Phyllis responded slyly.

Time got away from them. The champagne went straight to her head. That was her excuse.

"Oh! Yes! Okay! Yes!" she said passionately.

Phyllis's skirt was hiked up around her hips. One of her shoes had fallen off and landed on the floor behind him. Her blouse lay strewn on her chair, her bra landed on top of her computer monitor, and Jeff Lang's pants lay crumpled on the floor around his ankles.

Phyllis sat bare-assed balanced on the edge of her desk while Jeff pumped eight wonderful inches of man-flesh in and out of the folds of her hot, wet, and needy self like a man possessed. And she loved it! She loved every aching, reckless moment, tossing back her head, closing her eyes, moaning and groaning loud enough to wake the dead.

"Oh my gaaahd . . . Awwww!" Phyllis lay back and let her head fall over the opposite edge of her mahogany desk, grabbing handfuls and pulling at her own hair. It was a moment of madness, the likes of which she'd never experienced before in her life! He held on tight to her hips, pulling and pushing her back and forth across spreadsheets and Power-Point presentations scattered across her desk, penetrating her deeper with each magnificent thrust.

Phyllis raised her knees high in the air. She stared longingly into his eyes and licked luscious thoughts from her lips.

"Yessss!" he hissed, staring back at her.

Her eyes filled with warm, moist tears of gratification. How long had it been since she'd made love to anything that wasn't plastic?

"I'm cumming!" he said desperately. "Oh, I'm . . ."

"It's okay," she whispered. "I already did."

He convulsed, shuddered, seized, releasing a crescendo of his orgasm like a tenor at an opera, and then finally he collapsed forward, still throbbing inside Phyllis's sugar walls.

Together they rested in the satisfaction of the unexpected but splendid moment, settling their heartbeats and catching their breath between tender, sweet kisses of gratefulness. But in that instant, Phyllis gazed into the eyes of this man, and slowly, who he was began to come back into focus, and what the two of them had done rocked her foundation like an earthquake.

"Oh, my God," she suddenly gasped. Disbelief filled her.

"What?" he asked, out of breath.

"Oh, my God!" Phyllis screamed. "Get up!" She shoved him in his chest. "Move!"

Jeff did as he was told and stumbled backward. "What?"

Phyllis jumped down from her desk, hurried around behind it, and picked up her blouse. "What?" she said, her face twisted. "What!"

"What?" he blinked, confused.

"You're my boss, Jeff!" she said angrily. "That's what! And I don't have sex with people I work with!"

"Neither do I!" The realization of what they had just done finally hit home with him. "I'm sorry! Shit, Phyllis. I'm really sorry."

Phyllis struggled to put on her bra and slide down her skirt at the same time, causing her to fall backward into her chair. "What the hell is wrong with me?" she asked, appalled. "What the hell is wrong with . . . what did we just do, Jeff?"

The man was speechless, and suddenly, he seemed to transform from a grown man into a gawky and awkward teenager right before her eyes.

Phyllis started to feel faint. "Oh, no!" she said, clutching her head between her hands, trying to squeeze out the migraine coming on from that cheap champagne, the overwhelming guilt she felt from fucking the boss, and the burdensome shame she felt for molesting a child! "Oh, no! No! Noooo!"

"Phyllis," he took a step toward her, but she shot a look at him and put up her hand, which stopped him dead in his tracks.

"Don't! Don't."

Jeff wasn't a complete idiot, although he pretty much felt like one at the moment. He'd fucked up in a big way. He'd crossed a line he'd promised himself he'd never cross under any circumstances. "I'm sorry," he said, quietly, pulling up his pants and backing his way toward the door.

28

Fifteen years after leaving the force, Avery still had connections in the Denver Police Department. Isaac Sanders had been his partner for a few years, and the two of them still met up a few times a year to talk about old times over beers. Isaac worked vice now and had been grumbling his way toward retirement since Avery resigned.

Avery had asked his friend to run a check on Renetta Smith and Jones for any priors, and to check on her husband Vincent while he was at it. Renetta hadn't admitted to anything, but the longer he thought about it, the more his imagination took hold of what he believed she'd implied.

"We've both gotten exactly what we deserve . . . mind your own business."

Avery couldn't just let it go. Maybe he should've, but it just wasn't in his nature to let a perfectly good implication go without checking it out.

"Other than a few complaints from neighbors, I didn't

come across anything on either of them," Isaac explained over the phone.

"What kinds of complaints?"

"Domestic disputes, mainly. A few times, neighbors called complaining about loud arguments or fighting coming from the house. In one incident, one was said to have witnessed Mr. Jones dragging Mrs. Jones from the house by the collar of her shirt and then kicking her in the side or back right there on the front lawn."

Avery got a visual that didn't sit well with him. "You sure it was her and not another Mrs. Jones?"

"Renetta Jones, bro. Tall, heavyset. By the time the cops showed up, Mr. and Mrs. Jones were back inside the house, claiming that they'd had a slight disagreement but nothing nearly as violent as what the neighbor had claimed to witness."

"So no charges were filed?"

"Nope. Not one. I called down to that nursing home in Pueblo, told them I was a cop and was looking for a person who'd been reported missing."

"Vincent Jones."

"Yeah, and they confirmed that he was still there. Safe, sound, and practically a vegetable."

"Any visitors?"

"Twice a year, from his wife on his birthday and Christmas."

Avery took notes to help him process the information Isaac reported to him. The Renetta he knew was too strong-willed to have ever been physically abused by anyone. Renetta was confident and in command of every aspect of her life, down to the sex. So, her old man ends up having a stroke, all of a sudden she's a free woman, and—and starts a new life, a better life without her husband. Coincidence? Or just good old-fashioned luck?

"Were you able to dig up anything on them when they lived in Arkansas?" Avery probed further.

"As a matter of fact, there was one thing," Isaac continued. "Credit card fraud."

Avery sat up straight.

"It seems that Mr. Jones filed a complaint with the police department about fraudulent charges against his bank account from some online company that sold herbs."

Avery frowned. "Like weed?"

"No. Like herbs. Apparently, there were several debits from his account to buy some kind of obscure shit from Africa called yohimbine." He pronounced it slowly. "It's supposed to help with impotence, like Viagra or something. The police told him to report the problem to his bank."

"Maybe the wife was buying it," Avery surmised, knowing firsthand how aggressive Renetta was sexually. Maybe the old man was slowing down and couldn't keep up.

"Or he did and just didn't want to admit that he'd been having trouble getting it up," Isaac laughed. "He probably bought the shit; it didn't work and then decided that he didn't want to pay for it. Filed a claim of fraud with the credit card company, and the police for good measure, to try and get his money back.

"Nothing ever came of any of it, though," Isaac continued. "And a couple of years after that, the two of them moved back here to Denver."

Avery sat quietly on the other end of the phone.

"So what's the problem?"

"I don't know yet," Avery responded.

Isaac sighed. "Look, man. I know how you think, and I think you need to slow it down and stop making up shit in your head."

"I'm just contemplating, Isaac. Trying to make it make sense."

"Yeah, but that's the problem. That's what made you a bad cop. You never look at the facts, Avery, man. You look past them to the shit that makes life more interesting for you. Pretty cut and dry if you ask me. The man had a stroke. Period."

"But why would she dump her husband in a nursing home all the way down there in Pueblo if there wasn't more to this?"

"Why wouldn't she? If he was beating her ass on the regular, which I'd be willing to bet he was, then why keep that mean motha-fucka in the house, or even in the same city?"

"Why not just divorce him?"

"Hold up! You trying to tell me that you've got me out here chasing rainbows on this woman and wasting my time because you can't figure out why she's not divorced?"

"I don't know, man. I've just got a feeling."

"Based on what?"

"Based on . . ."

"A feeling," Isaac said, finishing the sentence for Avery, and yeah, it sounded silly.

"You doing her?" Isaac blurted out.

"What makes you think that?"

"Come on, man. It's me. Talking about having a feeling, I have a feeling that you might have something going on there with this chick."

"She just doesn't strike me as the victim type."

"Now see, domestic violence survivors everywhere

would be stoning your ass right now if they heard you say that. What type is a domestic violence type, man?"

"She's just . . ."

"You are doing her," Isaac laughed.

"Whether or not I am has nothing to do with what we're talking about, Isaac."

"I think it does."

"How's that?"

"I think you've got commitment issues, Avery, but I've told you that already."

"Oh, here we go. Man, don't pull that Dr. Phil shit on me."

"You tend to wanna get with women you can't have: married, lesbians, too old, too young, and in this case, a potential ax murderer."

Avery grimaced. "You need to stop watching those talk shows, man."

"I'm just saying, it doesn't take a psychiatrist to figure out what's up. You want what you can't have, and then you walk away with nothing, and I think you dig that shit. If you're feeling her then just go with it."

"Even if she does turn out to be an ax murderer?" Avery asked dryly. "That means I could be next, Isaac."

"I think you're overreacting and looking for something that's not there. You're paranoid because it gives you an out when you decide it's time to tuck tail and run the other way. No offense man, but it makes you sound kinda weak. Like a—a sissy."

"Fuck you, Isaac," Avery chuckled.

"You digging her, right?"

"I don't feel one way or another about her. We're just kicking it."

"You sound like you're sixteen, Avery. Grown men and grown women don't need to be kicking it. You either dig her or you don't."

"I'm not romantic like you, brotha. I'm truly kicking it and so is she."

"Yeah, well . . . kick it and enjoy yourself, but Vincent Jones is where he is because of karma. He probably brought that shit on himself, and now she's reaping the benefits of it, which, if he was whooping her up, is justice. Stop looking for shit, because you and I both know, if you look long enough, hard enough, far and wide enough, everybody's got shit to hide. Sometimes, though, you just need to let it rest, man, and just take it for what it's worth."

Isaac was probably right. And Avery was probably over-reacting. Admittedly, he was a man who thrived on drama and, if there wasn't any, he was notorious for stirring some up. He needed Renetta to be complicated, a puzzle, so he was no doubt trying to turn her into one. That's all it was. Of course, there was still the possibility that she could very well have been Tasha Darden's birth mother. Tasha seemed like she'd disappeared from the face of the Earth. She hadn't called or stopped by his office. Not that he'd expected her to, but for some reason, his business with her still felt unfinished.

Renetta hadn't mentioned anything about a long-lost daughter coming back into her life. As secretive as she was, however, he wasn't surprised. Hell, Avery was a piece of ass to that woman, and since when did you tell ass every intimate detail of your life?

Full of Fire

29

❦

Instinct warned Tasha that she was going too far. Any rational thoughts she'd had had gone up in smoke and Tasha was fueled by pure resentment. To anyone looking at her, Tasha looked like a well-adjusted, reasonable young woman. But inside, Tasha was an anxious and overwrought ball of confusion.

Jeff Lang was a means to an end. He was just a pawn in a game he didn't even know was being played. He worked with Phyllis. He was her boss. Tasha had connected to Freddie's lifeline, her family. Jeff Lang was Phyllis's lifeline. It was a crazy theory, but it wasn't. It was enough to keep Tasha moving in the direction she needed to go, toward the truth and her version of justice.

She was losing him. Jeff had been preoccupied since the two of them had sat down for drinks, and the more Tasha worked to try to keep a conversation going, the more restless and uninterested he seemed.

"Work's got you pretty busy, I suppose?" she asked, fishing for what could be bothering him. In the half hour they'd sat down at the bar, he'd finished two gin and tonics but had hardly completed two sentences.

Tasha had come prepared to entice, wearing a low-cut tank top, the tightest jeans she could find, and four-inch high-heeled sandals.

He shrugged. "As usual."

She waited for him to elaborate, but he didn't.

She reached across the table and placed her hand on top of his. Jeff looked up at her, and Tasha smiled. "Should we do this another time?" she asked seductively. "You look like you've got a lot on your mind, and if you'd like to get together some other time, I understand."

Get him to want you, Tasha, she'd commanded herself. *Get him to want you and then tell her who you are and watch the bitch squirm in her designer shoes, trying to figure out how to pick up the pieces of her perfect world.*

She was beautiful. And Jeff was an idiot. Things had definitely gotten out of hand with Phyllis, and he'd been kicking himself ever since. Jeff hadn't gotten to where he was by making mistakes or letting emotions get the best of him. His career had been carefully orchestrated since he first set foot in the advertising business, knowing full well where he was headed, straight to the top. And he'd put all that in jeopardy in one stupid move.

"I didn't mean to bring my problems with me on this date," he said apologetically.

"Anything you want to talk about?" she asked sincerely.

Jeff smiled. "That's what happens sometimes when you're married to your job. The problems at the office spill over into your personal life, and before you know it, you're living and breathing the office twenty-four-seven."

"Sounds exhausting." Tasha leaned back in her chair, and Jeff's gaze lingered at her bustline far longer than he'd intended.

He quickly took another sip of his drink and flagged down the waiter for another one.

Tasha picked up her purse and prepared to leave. "Look, why don't I just go, and we can get together another time, Jeff."

"No," he said, reaching out to take hold of her hand. "I don't want to do it another time, Tasha. I mean"—he grinned—"you know what I mean."

"I hope so," she said, smiling back. "So, why don't you tell me what's bothering you?"

Jeff waited for his drink before starting to explain. "I screwed up," he said simply. "Which, if you knew me better, you'd know that I don't ever screw up. And I'm not bragging," he quickly added. "I'm just careful."

"We all make mistakes, Jeff. Maybe you're being too hard on yourself."

He shook his head. "In this case, I should be hard on myself. It was a stupid mistake, one that could've been avoided, and I let it get away from me."

"Does your boss know?"

He sighed. "No, it's nothing like that. It has to do with a coworker." Jeff stared at the woman sitting across from him and knew that he couldn't go into any more detail than that. He was interested in Tasha, and she was obviously interested in him. The last thing he needed to do was to confess that he'd had sex with another woman.

"But you can't tell me what happened, exactly?"

"I'd rather not. Just that it shouldn't have happened."

"Have you spoken to this person about it? Maybe it was some sort of misunderstanding? Or maybe it's not nearly as bad as you think."

He loved watching her mouth move when she spoke. Tasha's full, pretty lips were intoxicating to watch.

"You know what? Let's talk about something else."

She laughed. "Nice way to change the subject, Mr. Lang. Smooth."

"When I'm not tripping I can be smooth, Miss Darden. Believe that."

Jeff was an intelligent enough man to know when to shut up. What had happened with Phyllis was an issue that would need to be dealt with, but not here and not now. What happened with Phyllis was an error in judgment for both of them, and she was probably as torn up about this mess as he was. The two of them would gather their thoughts and they'd get together, talk it through, and probably agree to pretend it never happened. But right now, Jeff was sitting across from a gorgeous woman, and he needed to stop crying in his drink and savor this opportunity before he let this opportunity get away from him.

"You look beautiful. Did I tell you that already?"

She blushed. "You just did."

"Thank you," he said, earnestly.

"For what?"

"For agreeing to meet me for drinks. For being patient as I processed my way through this foul mood, and for luring me back to this moment."

. . .

He loved to kiss. Tasha always hated kissing, until now. Jeff held her close the whole time, and Tasha hated being held close, until now. She'd always made love on her terms, her way. But he'd taken the lead, and she'd followed, and Tasha hated giving up the lead, until now.

30

Don snuck up behind her, lifted her up off the ground, and nuzzled his face in her neck.

"Grrrrrr!" he growled like a bear.

"Put me down!" Freddie fussed, slapping his shoulders. "Don Palmer if you don't put me down . . . !"

He did as he was told. "When you gonna come bowling with me, baby?"

Don had on his orange-and-white bowling-league shirt. He hovered over her as she finished up the dinner dishes in the kitchen.

"You know I've got my writing class on Thursdays," she reminded him.

He sighed. "Can't you miss it every now and then and come spend time with your husband?" He tickled her.

Freddie yelped. "Get back!" She pushed him with her behind.

"You used to love to go bowling with me."

"I still love bowling, Don," she said, consolingly. "But this is important to me, and I just need to do this for myself." Freddie turned to him. "Can't you understand that?"

"Of course I understand it. I just miss my bowling buddy. That's all."

Freddie couldn't believe what she was about to do. She had told Don an outright lie tonight, and she'd let Bianca talk her into going some place she would've never gone on her own. She drove slowly through the streets of lower downtown Denver, looking for a place called the Reformatory, which according to Bianca was the best kept secret west of the Mississippi.

"From the outside, it looks like an old warehouse," Bianca had explained earlier. "There are no signs on the outside, and the building looks completely dark."

"Well, how am I going to know which one it is?" Freddie argued.

"You'll see me standing outside, waiting for you."

And there she was, wearing dark glasses, a floor-length black trench coat buttoned to her neck and cinched at the waist with a wide belt, looking like something out of *The Matrix*.

Freddie parked half a block away. She found herself almost running toward Bianca, but those high-heeled boots would only let her move so fast. She wore her coat pulled tightly around her, feeling like a complete and utter fool for what she was wearing.

Bianca smiled when she saw her. "I was worried that you'd had a change of heart."

Freddie smiled back nervously. "I did. Several, as a matter of fact."

They went inside, and Bianca handed the doorman a gold business card. She took Freddie by the wrist and led her up a narrow flight of creaking stairs to another door, painted red. She knocked twice, and moments later, the door opened slowly. The haunting sound of a sitar streamed from speakers anchored in every corner in the room. A tall, taller-than-Bianca-tall, lean but muscular woman answered, wearing a spiked leather collar, and a red shiny latex strapless body suit. Her lips matched the color of her outfit. Fiery red hair, straight and loose, hung past her shoulders. She stepped aside and let them both enter.

Freddie walked inside and stifled a startled gasp. The place was an absolute freak show, and she knew the instant she'd walked into that place that she had sinned and trespassed on everything that was holy in the world. There was a man hanging upside down in the middle of the room, bound in what looked like a leather straitjacket, and a woman naked from the waist up knelt on all fours in one corner of the room at a man's feet, barking like a dog. People sat at the bar, clad in everything from business suits to medical scrubs, drinking and holding conversations like they would at any other bar in any other place in the country.

Bianca pulled Freddie through the crowd and led her through heavy purple drapes in the back of the room, and then she took her into a small room and closed the door.

"Show me," she commanded, staring excitedly at Freddie.

Was it too late for second thoughts? Because Freddie certainly had plenty. "I think I need to go home," she said, starting to push past Bianca.

"Oh, come on, Freddie," Bianca whined.

"I feel like a fool!" she argued.

Bianca laughed. "Did you see those people out there? Talk about foolish."

"I shouldn't be here, Bianca," Freddie reasoned. "I let my curiosity get the best of me with all this, and—I should be bowling with my husband." She really felt like she wanted to cry.

"You can bowl anytime, Freddie. Look, I certainly don't expect you to go out there and start paddling somebody. I brought you here just so that you could get a glimpse of a world a million miles removed from your own life. You've seen bits and pieces of it in my basement, but there's so much more to it than that."

"Maybe I don't need this kind of experience."

"And maybe you don't. Maybe you'll walk out of here tonight and make up your mind that you never want to see me or any part of my crazy life ever again, and I would respect that."

"Then that's what I'll do."

"But all I'm asking you to do is to have an open mind, Freddie, because the best writers have open minds. They may not agree with everything or everybody they write about, but they are skilled enough to know when to push aside their own ideas in order to make room for their character's. And to do that, they have to be willing to detach themselves from themselves and step into someone else's shoes, even if it's just for a short while."

"So this is like research?" Freddie asked meekly.

"That's exactly what it is," Bianca exclaimed. "So come on. Take your coat off and let me see it."

Reluctantly, and slowly, Freddie removed her coat.

Bianca clasped her hand over her mouth, her eyes grew wide, and she was speechless.

"I look ridiculous!" Freddie started to put on her coat and leave, but Bianca stopped her.

"You look beautiful, Freddie!" she said sincerely. Bianca turned Freddie to the mirror behind her. "Oh, my goodness!" she said, almost tearing up. "Sweetheart, you look absolutely wonderful."

Freddie stared despondently at her reflection, dismayed by the fact that she was nearly fifty years old and a grandmother and an expert bowler. Bianca had insisted that the electric blue latex square-necked bodysuit with black lace-up stiletto boots would be a perfect fit on Freddie's short, plump, and curvy frame. That thing hugged every unwanted lump and bump in place, better than any girdle she'd ever owned. Her full breasts exploded from the top, looking like plump, ripe, youthful melons, and even she had to admit, right at this moment, she looked different.

"You need lipstick," Bianca muttered, standing behind her. She reached into one of the pockets of her coat and pulled out a tube of lipstick so red it looked almost black. Freddie spread it over her full lips, pressed them together, and looked at Bianca.

"Fabulous!"

"I'm a nervous wreck," Freddie's voice quivered.

"That's because when you walked in here," Bianca explained, "you were Freddie Palmer."

Freddie looked perplexed. "Who am I now?"

Bianca turned her to face the mirror again. "You are . . . Fionna Blue." She smiled, having just made up that name on the spot. "*Mistress* Fionna Blue."

Bianca slithered back into that room like a cobra, and Freddie trailed behind her, following suit. She shuffled over to the bar with Bianca, drank what Bianca drank, and smiled politely to anyone looking at her and wondering who the hell she was.

"Pretend you're someone else, Freddie."

"But I thought you said this lifestyle wasn't a game to people."

"It's not a game to them. It's not a game to me. But to you, sweetie, that's all it is."

Freddie knew that Bianca told her that to keep things in perspective for Freddie. She was learning how to pretend. If she wanted to become a great writer, then she'd have to learn how to pretend to be this Fionna Blue person. And if she could pull that off, then she could pretend to be any character she decided to write about from that moment on.

An hour after arriving, Freddie began to realize something. She began to realize that she wasn't as jittery as she'd been when she first walked in. No one bothered her, people were very nice, and other than the weirdness around her, she could've been in any bar in the city. Gradually, she felt herself begin to detach herself from her nervousness and just be who she truly was, which was nothing more than a spectator, more objective than she'd been an hour ago, detached, but able to take it all in in small doses. Of course the two cosmopolitans she'd had certainly helped.

"Have you ever been a submissive?" Fionna Blue whispered to Bella Donna.

"Oh, yes," she exclaimed.

Fionna looked shocked.

"To be a good dominatrix, Fionna," Bella explained, "one must also master the art of the submissive."

"The art of the submissive." Fionna twisted her face.

"Dominants respect the submissives, Fionna. To outsiders, it may not appear that way, but think about the strength it takes to willingly allow someone to dominate and control you? Our natural instinct revolts against the very idea, but it takes discipline and a brave and daring heart to be a good submissive."

The alcohol must've been getting to her, because for a moment, she actually understood Bella Donna's point.

Half an hour later, Mistress Bella Donna excused herself to the ladies' room, and Freddie—Fionna Blue—found herself sitting alone at the bar. She needed to be home no later than eleven. Don would worry if she wasn't there by then. Fionna glanced around the room looking for a clock, but of course there was none.

"May I help you with something, Mistress?"

Goodness gracious! she shrieked in her mind. *A brotha!*

"What?" Fionna asked, looking stunned.

And a good-looking one too—tall and handsome, wearing what looked like a very expensive suit. He immediately averted his eyes to the floor when Fionna looked up at him.

"I apologize, Mistress," he muttered. "You seemed to be looking for something. I thought that maybe I could be of service to you."

Be of service? Fionna started to laugh and then caught herself. He obviously had her confused with somebody else.

"No. No, I'm fine. I was wondering . . . do you have the time?"

He glanced at his Rolex. "It's not quite ten, Mistress."

"Thank you." Fionna took another sip of her wine, wondering why the man was still standing there in his expensive suit with his head hanging down. The moment was awkward to say the least, and she'd had half a mind to get up and walk away, when suddenly a thought came to her. It was a crazy thought, absolutely ridiculous, but then here she was sitting in an S&M club, wearing an electric blue rubber suit, when she should've been bowling with her husband—so what about her evening *wasn't* ridiculous?

"You may go," she said, half expecting a backlash of protest and laughter from the handsome gentleman.

He bowed deeply at the waist. "Yes, Mistress." And with that, he shuffled away.

It took everything in her not to burst out laughing.

The man never strayed more than ten feet from Fionna Blue. She tried to ignore him, but despite her best efforts, it was hard to do.

"What is up with this fool?" she asked Bella Donna when she came back.

"Who?" Bella asked.

Fionna leaned her head in his direction. "He's been hovering around me since you left," she muttered.

Bella Donna studied him and then looked at Fionna. "He's interested in you," she said, smirking.

"For what?"

Bella laughed. "Look at him. He's lonely and he needs a mistress. I think he wants you."

Fionna stared at Bella like she was crazy. "You need to stop."

"Humor him, Fionna. Just for tonight. It'll be fun." She smiled wickedly. Bella Donna stepped past Fionna Blue and walked over to the stranger. "What's your name?" she demanded to know.

He didn't respond.

Bella Donna suspected that he wouldn't, without permission. Fionna was standing close behind her, and Bella Donna nudged her in the gut with her elbow.

"What?" Fionna whispered.

She whispered back. "Tell him to answer me."

Fionna looked stunned, but what the hell? "Tell her your name," she said politely.

"Joe, Mistress," he hurried to say.

Fionna almost fell over backward.

Bella reached behind her to Fionna, and switched places with her. "Talk to him, for crying out loud," she told Fionna.

"What do I say?"

"Whatever you want."

Fionna cleared her throat and then just decided to ask the obvious. "Why have you been following me all night?"

"I think you're beautiful, Mistress," he responded sheepishly.

"Really?"

Bella nudged her in the back.

"I mean . . . *really.*"

"I didn't mean to offend you, Mistress," he added, quickly.

Okay, so now what?

Bella leaned in and whispered, "Tell him that he needs to show reverence to your beauty by kneeling when he speaks to you."

Fionna shook her head, but Bella urged her on.

"Well," she started hesitantly, "if you really think I'm so beautiful, then you should kneel when you speak to me."

That man hit the ground hard on both knees in an instant. "Forgive me, Mistress . . ."

"Fre—Fionna," she told him. "Fionna Blue."

For the next hour, he followed her around the room, walking on his knees, which Freddie found absolutely hilarious. If Don saw this he'd fall over laughing. As she and Bella Donna were leaving, the man followed her to the door.

"Excuse me, Mistress Fionna Blue, but will you be coming back?" he asked desperately.

By this time, Fionna Blue was operating in full force and had been pleasantly amused all evening by this man's antics. She was beautiful to him, and he had been willing to do anything she asked. Talk about a rush!

"Oh, I don't think so," she said, magnanimously. "But if you're a good boy," she added, "perhaps."

She laughed so hard on the drive home she nearly peed on herself. Don was asleep when she arrived, thank goodness. She'd had the good sense to stop at the Burger Palace around the corner from the house and change back into her jeans and sweater. She'd put her Mistress Fionna Blue outfit in a gym bag and stuffed it deep into the trunk of her car. If she ever put that thing on again, it would be for Halloween or something, but she had no plans of ever going back to Bianca's special club. The experience had been a memorable one, though. Freddie had had her own private little adventure, one that no one who knew her would ever believe, even if she ever did tell them about it. Maybe next Thursday she'd go back to being normal and take Don up on his bowling offer.

31

Phyllis hadn't seen Jeff since the night of "the incident." The week following "the incident" she called in and told her assistant to let everyone know that she wasn't feeling well and would be working from home. A week later, however, she had to come into the office, because a migraine can't last forever and, besides, she had clients coming in to meet with her.

As soon as she got off the elevator she spotted Jeff standing at the end of the hallway chatting with one of her coworkers. Her cosmic aura must've been powerful because he glanced over in time to see her too. Phyllis hurried to her office, closed the door, and braced herself against it, taking several deep breaths to try to calm her nerves.

She'd spent the last week trying to forget it ever happened, throwing herself into her reports, working out on the treadmill, rapping loudly to any song Eminem had ever recorded, and watching every reality show known to man or woman, and still the images haunted her. Physical and lustful images that had caught her up in a cyclone of passion, the likes of which she hadn't experienced in ages. Sure, she'd had sex since divorcing Marcus, but nothing as spontaneous, careless, or as fevered as the sex she and Jeff had in her office. Sexual encounters for Phyllis had always been well thought out, planned, orchestrated events specifically scheduled to avoid rocking boats or creating unnecessary drama in her social or professional life. That episode with Jeff had left her feeling nauseated since it had happened and left Phyllis on edge, expecting that proverbial hammer that would surely come crashing down on her head at any moment.

She stood staring at her desk, seeing ghostlike images of herself, legs raised in the air, blouse strewn over the chair—and him, pushing and pulling, his gaze locked on hers, just . . . doing the damn thing! "Oh goodness," she sighed, suddenly overcome with another hot flash. They'd been coming more often now but were especially more intense when she was stressed.

All of a sudden she felt dizzy thinking about it. This wasn't going to work. A dark and dismal realization engulfed her, and she knew that there was no way the two of them would be able to work together under the circumstances. Phyllis stumbled to her desk and managed to sit down before actually fainting.

Moments later Jeff opened her door, walked inside, and closed it. She stared at him, appalled. "What are you doing here? What are people going to say if they see you in here with the door closed?"

Jeff tentatively approached her with his hands raised in surrender. "I'm just going to be in here for a few minutes," he assured her.

Phyllis stared wide-eyed at the man, numb and unable to move.

"I made a mistake, Phyllis." He spoke quickly and quietly. "I know this, and I'm sorry. It was bad judgment on my part and definitely out of line."

Out of line? she shrieked in her mind. *Out of fuckin' line?* He had just made the understatement of the century.

"What we did, Jeff," she spoke slowly, "was to obliterate any so-called line entirely. We didn't just cross it. We fuck-ing erased it."

"Of course." He shifted uncomfortably. "But we're adults, Phyllis, and we're professionals. We can put all of this behind us if we set our minds to it."

Jeff's blind faith was mind-blowing. Phyllis desperately wanted to buy what he was selling. Life could go back to normal if he was right and the two of them could move past this like grown folks, but the moment she was starting to come to terms with moving beyond "the incident," a picture of Jeff suckling on one of her boobs flashed in her mind. Phyllis cringed.

"There's only one thing left for me to do," she said, as calmly as she could. "I'll have to resign."

Jeff straightened his back. "No, Phyllis," he said, sternly. "No."

"What else can I do?" she said. "Jeff, we just . . ." She pushed back away from her desk. ". . . Here, and we . . ." She shuddered. ". . . All over my . . . and we . . ."

"We've both worked too hard to get to where we are, Phyllis." Jeff stared her in the eyes. "We know how to pick up the ball and recover from our mistakes better than anyone in this division, and we know how to keep it moving in the right direction."

Jeff stood across from her looking every bit the vice president of this division.

"I know it won't be easy," he continued, "but I don't want to lose the best director I have. I don't want to lose my job, and I know you don't want to lose yours."

She cleared her throat. "I don't. I've worked too hard for this."

"I know you have, and you deserve to be here, Phyllis. We screwed up, but it was a moment. That's all it was. And in the grand scheme of things, I believe that it's in our best interest to move past that moment and do what we do best, which is making this the highest revenue-grossing division in the whole fuckin' company. You're the key to that, Neville. And you know it."

Phyllis watched him walk out. She composed herself and let what he'd said start to sink in. She'd always had loftier goals than just a corner office and director's position. So she'd given in to temptation. Phyllis had always been a very disciplined and controlled woman where her career was concerned. But in a moment of weakness, she'd let go of all of her self-control, which resulted in a terrible lack of judgment on her part. Hell, she was human, and far from perfect. People made mistakes all the time. Phyllis needed to stop being so hard on herself and accept that she'd fallen prey to a moment of weakness. She and Jeff had made a mistake, but what was done was done. She thought about it, and then reminded herself that she was better than most when it came to moving past her mistakes. Phyllis had done it before and she knew damn well she could do it now.

. . .

Jeff felt a huge sense of relief. After his conversation with Phyllis, it was business as usual, and by the afternoon, it was like nothing had ever happened between them. And to top if off, he was sitting across from the lovely Tasha Darden, enjoying his dinner and definitely looking forward to dessert.

She caught him staring and smiled. "You're looking at me like you think you're going to get lucky or something," she teased.

He grinned. "I've had a fabulous day so far. I'd be lying if I said I wasn't hoping to have a great evening."

"Maybe I can help you out with that." She smiled.

"Maybe you can," he said, leaning in for a kiss.

"You taste like steak sauce," she laughed.

"And you just taste good."

She was just leaving the restaurant when she saw them. Phyllis stopped in her tracks and watched in unexpected jealousy as she saw Jeff kissing and canoodling with another woman.

"Miss?" the hostess came over to her. "Is there a problem?"

Phyllis didn't even acknowledge the woman. She turned to leave before he saw her, but after taking a few steps, she stopped.

"Miss?"

With each step in his direction, she reminded herself that there was nothing between her and Jeff except for a professional working relationship. The two of them had come to terms with that and she had been relieved. So, what was this feeling stirring in her gut? Whatever it was, it wasn't supposed to be there.

"Jeff," she said, finding herself standing over him at the table.

Jeff was startled. "Phyllis?" He wiped his mouth, cleared his throat, and stood up. "Phyllis."

Phyllis stared at him, wondering what in the world she'd come over to say.

"Jeff," she finally said.

The awkward silence was eventually broken by the sound of the woman he was with clearing her throat.

"Phyllis," he said. "This is . . . a friend of mine," he said carefully. "Tasha. Tasha Darden."

Phyllis's gaze fell on this Tasha. She was young. Very young, and lovely.

"Tasha, this is Phyllis Neville. She's one of our directors at the company."

The two women stared at each other, but neither of them said a word.

Phyllis turned her attention back to Jeff. "I didn't mean to interrupt," she explained uneasily.

"It's fine, Phyllis. Would you care to join us?" He said it, but she knew good and damn well he didn't mean it.

"No, Jeff. I just wanted to say hello."

"Hello, again," he smiled uneasily.

"Well, I guess I'll see you at the office tomorrow."

"Of course," he quickly said.

Phyllis stood frozen in the uncomfortable silence between them before finally turning to leave.

"Enjoy your dinner." She glanced briefly at the young woman.

Phyllis hurried away and disappeared from the restaurant.

Jeff was less talkative, much to Tasha's relief. She needed her own time to process what had just happened. Phyllis Neville had hardly glanced in her direction, but Tasha had been unable to take her eyes off of the woman.

The tension from the encounter still lingered in the air. Jeff and Phyllis had tried to be careful, but Tasha had a feeling that they hadn't been careful enough.

32

"Japanese-clover nipple clamps," the saleswoman with the pierced lips, nose, and brow explained, "they're all the rage. One of our most popular items."

Freddie reluctantly took the package from the woman and studied it. "Do men use these as well?"

The woman laughed. "They're for anyone with nipples."

"Freddie?"

Freddie turned quickly and stared shocked into Renetta's curious expression. "Hi," she said, hiding the package behind her hip and forcing a smile. "Renetta. How are you? How have you been?"

"Fine. I've been, I *am* fine. You?"

"Good. I'm fine, too."

"What do you have there, Freddie?" Renetta's eyes twinkled.

"What?" Freddie looked frightened all of a sudden.

"What do you have in your hand?"

"Oh," Freddie's voice quivered. She shrugged and held the package for Renetta to see. "It's, uh . . . well . . . it's . . ."

Renetta took it from her and smiled. "Nipple clamps?" She nodded introspectively. "Interesting." She handed the package back to Freddie. "You and Don like . . . nipple clamps?" she asked slyly.

Freddie put them back on the counter. "No," she said, composing herself. "I was just curious."

"Research for that book you're writing?"

Freddie looked confused but then remembered that she was supposed to be working on becoming a published writer. "Yes. Exactly," she said sheepishly.

Renetta decided to let Freddie off the hook and turned her attention to the sales clerk. "Hi. I called earlier about the pink, fuzzy handcuffs."

"Pink . . ." Freddie looked dumbfounded.

Renetta looked at her and smiled. "Handcuffs," she winked. "I like handcuffs." Actually, they were for a photo shoot, but Freddie didn't need to know that.

"Oh."

After paying for her merchandise, Renetta managed to talk Freddie into having tea together at a small shop across the street.

Freddie was as nervous, as the old saying goes, as a ho in

church, and Renetta was getting a kick out of it. She leaned closer to Freddie. "Soooo, Mrs. Palmer," she said menacingly, "wanna tell me what you were really doing in a fetish shop?"

"You figured it out. Research for my book."

"Your erotica book."

"Yes." Freddie sipped her tea. "Why else would I be in a place like that?"

Renetta smiled. "Every marriage needs a little spice from time to time, Freddie. Nipple clamps seem freaky cool to me. Maybe I'll go back and pick up a pair for myself," she teased.

Freddie blinked innocently. "I was in there just looking around, Renetta. That's it."

Renetta stared intensely at her. "Alright, then all I can say is that that's going to be one hell of a book, and I can't wait to read it."

On the drive home, Freddie started to laugh hysterically. She really could've told Renetta the truth about the way she'd been spending her Thursday nights lately, but the woman would've just thought she was crazy. Nobody could've ever imagined her going to a place like the Reformatory, and absolutely no one would've believed how easily she'd fallen into the role of Fionna Blue.

"What do you mean you're not going back? Of course you're going back."

Bianca had handed Freddie a gold membership card to the Reformatory that would give her VIP access for an entire month. Freddie had no idea how much Bianca had paid for this card, but she suspected that it wasn't cheap.

"How much do I owe you for this?" Freddie asked, reaching into her purse.

"I don't want your money, Freddie," Bianca said, disappointed. "And what do you mean you're not going back?"

"I insist on giving you back your money for this, Bianca. And I'm sorry. I had a nice time, it was interesting, but that place isn't for me and you know it. How much did this cost?"

"Five hundred dollars," Bianca responded casually.

Freddie's eyes widened. "Five hundred dollars?"

"I thought you enjoyed yourself," Bianca continued.

"I did."

"Then why not come back, and bring Don with you? Maybe you'll feel more comfortable with him there."

Bianca was a fool if she thought that Don would be caught dead in a place like that.

"No. Now I told you that I'd go once and I did. I'm just not cut out for that kind of lifestyle. You know that even better than I do."

Of course, Freddie had won her argument and the expression on Bianca's face confirmed it.

"Okay." Bianca sat back and sighed. "You're right. You agreed to go with me and you kept your word, and I respect that."

"It really was my pleasure," Freddie smiled, relieved.

Bianca raised her cup of tea in the air. "Well then, let's pay homage to Mistress Fionna Blue one last time. She was one hell of a woman and will be sorely missed."

Freddie raised her cup, too. "And she made blue latex look better than any damn body," she laughed.

She left Bianca at the coffee shop with a promise to stay in touch and to hang on to that gold card, just in case she had a change of heart and decided to resurrect the illustrious Fionna Blue and make an appearance at the club.

That should've been that, but it wasn't. When Thursday night rolled around the next week, Freddie had every intention of going bowling with Don, but he'd surprised her and made other plans.

"Sorry, babe. Heading down to the sports bar. Gonna play some pool, polish off a few beers, a couple of slabs of ribs and as many hot wings as is humanly possible. No girls allowed."

Half an hour after he left, Freddie dialed Bianca's number. "Are you going to be there tonight?" she asked, sheepishly.

"I'll be there. See you in an hour?"

"Sure."

Boredom wasn't enough of an excuse to do something she knew she shouldn't have been doing. Freddie just saw an opportunity and took it. And besides, Bianca had paid five hundred dollars for that gold card. It would've been rude not to use it. At least, that's what she told herself.

"Crawl, Joe," was all she said, and that man hit the deck like gunshots were being fired overhead. For the next two hours, he quietly and obediently trailed behind her, leaving Fionna feeling quite uncomfortable but surprisingly empowered.

Mistress Bella Donna, wearing a figure-hugging man's suit, complete with tie and a fedora, snaked through the crowded bar area of the club with Mistress Fionna Blue in tow, who'd gone back to the shop where she'd seen Renetta the other day and picked up those nipple clamps.

It was amateur night in the Cave at the Reformatory. The Cave was the room behind a purple door in the basement, and only platinum-carrying card members were allowed in the Cave, except on amateur night. Fionna gasped out loud when she entered that massive room, its walls painted black, with red paint splashed on the concrete floors. Blindfolded and gagged, leather-bound half-naked bodies hung over her head in steel cages. A grown, fat, pasty-complexioned man sucking on a pacifier and wearing a diaper waddled past Fionna and Bella, making his way to a petite, buxom blond wearing a nurse's uniform, waiting for him with open arms.

A woman bent over a piece of furniture that looked like something a gymnast would somersault off of, wearing nothing but a short skirt, bra, and handcuffs that anchored her to the legs of that thing, breathlessly confessed to the woman standing behind her dressed like a member of a notorious motorcycle club, "I've been bad, daddy! I've been so bad!"

The woman behind her raised a wooden paddle in the air and brought it down hard on the other woman's behind.

Fionna jumped and stumbled, catching herself before she toppled over.

"I see an old friend," Bella Donna said over her shoulder to Fionna Blue. "I'll be right back."

Bella looked past Fionna to Joe, who knelt down in a corner on all fours, wearing another one of those expensive suits.

"You go play with your toy, Mistress Blue," Bella said, walking away. "I'm going to go and adjust the shackles on mine." She winked. "He misses Momma."

Fionna's "toy" stood a respectable distance away from her, waiting patiently for her to beckon. She decided to ignore him.

"Yes!" the woman bent over the gymnastic equipment yelped. She'd started to sob, and Fionna stared horrified at the woman whose bottom burned bright red. "I should be punished! I need to be—"

The paddle came down again, and the woman moaned in ecstasy.

Hysterical laughter suddenly drew Fionna's attention, and in one corner of the room, a man lay on a long table, his arms stretched and bound over his head. His feet were clamped at the ankles in leather shackles. He had tears sliding down the sides of his face, he laughed so hard, while an Asian woman tickled his feet relentlessly.

"Mistress?" Joe in the good suit suddenly appeared at her feet, looking up at her with sad and desperate eyes as if pleading, *Pay attention to me.* When she looked down at him, he quickly lowered his gaze to the floor. "I was hoping to see you again," he confessed. "I-I've missed you."

And with those words kneeling vulnerable on the floor in front of her, Mistress Fionna Blue came to life, dismissing Freddie Palmer to a small corner of herself. She was in character now; Freddie had immediately slipped into the role she'd been playing for weeks now. Gone were the short, plump, and plain wife, mother, grandmother, and the boring court clerk. This woman was bold, dominant, and desired. She lived the kind of life Freddie Palmer couldn't fathom. She trespassed and trampled all over every moral and decent fiber of that woman, daring to see and do whatever she wanted. This man crawled to her on his hands and knees and practically begged her to spend the next few hours of her time with him, even if it meant telling him to stand in the corner with his nose touching the wall until she told him not to, which she'd done last week for half an hour and he'd done it. Mistress Fionna Blue had it like that.

She stared down her nose at him. "Sit up."

Joe in the good suit obediently sat back on his knees.

She'd gone back and bought these things on a whim, never fully committed to using them but never fully against it either.

"Unbutton your shirt, Joe." Freddie fought to maintain the authority in her voice.

Joe quickly did as he was told, his hands trembling in the process.

Fionna blew breath from between her pursed lips, her thoughts flip-flopping over and back again on whether or not she should do this. Maybe it was too much and for her to do this would be going too far. The fact that she was even considering this was beginning to feel overwhelming, and Fionna was two seconds away from turning and running full speed out of this building, jumping into her car, and forgetting she'd ever laid eyes on Joe in the good suit, the woman bent over the gymnastic apparatus, the man being tickled to tears, or nipple clamps.

She reluctantly pulled the nipple clamps from the bottom of her purse, held them in her hand, and stared at them. No. This was crazy. These things looked like torture devices, and there was no way she'd be able to inflict that kind of pain on another human being.

She happened to glance down at Joe, who stared at what she held in her hand with eyes lit up as if it were Christmas morning.

"I want you to sit there, Joe." She knelt down in front of him, sat her purse on the floor beside her, and tried to remember how the hell these things worked. "And don't you move a muscle."

33

❧

Tasha couldn't keep doing this to herself. It was time to confront the issue head-on and do what she should've done a long time ago. She was driving herself crazy with speculation and doubts, and putting herself through hell when all she ever had to do was to go up to one of those women and tell her who she was.

For some reason, Freddie had come to mind first, and if she was going to get this thing moving with any of them, she decided right then and there that it would start with Freddie. Tasha sped down the highway, more determined than ever to get to the bottom of this mystery ruling her life.

"Freddie Palmer," she said out loud in the car, rehearsing her speech. "My name is Tasha Darden, and I have reason to believe that you could very well be my . . ." Tasha didn't like it. It sounded fake—too damn cordial, like she was trying to sell the woman insurance or something. This situation didn't call for fake. It called for keeping it real. "Don't you know who I am?" she said, to herself, imagining Freddie's eyes as big as saucers when she stared at her for a few minutes, before realizing who Tasha was. "That's right, bitch!" Tasha continued reciting her lines as she drove. "It's me. I'm the one you left behind, and now I'm back! How's that for your ass?"

By the time she made it to Freddie's house, she was all riled up and ready to nip this shit in the bud tonight. She'd start with Freddie, and then hit up the rest of them one by one, turning all of their worlds topsy-turvy, upside down, and inside out in a fuckin' flash.

Tasha had parked across the street from Freddie's. She took a few deep breaths to compose herself, and just as she was about to climb out of the car, she suddenly saw Freddie coming out of the house, wrapped in a trench coat and six-inch thigh-high boots.

"What the . . ."

The woman put a gym bag in her trunk, climbed into her car, and pulled out into the street. Tasha ducked down in her seat to keep from being seen. When she sat up again, she spotted Freddie's car stopped at the corner, signaling to turn. Tasha started her car and followed Freddie.

Twenty minutes later, she pulled into a parking space half a block behind where Freddie had parked, and watched in awe as the woman got out of her car, walked up and embraced a tall, sexy-ass brunette, and disappeared through the doors of a building that looked as if it should've been abandoned.

Tasha waited and watched as more people came and went, wearing all sorts of weird outfits. *Is this some kind of punk-rock club or something?* She wondered. Eventually, she got out of the car and headed towards the building, too. She followed a small group of people inside the large, black outside door, down a narrow corridor to the stairs. At the top of the stairs was a giant black man in a dark gray suit and sunglasses, next to a red door. He let everyone in front of her in without incident, but when it was Tasha's turn, he stopped her.

"Card?" he asked soullessly.

She looked at him, confused. "I don't . . . Uh . . . how much to get in?"

"No card, no entrance."

The brotha looked serious, and she knew that arguing with him would be a moot point. Tasha left the way she'd come in, went back out to her car, and waited.

For the next three hours, Tasha stared at that door, waiting for Freddie to finally emerge. She was just about ready to give up and go home when her prayers were answered—Freddie got into her car and drove away. Tasha followed her to a convenience store not far from Freddie's house and watched Freddie take the bag from the trunk and disappear inside. Several minutes later, she emerged wearing a gray sweat suit and sneakers. After that, she drove straight home, and a few minutes later, Don pulled into the driveway.

Tasha had to sit there for a few minutes before she attempted to drive.

"What the hell just happened?" she muttered, shaking her head.

34

"There's your baby, Abby," the doctor said, smiling.

Phyllis stood next to Abby, holding her hand, staring at the ultrasound screen and at the image on it of a very real fetus.

"Oh, my goodness," Abby gasped, squeezing her mother's hand. With tears in her eyes, she glanced quickly at Phyllis's stony, expressionless face. "It's my baby, Mom," she said and laughed.

Phyllis reached down to her toes to pull up the muscles she needed to force a smile.

"I can't believe it's real," Abby squealed. "It's so beautiful!"

"Do you want to know the sex?" the doctor asked.

"Yes!" Abby shot back. "No! Mom?"

Phyllis was literally speechless.

"Mom? Should I let her tell me?"

Phyllis swallowed hard. "Sure."

Abby stared anxiously at the doctor, who studied the screen and finally made the announcement.

"It's a boy, Abby," she said warmly. "You're carrying a little boy."

Phyllis had taken the day off and driven the hour south to Colorado Springs to spend the day with her daughter. Abby was twenty-seven years old with a college degree and a full-time job with benefits. She'd been living on her own for years and had taken care of herself just fine without any help from either of her parents. Every day, young women from all walks of life had children of their own and had done just fine with or without husbands. So why did Phyllis feel like Abby was making the biggest mistake of her life? Why couldn't Phyllis be happy for her daughter? Why couldn't she say *grandmother*, as it applied to her, without damn near choking to death on a word that swelled to the size of a watermelon in the back of her throat?

After the doctor appointment, the two of them decided to stop for ice cream and do a little shopping for the baby.

"The good thing about knowing that it's a boy is that now I know what color to buy," Abby said. She'd been talking nonstop about the baby since they'd left the clinic, and Phyllis let her, without any interjections about work or accounts or fucking a company vice president.

"I don't want to overdo the blue thing, though. Maybe I'll paint his room a nice baby green or something. What do you think, Mom?"

Phyllis struggled internally to conjure up a strong dose of maternal instinct, and it must have showed on her face when Abby looked at her, because disappointment quickly washed over Abby's.

"You're really not feeling any of this, are you, Phyllis?"

Shit. Abby only called her Phyllis when she wanted to make her feel like shit instead of her mother.

"Of course I am, sweetheart," she said, sounding unnaturally sincere. "I'm happy because you're happy."

Abby studied her mother and shook her head. "It's the grandmother thing. Isn't it?"

Phyllis raised her eyebrows. "What you mean?"

"Mom," Abby said, exasperated. "I know you better than you give me credit for. You wear your emotions on your sleeve. You always did. You don't want to be a grandmother."

Phyllis stood there with her mouth hanging open, about to say something, but she had no idea what, so she didn't say anything.

"It's always about you, and it's always been about you," Abby said, sadly.

"That's not true, Abby."

"Sure it is, Phyllis."

"Mom!" Phyllis interjected.

Abby stared at her. "I've stood back my whole life, trying to stay out of your way, watching you do your thing. Do you know how hard that is for a kid?"

"Wait a minute, baby." Phyllis felt her defenses start to kick in. "You make it sound like I've never been there for you, and that's not true."

"You were there, but only on your terms," Abby stated severely. "I was lucky because Daddy was there, and he always made sure that I had the attention I needed. He was there to help me with homework and to drive me to volleyball practice, but sometimes I really wished I had you too."

"I was there," she said, starting to get angry. Was it hormones or was this girl talking like Phyllis lived on another planet? "I chaperoned at sleepovers, Abby. I went shopping with you for your prom dress, went to your volleyball games."

"Only when it didn't interfere with your schedule," Abby argued. "And now I need you, Mom. I really need you, more than I ever did for prom dresses and sleepovers." Abby started to cry.

"And I'm here!"

"But you don't want to be! What is it? Guilt? A sense of obligation? You're getting old and you're trying to get into heaven now? What?"

"Getting old?" Phyllis asked, appalled.

Suddenly it was like someone had turned on a lightbulb, and Abby wasn't in the dark anymore. "That's it, isn't it?"

Phyllis swallowed hard and took a deep breath to calm herself down. "I'm not getting old."

Abby stared quizzically at her mother and then shook her head. "Out of everything I've just said, that's the only part of the conversation that hit home with you?"

She brushed past her mother and headed out of the store.

Half an hour later, Phyllis was back on the highway, headed home. She'd tried having a conversation with Abby as they drove back to her apartment, but the girl wouldn't say a word. She was like her father in that respect. He used to give Phyllis the silent treatment too when the two of them had a disagreement. He'd spoiled that girl, Phyllis concluded angrily. At what point in her life had she been made to believe that the world revolved around her? And at what point in her life was she going to finally grow up and realize that everything Phyllis had done and hadn't done for her when she was growing up had been in her best interest? If Phyllis had denied herself her own ambitions, Abby would've been the one to suffer for it in the end, because Phyllis would've been a bitter, angry woman, weighted down by regret that she hadn't pursued her own dreams. She left her husband, her marriage, but never her child. And Abby had conveniently decided to forget all the times she'd called her mother in the middle of the night when she'd had a bad dream or when she wasn't feeling well. She and Phyllis had spent summers and spring breaks and holidays together, traveling and giggling like sisters, staying up till all hours of the night, painting each other's toenails and eating home-baked cookies. Phyllis might not have lived in the same house with her, but she had been there for her daughter.

Tears filled her eyes as she drove, and out of the blue, Phyllis hit the Bluetooth button on her steering wheel and dialed Abby's number. Of course she got her voice mail.

"I know you're mad at me," she said, choking back a sob. "But I've been there for you, Abby. Maybe not the way you wanted, but I have been there." She thought of hanging up after that, but Phyllis had one more thing to add, hopefully, convincingly: "Call me."

35

Avery came downstairs from Renetta's bedroom and followed the trail of voices into the kitchen. His eyes lit up at the sight of three beautiful young women sitting around the kitchen table, and at Renetta in jeans and a T-shirt, looking more like the older sister than den mother.

"Hey," she said when he came into the room. "Come on in and have a seat. Breakfast is still hot."

He stood in the doorway, expecting to wake up from what had to be a dream.

"Come on," Renetta coaxed. "Don't be shy."

Avery took a seat at the table. One of the girls filled a glass with orange juice and sat it in front of him.

"Thanks," he said.

The girl blushed. "You're welcome."

"How do you like your eggs?" Renetta asked.

"Fried, hard," he answered.

Two of the girls looked at each other and giggled.

"Alright you two," Renetta scolded gently. "You're making my guest uncomfortable."

"It's alright," Avery said, getting a kick out of all of this. "I'm a big boy. I can handle it."

"No, it's rude. And my girls know I don't allow rude behavior in my house." Renetta cut her eyes at the girls, but it was easy to see that her bark was much worse than her bite.

"You want grits, Avery?"

Avery looked at her. "Grits? What do you know about making grits?"

Renetta laughed. "Shoot, boy, I'm a grits-making queen."

"We're talking grits, and not Cream of Wheat, right? I don't put no sugar and milk on grits, Renetta."

Renetta set his plate down in front of him covered with cheese. "Salt and pepper's on the table," she said slyly.

Avery found out that the women at the table were some of Renetta's models. One of them had spent the night in her spare room, and the other two showed up for breakfast and to give the other a ride back to the campus in Fort Collins. Being the only man at the table, he was the center of attention, and the subject of speculation. None of them came out and said it, but all three were fascinated with the fact that he'd spent the night and that he'd spent the night in Renetta's room. A few hours later, the young women all gathered their things, thanked Renetta for breakfast, and kissed her cheek as they left.

"How come you didn't warn me there'd be a house full of women waiting on me at breakfast this morning?" he joked.

"I figured you wouldn't mind," she winked.

"They were gorgeous," Avery confessed. "And young."

"They're babies. Gorgeous babies."

"With a gorgeous mother hen watching over them," he said smiling.

"Those girls are the closest I've got to children. Want some more coffee?" Renetta asked, getting up to make another pot.

He wasn't interested in more coffee, but Avery wasn't ready to leave either. "Sure." Avery thought about Tasha. He hadn't heard from her since he identified the women in the photograph for her. Based on what Renetta had just said, he concluded that either Tasha still hadn't gotten around to making contact with Renetta, or that she had reached out to her and determined that Renetta wasn't her mother. He studied her while she made a fresh pot. Every move she made was as graceful as a dancer, and he looked for hints of the woman Isaac had told him about, the one sprawled out on the front lawn after being dragged there by her husband.

Renetta turned to him and smiled. "You're staring."

"You're lovely."

Renetta sat back down at the table. "Thank you."

An hour after he left, Renetta sat in her garden thinking fondly of Avery. Since when had she felt sincere fondness for any man, she wondered, smiling. He was nobody in particular. Renetta had been courted by successful businessmen, politicians, even dignitaries. Avery wasn't a man who would stand out in a room, except to look uneasy and out of place. For some strange reason, she found that charming.

Had she met someone like him instead of Vincent, her life might've turned out vastly different. She and Avery could've had children together, allowing her an opportunity to atone for her sins. She wouldn't have had to spend a life wondering "what if." He would have been the kind of man she'd have felt comfortable sharing all her secrets with, and perhaps Renetta wouldn't have had to spend a lifetime looking over her shoulder and expecting the police to finally catch up with her.

36

~⁘~

"I'm sorry I'm late," Tasha said, climbing into Jeff's car. "I had to make a quick call."

"Got everything?"

"Yep."

"Let's hit the road."

Spending an evening with Jeff was one thing, but spending an entire weekend was something she wasn't sure she could handle.

"I like to get away from time to time. Got a little place up in the hills where I go to unwind, and I'd love it if you joined me."

Tasha's first inclination was to refuse. It was easy to string along a conversation over dinner and, of course, conversation during sex was hardly an issue. This was going to be a challenge. Jeff had made it clear that he had planned on using this opportunity to "get to know her better." Tasha worried about him getting to know her too well.

He knew the basics, that she never knew her parents, was raised in the foster care system, and had hired an investigator to help find her mother. She just avoided telling him that her mother could very well be one of his employees.

Spending the weekend with Jeff was risky for Tasha. The more time the two of them were together, the more she risked giving in to her vulnerability. Jeff was an attractive man, inside and out. He was easy to talk to, and if she wasn't careful Tasha could open up and run the risk of telling him more than he needed to know.

The encounter she'd witnessed between him and Phyllis the other night over dinner was strange. The vibe between the two of them transcended the line of two people who happened to work together. The look on that woman's face had struck Tasha as odd and Jeff's usual cool demeanor was visibly shaken when he saw her.

It could've been a case of Tasha letting her imagination get away from her, but she didn't think that it was. Would he come out and admit that he and Phyllis were sleeping together? No. But Tasha was very astute in reading between the lines and this weekend, she'd planned on reading him.

The drive up to Aspen was scenic and relaxing. Jeff seemed to like the serenity of the ride, too, as they both were content to enjoy the sound of smooth jazz filling the SUV.

It was a shame that she'd spent her whole life living this close to the mountains and yet could count on one hand how many times she'd actually ventured into them.

. . .

The sun was starting to set, and the two of them had just finished having dinner out in town. Jeff's condo was sleek, modern, with magnificent mountainside views. The two of them had settled into the hot tub and shared a bottle of wine.

"I love it up here," Tasha said.

"Coming here helps keep me sane," he explained, smiling.

"Why do you do that kind of work if you hate it so much?"

"Who said I hate it? I love what I do."

She laughed. "Oh, really?"

"You don't sound convinced." He grinned.

"Hey, if working eighty hours a week is your thing, more power to you. Personally, I'd rather have a life."

She expected him to be offended, but he wasn't. "Look around you, Tasha," he said confidently. "This is my life. I have another condo in Miami, and I'm thinking of buying a flat in Europe, so . . ."

She laughed and raised her glass. "Well, alright then."

"So, what about you?" Jeff asked. "What else do you do with all that life you have?"

His question struck a nerve and caught her off guard. The truth was, Tasha wasn't doing a damn thing with her life, other than obsessing over a situation that haunted her morning, noon, and night. But instead of admitting that, she opted to continue to play the role she'd been playing since she'd met him.

"I like to travel." She and Robin had gone to Vegas for a weekend once, a few years back.

"Really? What's your favorite destination?"

Of course her mind went blank. "Puerto Rico," she blurted out.

"Puerto Rico's great," he said, grinning. "Where'd you stay?"

Fuck! Really? Did he really just ask her that? "A quaint little village near the beach," she said, casually.

Jeff nodded. "I've been to San Juan a couple of times. Loved it."

"Yeah," she smiled and quickly sipped on her wine. Tasha was tired of talking and Jeff seemed determined to get her to open up. Tasha decided to take matters into her own hands and change the subject.

One kiss led to a longer kiss, and then to lovemaking in the hot tub. Eventually, they moved the fun and games into the bedroom, and finally lay spent and satisfied in each other's arms. Every now and then, Phyllis's face crept into her thoughts, but Tasha focused on the task at hand until it faded. This weekend belonged to her, not Phyllis, Renetta, or Freddie. But her curiosity about the nature of the relationship between Phyllis and Jeff had been nagging at her.

"That woman I met? Your coworker, what was her name again?"

Naturally, Jeff was exhausted after they made love, and drifting quickly off to sleep. He moaned.

"You know. The one we met at dinner last week," she probed.

Jeff wrapped both arms around her, kissed her tenderly on the forehead, and squeezed. "What about her?" he asked groggily.

"She didn't seem too happy to see you with me."

He didn't respond.

Tasha knew she was pushing the envelope. But that's why she decided to make this trip with Jeff. It was all about pushing envelopes.

"Jeff, is there something going on between the two of you? I'm not prying," she said. "I just need to know the boundaries."

Jeff never opened his eyes. He never answered the question and she soon realized he'd fallen asleep, or maybe he'd just pretended to.

37

❧

"Freddie Palmer. I'd tell you my name but it wouldn't matter. I know who you are, and I know the others. One day we'll meet and one of you can finally tell me which one of you is my birth mother."

After listening to that message the first time, Freddie reluctantly played it again, and then again. Alarm washed over her. Nothing could've prepared her for this. You can't hide from your mistakes. She'd known that her whole life, and now the biggest mistake she'd ever made had come back to prove her right.

"We need to talk, Renetta," Freddie told her over the phone.

"What's wrong?"

"Are you home?"

"Yes, but . . ."

"I'll be there in twenty minutes." Freddie's voice shook.

After she hung up the phone, she sat behind her desk

trying to calm her nerves. There was no way she could drive like this. She waited a few moments, clasping her hands together until they finally stopped shaking.

Moments later, she hurried out of her office and left a message with one of her coworkers that she wasn't feeling well and had to go to a doctor's appointment.

"Hope you feel better, Freddie," her coworkers said.

Her life had changed direction on a dime and she knew without a doubt that it would never be the same again.

Renetta answered the door and immediately panicked when she saw the expression on Freddie's face. "What's wrong, Freddie? You look like you've just seen a ghost."

Freddie hurried inside. "*Heard* one, is more like it."

She was still shaking. Freddie fought desperately to control the quiver in her voice.

"Sit down." Renetta led Freddie into the formal living room. "Tell me what's going on, sweetie."

Tears suddenly flooded Freddie's eyes. "I got a phone call." Her voice trailed off. "Jesus, Renetta." She stared helplessly at her.

"What? Freddie," Renetta pleaded desperately. "What happened, honey? Tell me."

Freddie stood up and began pacing the room. "I can't believe this is happening! I can't believe it, Renetta!"

"What? For goodness sake! Please! Tell me what's going on."

"She called me!" Freddie blurted out.

"Who? Who called you?"

"The woman! The baby who was . . ."

"You're not making any sense, Freddie. Calm down and tell me what you're talking about."

"A woman called, claiming to be the child that we left in that hospital, Renetta." Freddie's eyes bulged. Beads of sweat formed at her temples. Suddenly the room felt like an oven. She unbuttoned the top two buttons of her blouse. "I need something to drink. Renetta? Please. Can I have some . . . water . . . some . . ."

Renetta sat frozen for several minutes before finally getting up and stumbling into the kitchen. She came back a few minutes later with a glass of water. "What did the woman say?" she asked, her heart racing. "How do you know she was telling the truth?"

Freddie finished the glass of water in one gulp. She took several deep breaths and finally composed herself enough to explain.

"She was . . . telling the truth," Freddie said, unfaltering. "I know she was."

Renetta looked uncertain. "What exactly did she say?"

Freddie stared unblinking at Renetta. "That she knows who I am . . . who we all are," she whispered. "She said we'd meet someday and that," Freddie swallowed, "we could finally tell her who her mother was. The message was on my voice mail when I got into the office this morning. She left it on Friday, after I left work."

Renetta didn't want to believe it. She fought internally not to let this be as real as it looked in Freddie's eyes. "Maybe it was somebody just fucking with you, Freddie," she mumbled. The whole world felt like it was shrinking.

Freddie shook her head. "It was her," she said softly.

"Somebody's playing some kind of prank," Renetta insisted.

"It was her, Renetta."

"How do you know?" Renetta yelled. "Did you actually talk to this woman?"

"She left me a message at work!"

"This is some kind of mistake, Freddie." Renetta stood up and started pacing the room.

"I don't believe it is."

"It's a joke. A sick, twisted joke and somebody needs their ass kicked for pulling a stunt like this."

"It's not a joke! My God, Renetta! Will you listen to yourself?"

"Will you listen to *yourself*? What did she say her name was?"

Freddie didn't respond.

"She didn't leave a name?"

"No," Freddie said, dejected.

Renetta threw her hands up in frustration. "If that woman is who you think she is then don't you think she'd have told you her name?"

Freddie shrugged, pitifully. "If it's not her, then who else could it be?"

"It could be anybody! I don't know! Maybe it's somebody with too much time on her hands who came across the article in some library archive or something. Maybe it's somebody the who thinks they can get money out of us. I don't know!"

"Nobody was ever able to identify the girls in that article, Renetta," Freddie finally said.

"Nobody that we know of. Maybe somebody did, and—"

"And what?" Freddie asked, appalled. "If they ever found out who any of us were, Renetta, they'd have come knocking on our doors—the police, social services, somebody would've confronted us about it."

"Okay, so you've just made my point! If no one else has ever identified us, then how in the hell could . . . she?"

Freddie stared intently at Renetta. "I'm not crazy," she said quietly.

"I never said you were," Renetta responded firmly.

"And I don't think this was a prank or a coincidence or some twisted fluke."

"I don't know what it was, Freddie, but I'd be hard pressed to think that . . ."

That the child they'd abandoned had found them. Renetta hadn't said it, but Freddie knew she'd thought it.

Both of them sat in silence for several minutes, trying to make sense of their worst fears.

"What if it *is* her?" Freddie finally spoke up and asked. Renetta turned to her. She looked as scared as Freddie felt. "What if it is, Renetta?"

Renetta didn't know what to say, so she didn't say anything.

38

❧

It was Monday night and Phyllis had done the unthinkable. She'd left work right at five. She'd been home for nearly two hours and still hadn't cracked open her laptop. Her last outing with Abby had made her stand up and take notice. Phyllis had argued and justified her mothering with Abby, but ultimately she had to admit that she'd fallen short in that child's life. Abby had been right. Phyllis had played mommy, but only when and how it fit into her own plans.

"I'm sorry, baby, but I have to go out of town on business. I'll come and get you when I get back, and we can spend next weekend together. Promise."

"Abby, Mommy just got out of a long meeting. But I'll come to the next game, sweetie. Promise."

"This is not a good time right now, honey. Call me tomorrow after school, and we'll talk about it then. Promise."

"No, Abby. Mommy isn't ready to be anybody's grand-anything right now, so why don't you just wait and have another baby in say, oh, five or six years, and I'll be a fabulous grandmother. Promise."

Her phone rang, and Phyllis debated whether or not to answer it. "Hello?"

"Phyllis." She recognized the sound of his voice immediately. "Marcus."

She sat straight up at attention, shocked by the fact that

he'd called. Something was wrong. Panic shot through her as she immediately thought of Abby. "Marcus. What's wrong?"

"Nothing. Nothing's wrong," he said quickly, hearing the panic in her voice. "Everything's fine."

Really? Nothing was wrong? Then why in the world was he calling?

"Look, I'm in town on business and I was wondering if you'd be interested in a late dinner." He lived in Colorado Springs too, not too far from where Abby lived.

She hesitated for a moment, attempting to process what he'd just said. "With you?" she asked without thinking.

"No, Phyllis. With this dude standing next to me. Of course with me."

"Oh . . . well, I—"

"I thought this would be a good opportunity to talk about Abby," he explained.

"Abby. Sure."

"I'm staying over until tomorrow, and I just thought . . ."

"Yeah, that's fine. I could meet you somewhere."

"You already know what I'm going to say."

Phyllis laughed, because he was right. "I can be there in an hour."

Marcus was already seated when she walked into his favorite restaurant, the Greek Town Café on Colfax. Phyllis ordered a glass of water and a Greek salad. Marcus ordered his usual souvlaki plate with Greek potatoes.

"The truth is, she's a grown woman," he reasoned. "Grown enough to have a child if she chooses."

"That doesn't mean I'm not still worried about her," Phyllis explained. "Being a parent is hard enough, Marcus, but being a single parent?" she said, concerned. "It's not going to be easy for her."

"No, it's not going to be easy," he said matter-of-factly. "But it's her choice. We can't tell her what to do anymore."

"Who made up that rule?" Phyllis muttered, frustrated.

Marcus laughed. "Somebody who never had kids."

"Yeah, well, maybe this wouldn't have happened if I'd been a better mother."

Marcus looked at her like she was crazy. "What?"

She sighed. "Our daughter thinks I'm a terrible mother."

"Oh really?" he said, not sounding the least bit surprised.

She studied him, and prepared to get her feelings hurt. "You sound like you agree."

"I didn't say that."

"But you were thinking it," she said, sounding surprisingly vulnerable.

"No, but obviously you were."

She shrugged. "Well, maybe she's right."

"If you say so."

"What's that supposed to mean?" she asked, offended.

"I'm just saying she's always been pretty good at making you feel guilty. Abby has always known how to push your buttons, and you've always been good at letting her."

Another time, another place, and she would've argued with him, but not this time. "Maybe she has a right to push my buttons."

Marcus stared at her.

"Let's face it, Marcus. I'd never win Mother of the Year," she said regretfully.

He put down his utensils. "Phyllis, don't."

"Don't what? Don't tell the truth? Come on, Marcus. You know like I know and like Abby knows that I wasn't there for that child like I needed to be."

"That was a long time ago. Abby wasn't some poor neglected kid who grew up without parents or people who didn't care about her," he argued. "You did the best you could," he shrugged. "Like I did the best I could."

"Your best was better," she said sadly.

"It wasn't a competition, Phyllis. Did I make mistakes? Sure I did. Did you make mistakes? Yeah. But believe me. Abby's fine."

Was she fine? Phyllis wasn't convinced.

"She's pregnant," he said. "She's got terrible taste in men. But I'm hoping she'll grow out of that," he said, smirking.

Phyllis couldn't help but laugh. "Well, she didn't get her terrible taste in men from me. I've always had great taste in—" She stopped short of finishing that statement.

Marcus decided to make light of the awkward moment. "Well, I can't speak for all the other men you've been with, but I was the best thing you ever had." He leaned back, tilted his head, and popped his collar.

"Whatever, boy!" She tossed her napkin across the table at him.

She always felt so comfortable with him. With everyone else, Phyllis had a tendency to put on airs, but not with him. "Hard to believe we actually used to like each other."

He smiled. "A lot."

Sitting across from him now, living without Marcus Neville felt so unnatural. Why did she think that anything or anyone could make her happier than Marcus?

"I'm sorry, Marcus," she said solemnly. "I'm sorry for not appreciating a good thing when I had it."

"We both messed up our marriage, Phyllis. I think we were young, too young to know what it was we really wanted. By the time we figured it out, we were both miserable."

In some ways, Phyllis was still miserable. Back then, the grass was definitely greener on any side except the one she was on. Phyllis wanted a career. She wanted to get out into the world and show anybody who was paying attention that she could accomplish great things. And she'd done it. At moments like this, however, she realized just how much success had cost her, and he was sitting across from her.

"You're happy now, though, with what's-her-name?"

"You know her name," he said, smugly smirking.

"I know it," she confessed. "I don't like saying it, but I know it, and I know that she must be very good for you. You look happy."

"What about you, Phyllis?"

"What about me?"

"Who do you have in your life that's busy making you happy?"

Unexpected tears glistened in her eyes, but Phyllis smiled through them. "Oh, you know me," she said, triumphantly. "I'm married to my career. A match made in heaven."

He stared deeply into her eyes. "Is it?"

He always did have a knack for searching out and finding that softer side of Phyllis. The conversation between them flowed easily and Marcus plucked it like a flower and Phyllis let him.

. . .

If they'd driven back across to her place, they'd have both come to their senses, had second thoughts, and gone their separate ways. But neither of them wanted to risk missing this moment. Marcus paid the bill, took hold of Phyllis's hand, and led her across the street to the cheap motel on the corner.

"If you don't want to do this," he said hoarsely, "please say something."

Marcus stepped closer to her, his gaze locked on hers.

Phyllis never said a word. He cradled her face between his hand, pressed his lips to hers, and filled her mouth with his delicious tongue. Marcus tasted better now than she had remembered. Not enough time had passed. They remembered too much about each other, things that should've been forgotten and things that neither of them could ever possibly forget.

She lay straddled on top of him. Phyllis made love to him the way she used to, slowly, passionately, savoring every inch of him inside her. It was as if the divorce had never taken place and he wasn't married to another woman. Emotionally, mentally, they'd both moved on in so many ways in their lives, headed in different directions with different needs. Physically, time had stood still for both of them, as their bodies lovingly recalled the nuances of each other.

"I'm cumming, Marcus," she whispered, quivering.

"I know, sugah," he told her. "Come on."

39

It was late, but Renetta couldn't sleep. She sat in her living room on the chaise, her legs drawn to her chest, her mind still reeling from the conversation she'd had with Freddie a day ago.

"If it's not her, then who else could it be?"

What if that woman really was that child? Where had she been all these years? How had she been? What would she do when she actually found out the truth? Her mother had been a terrified young woman, unprepared and irrational to deal with the circumstances in her life. But would it matter?

"We never meant to leave her like that," Renetta muttered, rubbing tiredness from her eyes. "Not like that."

But again, would it even matter?

She took several deep, cleansing breaths to relieve the tension building in her muscles. Renetta then sat down on the floor with her legs folded underneath her. She inhaled deeply, stretched her arms above her head, and then slowly bent forward at the hips, settling into child's pose to stretch her spine.

The rational side of Renetta was her ruling side. That side of her warned her not to panic and reminded her that this might all turn out to be nothing more than someone playing a guessing game with Freddie. Renetta needed to slow her thoughts, calm her emotions, and let common sense do what it did best.

Freddie had been right. Absolutely no one had come for-

ward to identify any of them when that article had been published in the paper. No one. In thirty years, not a single soul
had come forward and said, "I know who that is." If that were
the case, then how could this woman possibly know? How
could she have solved the puzzle of those mystery girls thirty
years after that article had been published, when they had
been impossible to recognize?

"Take off that sweatshirt."

"But it's cold outside."

*"It's got the name of our school on it. Take it off and put
this one on, and make sure you put on the hood."*

*"What difference does it make? We're just going to take it
to the front desk, leave it there, and run. Right?"*

"It's not an 'it.' It's a her."

The sound of Renetta's phone ringing startled her.
"Hello," she said, clearing her throat.

"Hey, sweet thang," Avery said teasingly. "You in the
mood for some company?"

"Avery. Hey, no. No, tonight's not a good time."

"You alright?" he asked.

Renetta was far from alright. She was trying like hell not
to come apart at the seams.

"I'm not feeling well. It's been a long day, and I'm tired."

"Uh-huh. You need someone to talk to?" he asked, concerned.

Renetta sighed. "You and me don't do much talking when
we're together, and you know it."

"Well, what you don't know about me then is that I'm one
hell of good listener. I swear I can listen and not put my
hands on you."

Sad tears rose in her eyes, and the need to make a confession burned in the back of her throat. Her past was threatening to come dangerously close to her present, but maybe it was time for her to talk to someone. Avery was as good a someone as any. If this woman was that baby, then it was only a matter of time before the truth came to light and everyone would know what the three of them had done.

"I'll hold you to it," she said, relieved. "And bring wine."

Avery had conjured up his own version of the story of those young women from looking at the photograph. He'd put together the pieces Tasha had given him, which wasn't much. To hear the story firsthand from one of the only three people in the world who knew the truth was something else.

"We didn't mean to leave that baby like we did," she said, trying to keep from crying. "God, Avery! We panicked. We got scared and . . ." Renetta shrugged.

Avery was sitting in a hot seat if there ever was one. Should he tell Renetta that the woman who had called Freddie Palmer wasn't a lunatic? She was authentic and he'd been the one to put her on their trail. He didn't say a word. Avery sat there staring into the tearful face of Renetta, unable to utter one word of what he knew.

"We thought we knew so much," she said remorsefully. "The closer it got to graduation, the more we strutted through those hallways reminding anyone who'd listen that we were on our way to being grown." She half smiled. "But when it came time to be adults for real"—Renetta shook her head, and ran her hand over her hair—"shit, we were clueless."

He gathered enough courage to ask one question, one that

he never thought actually mattered, but maybe, eventually, it would: "Who's the father?"

Renetta took a deep breath and blew out a loud groan. "That's the really fucked-up part," she said, letting the tears flow like rivers. She'd stopped trying to dry them a long time ago. "Just a boy at school," she said quietly.

"Did he know?" He knew the answer to that without even having to wait for it.

She shook her head. "He never did," she said sadly.

"How could he not know?"

She looked at him and forced a smile. "He just didn't know."

Avery sat quietly wondering about the lucky bastard who had no idea that he was a part of this jacked-up puzzle. If there was a God, hopefully he'd be merciful and leave that poor fool out of it.

"What if it's her, Avery?" Renetta traced circles around the rim of her wineglass with her finger. She looked at him. "What if this isn't a hoax and that baby has come back to confront us about what we did?"

Avery had to have looked as dumbfounded as he felt. He sat there trying to appear detached and clueless, but inside, he was being torn to shreds. Obligation was kicking his ass, but obligation to whom? Renetta? Tasha? If Renetta knew that he'd been the one to find her, she'd hate him for it. Avery wasn't in love or anything like that, but it wasn't like he didn't care about her.

Tasha had been a paycheck. She'd been a client, and the two of them hadn't spoken since he'd handed her the three files on these ladies. But Tasha was the victim in all of this. Tasha had been the one who'd been screwed up by all of this, even if she never came out and said it. He sensed it to be true. He decided right then and there that the best thing he could do was to keep his damn mouth shut.

"I've spent my life looking forward," she said softly. "Never backward. The darkest years of my life started that night, and they lasted far too long." She looked solemnly at Avery. "My husband was abusive. Did I ever tell you that?"

He shook his head.

"He treated me like I was worthless, but I let him. Because that's how I felt. My penance, I suppose. Besides, having my ass beaten took my mind off other things," Renetta said, bitterly. "I just replaced one pain for another until it nearly went away altogether."

Renetta set down her wineglass then raised the sleeves on her shirt and showed Avery her wrists. Horizontal scars had long since healed. How the hell had he missed that?

"I cut the wrong direction," Renetta explained, studying them. "A serious suicide cuts vertically and deep," she explained. "Very deep."

Avery put his glass down, too, took her wrists in his hands, and raised them to his lips and kissed each of them. Renetta pulled them back, cradled his face in her hands, and pressed her lips to his, sobbing uncontrollably. Avery didn't know what else to do. He gathered her in his arms, lay back on that chaise lounge, and held her tight until they both drifted off to sleep.

40

⚜

"I've been calling, Tasha," Robin said, coming into Tasha's apartment. "Did you get any of my messages?"

Tasha scratched her head and closed the door. "Yeah. I've just been busy."

Tasha looked alright. She may have lost a little weight, but all in all, she looked fine, which for Robin was a relief.

"So, how's it going?" Robin asked, sitting next to Tasha on the sofa.

Tasha nodded and then shrugged. "Fine, Robin. It's going fine."

Robin stared at her, recognizing agitation in Tasha's expression. "I saw Dom the other night at Pierre's. He asked about you."

"Did he?" Tasha said impatiently.

"He said he'd called you, too."

Tasha fidgeted and bounced her knee. "He might have. I don't know," she said irritably.

"He still cares about you, Tash. I think he calls himself being in love," she chuckled uncomfortably.

"Yeah, well he's the only one, Robin." Tasha finally looked at her.

"What's wrong with you?" Robin frowned.

Tasha looked at her like she had two heads. "What the hell do you think is wrong with me?"

"Do you know who she is?" Robin asked hesitantly.

Tasha rolled her eyes.

"Have you even spoken to those women, Tasha?"

"Not yet," she muttered under her breath.

"What?"

"No, Robin!"

Robin stared frustrated at Tasha. "Oh my goodness. It's been months now and you haven't spoken to any of them?"

Tasha didn't answer.

"So you've just been sitting here wallowing in this shit all this time? Really, Tasha?"

Robin's frustration quickly got the best of her and she picked up her purse, bolted to her feet, and headed for the door. She turned to Tasha one last time before leaving and shook her head. "Do you have any idea how scary you are right now? Do you see what you're doing to yourself? You've managed to make a bad situation worse and I am so worried about you, Tasha."

"Bye," Tasha said dryly, waiting for her to leave.

Robin spun around. "You know, you're a fuckin' piece of work!"

Tasha stood up. "I'm a piece of work?"

"That's what I said!"

"Why are you still here? There's the goddamn door! Use it!"

"You know, Tasha, maybe I *don't* get it. I know who my mother is, and she didn't leave me in some gym bag next to the men's room. But I am your friend. I have been your friend since we were kids, and maybe I would get it, if you stopped being so strange and help me help you."

"I don't need your help, Robin," Tasha said, crossing her arms.

Robin was hurt, and it showed. "I get that you have no idea who your mom is. I get that. I get that the woman abandoned you when you were a baby and you had to be stuck living with that weird-ass Miss Lucy. I get that. What I don't get is why you've been acting like this. I don't get why you've been spending all that time on the Internet, pasting pictures on the walls, obsessing over which of those women gave birth to you when all you have to do is ask them. That's what I don't get, Tasha."

Tasha paced frantically back and forth, "Just ask," she muttered.

"Yeah."

"Ask, and one of them will tell me?"

"That's right. And then it'll be over."

Tasha stopped, turned to Robin, and glared at her with tears in her eyes. "See, that's the part you don't get, Robin." She chewed on her bottom lip.

"Then tell me, Tash," Robin said tenderly. "Tell me so that I can get it."

"Me finding out who my mother is isn't the end," her voice quaked. "It's the beginning."

Robin tried to smile. "Well, then that's a good thing. Right? You'll get a chance to build a relationship with the woman who had you, Tash. The two of you can start a new beginning, and you can have the relationship you always wanted but didn't have. That's what you want? Isn't it?"

Tasha stared coolly at her and shrugged. "Is it?"

41

❧

"Don't forget, Freddie. We're meeting with the new judge in an hour." Phil Morrison, her supervisor, stopped by her office to remind her. "The meeting's in his chambers."

"Sure, Phil. I'll be there."

She'd been feeling sick to her stomach ever since she received the voice mail message a few days ago. Now every time her phone rang, Freddie waited for the caller ID to show up telling her who it was, and when no caller ID was available, she'd let the call go to voice mail and check it later.

Freddie had always feared that something like this would happen. Back then, she had waited on pins and needles every single day, expecting the police to knock on the door of her parents' house or to show up at her school. It wasn't until she and Don moved to Germany that Freddie could begin to let her guard down, but it had taken years for her to actually become complacent.

Renetta could try all she wanted to pretend that this wasn't really happening, but Freddie knew better. The past hadn't vanished in the air like smoke. That child was as real now as she'd been back then, and she had found them. She'd found all three of them. They'd been spared the wrath of their actions long enough, and now it was time for them to own up to what they'd done once and for all. She knew she had no choice now but to finally tell Don. Through the years, she'd tried, but Freddie knew good and damn well she hadn't tried hard enough. There was no getting around it this time, though. Freddie couldn't put it off any longer, and tonight, after dinner, she'd tell him everything.

"Freddie Palmer"—her boss, Phil Morrison, didn't need to bother with an introduction, but neither one of them interrupted him when he did—"this is Judge Joseph Wagner." Phil grinned like a candidate running for office. "Judge Wagner, Freddie is the best clerk in the state of Colorado, sir, and she will be assisting you with getting settled into your courtroom and will show you around our facility. She'll take good care of you, sir, and please don't hesitate to let her know what you need."

Morrison excused himself, and Freddie and Judge Wagner stood staring unblinking at each other for what seemed like an eternity. The last time she'd seen him, Joe in the expensive suit, he was trailing behind her with clamps on his nipples and a painful but euphoric expression on his face, and she was bound in a leather corset with cleavage spilling out from the top like lava erupting from a volcano.

Now here they were, face-to-face in the real world, with their real jobs, looking utterly shocked at seeing each other again. Maybe, by some miracle, he wouldn't recognize her without the latex and leather. Maybe he'd think she just looked like someone he knew but couldn't possibly be, because Freddie was a dowdy court clerk, and the woman she resembled was a commanding and sexy vixen capable of making slaves of men. Freddie could hope all she wanted, but the truth was written all over his face.

Freddie cleared her throat. "I think it would be best if I got one of the other court clerks to help you get situated, Judge Wagner."

"I—this is a surprise," he said hesitantly.

"Yes, sir." Her voice quivered. "This is definitely unexpected, but I'm sure one of the other court clerks would be more than happy to work with you, Judge."

"Why would you think that, Mistress?"

Freddie stared at him, shocked by what he'd just called her. "Don't say that!" she said sternly.

The judge lowered his head like an admonished child. "Forgive me. I was out of line."

Freddie was appalled. "Stop it! Don't act like that around here. You don't—" She took a step closer to him and lowered her voice almost to a whisper. "I'm not Mistress anymore, Judge Wagner. I'm Freddie. Freddie Palmer—that's my name. I am a clerk of this court, a regular woman, and I expect you to treat me accordingly." Freddie stepped back, raised her chin, and regained her composure.

He raised his eyes slightly to hers. "Thank you for correcting me," he said humbly.

Lord have mercy! If there was ever a time for the Rapture, this was it and even if she'd sinned too much to be caught up, maybe Judge Wagner could go.

Her heart couldn't take much more. Panic burned like acid in her stomach. Everything seemed to have been happening at once, the call from that woman and the possibility that Freddie could crash and burn from the truth coming to light, and now all this mess going on between her and the new judge.

"I'll get you another clerk, Judge." Freddie started to walk away, but he stepped slightly into her path to stop her.

"That won't be necessary," he said quietly, finally staring back into her eyes. "I assure you."

She didn't like this. Call it instinct or woman's intuition, but every warning bell in her body started to ring at the thought of her and this man working together. They'd crossed some serious lines at the Reformatory, and because of that, the two of them had no business even being in the same courthouse together. "I think it would be best," she said severely.

"Forgive me, Mis—, but I prefer to work with you, and I am the judge." He said it as considerately as he could, but the underlying tone to what he really meant seemed loud and clear.

"I assure you, sir," she said, struggling to remain calm, "we have some highly experienced and wonderful clerks here that would be more than happy to assist our newest judge in getting settled. I'll see to it personally that the most competent and organized individual will be assigned to you." She smiled.

"But I chose you," he said abruptly, catching her off guard.

Freddie looked stunned. "What?"

"That night? I chose you," he said, slowly raising his gaze to meet hers.

She took a step back.

"I saw you walk in, and I knew immediately that I wanted you."

She looked appalled. "To do what?"

He smiled. "To manage me."

Freddie couldn't believe what she was hearing, and she certainly didn't want to believe that somehow she'd let herself be manipulated in all this. "Well, I can't manage you now, Judge Wagner," she explained cautiously. "Back then, that was just . . . I was . . . pretending to be someone else. I was playing a game. Acting."

His stone-faced expression caught her by surprise. "I assure you, Mistress Fionna, I wasn't."

Before she could say another word, a knock at the door interrupted them.

"Joe!" Another judge came into his chambers smiling and extending his hand for Wagner to shake. "Glad to see you finally made it."

Judge Wagner smiled. "You do know Mrs. Palmer, don't you?"

The other judge turned to her. "I haven't had the pleasure, but I've heard great things about you from my colleagues. It's a pleasure to meet you, Mrs. Palmer."

Freddie managed to work up enough composure to thank him for his compliment and to excuse herself from the judge's chambers. She walked back toward her office feeling as if she were caught up in a vortex, hearing nothing but the sounds of her own shoes tapping against the marble floors. *This isn't happening*, she tried convincing herself. *This is absolutely not happening.*

Freddie sat at the kitchen table next to Don, with too much on her mind and not enough appetite.

"What's wrong with you?" he asked with a mouth full of food.

Freddie barely heard him. "What?"

Don stared at her. "You been quiet all evening. Too quiet."

The thought crossed her mind to tell her husband every-thing: from the baby they'd left in that hospital, to the man she'd had following her around in a secret club hidden downtown, who, as it turned out, happened to be a judge and was now her boss. But then it occurred to her that Don was fifty, and even if his heart could survive hearing all of that at once, he'd surely want a divorce right then and there at the dinner table.

She really had no idea where or how to even begin to tell him everything.

"Long day," she sighed.

The thought had never occurred to her until now that she'd been cheating on her husband. Freddie had been as unfaithful to Don as she would've been if she'd actually had sex with the judge. That's how he'd see it, and he'd be right.

"A long day and what else?" Don finally asked.

Freddie just stared at him.

"Something's on your mind, Freddie," he said. "If you don't want to talk about it, just say you don't want to talk about it."

"There's nothing to talk about, Don," she said, softly. She'd done it again. Freddie had lost her nerve.

Don nodded and took another bite of his meatloaf. "Well"—he leaned back and rubbed his round belly—"when you do want to talk about something." He winked. "Let me know."

She loved him. Anything she'd have told him would only end up hurting him, and that was the last thing she'd ever wanted to do. Don went back to eating without missing a beat, and all Freddie wanted was to have the same peace of mind he did, that allowed him to keep his appetite so that he could eat his meatloaf without feeling guilty. It was all she could do not to run away from that table and into the bathroom to throw up.

42

It was late, and as usual Phyllis was still at the office. She hadn't seen or spoken to Marcus in nearly a week, and it was driving her crazy. Phyllis had dialed his number a dozen times, only to stop short at the last digit and hang up before she finished. Even if she had called, what would she have said? "I'm sorry for slipping and falling on your dick, Marcus?" There seemed to have been a lot of accidental slip-ups on her part lately, first with Jeff and then with her ex. No matter how hard she tried, though, there was just no getting over Marcus. With Jeff, it had been weird but eventually back to business as usual. At best she may have had a momentary crush on the man, but she was over it. But with Marcus, her heart was invested. There was no way around it. Phyllis loved him and that was all there was to it.

She sat there thinking that maybe she needed to be as fearless with Marcus as she was with her career moves. Yeah, he was married now and telling him how she felt was a risk. Marcus could very well laugh in her face and remind her that he was way more happily married with Sharon than he'd ever been with Phyllis. But Phyllis knew him better than she sometimes gave herself credit for. Marcus would never laugh at her. And deep down, he still felt something for her too.

"You called?" he asked anxiously.

Phyllis sighed. "You answered."

She'd dialed the last number this time. The two of them needed to talk about what happened. Period.

"I wanted to call," Marcus said.

"Why didn't you?"

"I didn't know what to say."

She laughed. "Me neither."

"I thought about it, but I'm not going to apologize."

"Good. I wouldn't want you to."

Neither of them said anything right away.

"So what did it mean, Marcus?" Phyllis felt vulnerable, and she hated feeling vulnerable, but if anyone could bring up that emotion in her, it was him.

"I have no idea."

She swallowed hard before asking a question that she wasn't sure she wanted the answer to. "Do you love her?"

He hesitated before responding. "I do."

"Do you love me?"

"I miss you."

Not quite what she was hoping for, but better than she expected. "But you don't love me?"

"I don't know, Phyllis. I honestly don't know."

"Well, either you do or you don't."

"There you go. Everything's not black-and-white, Phyllis. It's not that easy. You know that."

"Yeah, but maybe it could be easy if you just said you loved me," she said softly.

"Say it and mean it. Right? Do you love me?"

She held her breath, and then let it go. "Yes."

Marcus sat silently on the other end of the phone, and his silence deflated any hope she'd had that he felt anything for her besides missing her.

"I shouldn't have called," she finally said.

"Maybe I shouldn't have answered."

"I'd have just called again until you did and ended up asking the same dumb question and getting my feelings hurt."

He sighed. "I'm sorry. You know that's not what I meant to do."

"No, but you did. You told me exactly what I needed to hear. And as usual, your honesty is appreciated, Marcus."

"You're welcome."

She hung up expecting to feel like a fool, but she didn't. Phyllis wasn't as hurt as much as she thought she'd be, either. More than anything, she felt relieved, knowing that it really was time to let herself get over him now. She hadn't had any lasting relationship that had been worth a damn, because she hadn't fully come to terms that she needed to move on, even though he'd moved on years ago. Phyllis let her sadness wash over her, and then powered down her laptop to leave for the day.

"Hello?"

Phyllis looked up and saw a woman standing in the doorway of her office. "May I help you?" She didn't recognize this woman as being an employee of Skyland Advertising, and she had no idea how the woman had gotten past security to get up here in the first place.

The woman didn't wait to be invited in. She walked into Phyllis's office and sat down in the chair across from her desk. "You're Phyllis," the young woman said, staring at her like she was a ghost. "You don't remember me. Do you?"

"Should I?" Phyllis asked, not bothering to hide her impatience.

The woman pressed her lips together and blinked innocently. "Jeff introduced us a few weeks ago. Jeff. Your boss?" she explained nervously.

So, Jeff had introduced them. Phyllis stared back like it should matter. "I believe Jeff's gone for the day."

The woman nodded. "I know."

"Then you should be gone, too." Phyllis said harshly.

"I wanted to see you," she replied, obviously offended, staring at Phyllis.

"I don't understand. If Jeff's your friend what's that got to do with me?"

The woman started to speak, but then seemed at a loss for words.

Phyllis was beyond frustrated and ready to go home. "Okay, look . . . it's late and I was just getting ready to call it a night. If you want to see Jeff, I'd suggest you come back in the morning during normal business hours."

"My name is Tasha," she suddenly blurted out. "Tasha Darden."

"What the hell is this about?" Phyllis asked defensively. Something about her didn't sit right with Phyllis, and if Jeff had told her anything about their encounter and this heffa had come up here looking for trouble, then she'd found it in Phyllis. She'd never fought over a man, but she'd beat a bitch down to defend herself.

The woman started to visibly tremble. "I wanted to see you, Phyllis. I wanted to see you in private."

Phyllis glared impatiently at her. "You've got ten seconds to get out of my office, or I'm calling security," she threatened.

"Don't call security," the woman pleaded.

"If I were you I'd start walking now," Phyllis threatened.

"I sent the picture, Phyllis. I sent the picture from the article in the newspaper."

Phyllis froze.

"One of you gave birth to me." The woman hurried and said. Tears began to fall fast down her cheeks. "I don't know which one." Tasha couldn't miss the shock on Phyllis's face, and she almost relished it.

"Amazing," Tasha whispered, staring at Phyllis looking like a statue. "I didn't think I'd ever find the courage to actually say it to any of your faces."

The two women stared silently at each other. There was so much more that needed to be said, but this brief encounter had left them both speechless and numbed by Tasha's confession, and for now, she'd said enough.

Tasha stood up and left as quietly as she'd come in. It was a step. A big one, and one that had terrified her, but she'd finally started the process, and she was proud of herself. As for Phyllis, once the initial shock wore off, the bitch would begin to panic, and it served her ass right.

43

❧

The older he became, the harder it was for Vincent to maintain an erection.

"Shit! Come on! Alright!" he growled, gritting his teeth. Vincent lay on top of Renetta, cursing and humping, trying to force his soft, meaty lump of flesh into the space between her thighs.

Renetta lay still knowing that it was only a matter of time before he took out his frustrations on her. She was thirty-five and Vincent was fifty-three, and he wanted to still be able to fuck like he wasn't impotent.

"Maybe I should get on top?" she asked modestly.

Of course he glared at her like she was possessed by the devil, but desperation won out where pride once ruled and Vincent turned over on his back for her to mount him. Renetta did the best she could, trying to somehow resurrect his limp dick back from the dead, but Vincent didn't see it that way, and out of nowhere, his open palm landed flat against the side of her face with such force that he knocked her off the bed and onto the floor. Renetta sat up in time to see the blurred image of Vincent disappear into the bathroom. In that moment, she decided that she'd had enough.

Renetta managed to get to her feet, found the old tattered suitcase in the back of the closet, and then started to fill it with as many of her things as she could, as quietly as she could. She slipped out of her nightgown and into a pair of faded sweatpants and a dingy T-shirt. She grabbed her suitcase and sneakers and started for the door, then he came out of the bathroom.

"Where the fuck do you think you're going?"

Vincent moved across that room like a spirit.

"Vincent," she pleaded.

The first blow landed in her stomach, knocking all of the wind out of her. Renetta doubled over, fighting to stay on her feet. She could run if she could just stay on her feet.

Vincent grabbed her by the hair in the back of her head and dragged her over to the bed, then forced her down on her hands and knees on the floor in front of him. His fleshy, limp penis lay in his lap, and he pulled back her head and commanded her, "Put it in your mouth."

She tried shaking her head no. Renetta hated sucking him. Vincent wouldn't get hard, and it took him too long to cum. He'd hold her head down and make her do it until her jaws ached, and when he finally did ejaculate, he'd force her to swallow until she gagged and threw up all over the floor.

He held it next to her lips. "Suck it, Renetta! Or I swear I'll choke you with it."

She mouthed the word no.

He leaned close to her and spoke directly into her ear. "Oh, I see," he said, menacingly. "You too fuckin' good to suck cock now? You can throw a little baby away like garbage but you can't put your husband's dick in your mouth. Is that it?" He knew what buttons to push and when to push them. Telling Vincent had been the second biggest mistake Renetta ever made, and she paid clearly for it.

Tears slid down the sides of her face, and Renetta slowly opened her mouth.

. . .

Renetta used to cringe at her memories, but now they played out in her head like movies that she watched with a detached indifference. Death for a man like Vincent would've been too good for him. She believed that it would've been as much of a relief for him as it would've been for her. She believed that maybe he would've welcomed being set free from his despicable self as much as she welcomed it.

For a time, she got what she deserved from Vincent. He'd have treated her like shit whether she'd told him her secret or not, but the fact that she did tell him only fueled any excuse he already had for being abusive. Telling him the truth had been like adding gas to fire. It was a weapon, and he used it when it suited him.

She'd confessed to him not long after they'd first met, back when Vincent was charming and patient. Back when he'd actually made her believe that he was everything she'd ever needed in a man. Renetta told him because she needed to. Her relationship with her father was almost nonexistent, and her mother had cut out on them years before. Her two best friends were as confused as she was, and so Vincent seemed like someone she could trust.

She suffered abuse from him for years thinking it was what she deserved, but eventually, the shit got old. Eventually, she had had enough, and it was time to move past the vice that was Vincent Jones. Leaving him would have been the humane thing to do, but since when did she and her husband ever have anything humane between them? The years had changed her and turned her into something almost as wicked as he had been. Finding ways to make Vincent's life as miserable as he'd made hers gradually became a game to her, and it started with silly things like putting laxatives in his food, or purposefully spilling water on the bathroom floor, knowing he'd get up in the middle of the night to pee.

"Ugh! Shit! What the . . ."

Torture was fair play, and all was fair in love and marriage.

Karma never forgets. She'd seen how true that had been back then, and she was certainly living proof of it now. Renetta knew that it was only a matter of time before she came face-to-face with her destiny. Vincent was already looking his in the eyes every day that he lay in that nursing home with nurses having to come in and change his dirty diapers.

"Renetta?" a young woman knocked on the door to Renetta's home office, and smiled. "The two o'clock is here. Should we start the showing?"

Renetta smiled. "Go ahead and start, dear. I'll be right there."

44

It's amazing what you can find on the Internet:

"Yohimbine . . . used for the treatment of such afflictions as fevers, leprosy, angina, and hypertension . . . to increase sexual ability and pleasure. It has also been smoked as a mild hallucinogenic . . . widely used for more than 75 years as an accepted treatment for male erectile dysfunction."

Okay, he thought. *Not bad . . . so far.*

"Should not be taken by anyone who suffers from low blood pressure, diabetes, heart disease, liver disease, or kidney disease. Overdose can result in death. Side effects included seizures, kidney and liver damage, and heart failure."

Vincent Jones had reported that someone had been using his credit card. He'd called the police, who in turn directed him to report it to the credit card company. Apparently, he'd reported it lost. Someone had used it to order some of this shit. Why? If you find a credit card lying on the ground and you're bold enough to try to use it, why not buy a television, a stereo, shoes? Why go and buy something as obscure as yohimbine?

Avery's eyes burned from staring at that computer screen in his office for the last two hours. The more he discovered about this herb, however, the more questions he had than answers. So what was Avery thinking? That Renetta had bought this crap to try and kill her husband? The thought was vague at best, but most of Avery's success in this business was born of vague notions. Wives or husbands had the *feeling* that their significant others were being unfaithful. Bosses *suspected* that employees were stealing from them. Avery spent a lot of time playing hunches, and most of the time they played out to be true.

He leaned back and thought about this woman he'd been seeing. He thought about the things she'd confessed to him, from walking away from that child to living in an abusive marriage. Renetta was as gentle a woman as he'd ever known. He'd seen evidence of that in the faces of those young women she had working for her. She took care of them, even more than she exploited them.

"I told you, Serita," he'd overheard her telling one of the girls, "until you're back in school, you're not working for me. Your education is more important than this job, and I will not be the one to blame for you not stepping up and being the best young woman you can be."

And then he thought about good old Vincent. Any man who hit a woman was a beast no matter how you sized it up, as far as Avery was concerned. He'd tortured Renetta when they were married. He'd treated her like shit, and her guilty conscience allowed him to do it, and now the poor bastard was stuck breathing through tubes and shitting on himself for the rest of his life.

Avery was no doctor, but from everything he'd read about this yohimbine, yeah, enough of the stuff could've caused a stroke in the wrong person. Vincent could very well have been that wrong person. A man of fifty-five, which was how old he'd been at the time of the stroke, could've had high blood pressure, a bad heart, or bad kidneys. A man his age could've been impotent, could've heard about a drug like this, and might've been more than happy to put a little in his beer.

On the flip side, a desperate young woman, anxious to end the abusive treatment from her husband, who couldn't see any other way out of her situation, could've also found out about yohimbine and seen opportunity.

45

The annual Palmer Labor Day Bar-B-Que was in full effect. Children ran circles around the backyard, squealing and laughing, Felicia's boyfriend had taken it upon himself to play DJ, insisting that the only music allowed to flow through his speakers was hip-hop.

"Then take that shit back where you found it, son," Don commanded. "This is my goddamned house, and my electricity only plays soul music or jazz. That blinging, blanging rap shit got to go, and you can go with it if you want to! I don't give a damn!"

"Daddy!" Felicia intervened like she always did between those two.

"Daddy nothing! How you gonna tell me what kind of music to play in my own house?"

"Don, honey, the ribs are burning!"

Freddie hurried back into the house. Her head was pounding; all these damn people were getting on her nerves, and Freddie's life was falling apart around her. She turned off the eggs boiling on the stove for the potato salad and then hurried upstairs to her bathroom, closed and then locked the door behind her. *If she could just scream.*

She should've told him. Maybe if she had, they'd have canceled this thing. She and Don could be sitting here alone in this house hurt and angry, but they'd be alone, and she could at least hear herself think. Freddie wouldn't have had to smile when she didn't feel like smiling, or make conversation when she didn't feel like talking.

"Mom!" She cringed at the sound of Felicia's voice coming upstairs. "Mom, are you up here?"

Freddie wanted not to answer, but Felicia was her usual insistent self. She came into their bedroom and knocked on the bathroom door. "Momma?"

Freddie rolled her eyes and sighed. "What, Felicia?" she asked wearily.

"Dad wants to know if we have any more molasses?"

"Look in the pantry."

"I did. I didn't see any."

"Then there isn't any, Felicia," she said irritably.

"Okay then." Felicia tried not to say something smart; that girl knew better. "I'll send DJ to the store for some."

DJ, Felicia's brother, had taken his sweet-ass time leaving to get the molasses for Don's secret recipe sauce, so Don went himself and cursed under his breath all the way to and from the store, wondering why in the hell he insisted on doing this shit every year.

Don was just getting out of his car when he heard someone calling his name. He turned to see a woman coming toward him.

"Don?" The young woman smiled, approaching him.

It took a minute but he eventually recognized her. "Tonya?"

"Tasha," she corrected him.

He grinned. "I'm sorry. Tasha. How you doing?"

"I'm fine. I was just in the neighborhood waiting on the realtor to come show me the house, and I think I've been stood up." She smiled apprehensively.

"Aw, I'm sorry to hear that. Have you eaten?"

"No, I haven't."

"Well come on in," Don said, walking toward the front door. "We've got plenty of food."

Tasha had ended up here as if by magic. Lately, that was how most events seemed to unfold in her life. Jeff had gone to visit family for the Labor Day weekend. She and Robin weren't speaking and Tasha had too much time on her hands to think. She'd started with Phyllis and she had walked away from the introduction surprisingly unscathed and em-powered. Momentum was on her side, and momentum had led her here.

Felicia's response at seeing Tasha at her parents' house again was awkward at first, but Tasha quickly told her the same story she'd told Don about being stood up by the realtor.

"Next thing I know," Tasha smiled and shrugged, "your dad had invited me in for bar-b-que."

Felicia shook her head. "Why am I not surprised." She smiled and offered Tasha something to drink.

Felicia talked and Tasha half listened, nodding and re-sponding with an occasional "Mmmmm. Yeah, girl. I know what you mean," but Freddie was always in her line of sight. Anticipation swelled in her stomach. Tasha was still shaky from her confrontation with Phyllis, but she felt stronger too, because she'd faced her worst fear and walked away from it in better shape than she'd left the other woman.

"Granny! Granny!" A child ran up to Freddie and tugged on the hem of her tunic.

"Yes, baby. What is it?" Freddie asked, forcing the irritation from her face.

"Can we fill up the water balloons now?"

"Mom." A young man approached Freddie too. "I'm making another run to the store for Dad. You need anything?"

Freddie shook her head.

"Granny, can we?"

"You sure?" the young man asked.

"Granny, please?"

"Yeah, I'm sure, DJ, and no, Grace." Freddie's annoyance finally took over. "Not yet."

"But Granny," the little girl whined.

"I said no," Freddie said more firmly.

The child walked away pouting toward the other children. "She said not yet," the girl called out. All the children moaned their disappointment in unison.

Freddie disappeared back inside the house.

Tasha saw her opportunity. "Would it be alright if I used your bathroom?" she asked Felicia.

Felicia started to get up. "Sure. Let me show you where it is."

"No," Tasha said quickly. She smiled. "I remember where it is from the tour you and your dad gave me."

Felicia laughed. "Help yourself, girl."

The kitchen was the first room you entered right off the deck. Tasha half expected to see Freddie inside, but she didn't. Compared to the activity outside, the house was relatively quiet and empty. A couple sat in the living room, huddled together on the sofa, talking in low voices. They didn't even seem to notice Tasha. She cautiously ascended the stairs knowing that she had a good excuse for going up because that's where the guest bathroom was. Her heart was beating so fast and so loud it seemed to be the only sound echoing in her ears. Tasha made it to the top of the stairs, turned right, and bumped right into Freddie Palmer.

"I'm sorry," Tasha said anxiously. "I was . . ."

Freddie smiled and stared up at her with gentle brown eyes. "Looking for the bathroom?"

Tasha stared transfixed at the lovely brown face of this woman she'd only ever fantasized about. "Yes," she said softly. And then just as quickly, she decided not to delay the inevitable. She'd lose her nerve if she did. "No, Freddie."

Freddie looked confused. "Have we met?"

Tasha batted her eyes, unsure of how to answer that question. "Can we talk?" she asked, apprehensively. "Privately?"

This young woman's odd request made her feel uneasy, and Freddie was feeling uneasy enough as it was. "Who are you?"

The woman stared at her like she should already know. At first, she wanted to believe that she was one of her son's girlfriends who just wanted to get to know his mother better, or one of Felicia's friends hoping to get Freddie's recipe for banana pudding.

Freddie suddenly covered her mouth with her hand, stifling the gasp that rose up from the back of her throat when she realized who this woman was. Ever since that mystery woman had left that message at her job, Freddie had been looking over her shoulder, fully expecting that this moment would come.

Tasha's eyes filled with tears. "I think you know, Freddie," she whispered.

Freddie stumbled back away from this woman, fighting to catch her breath. "I'm sorry," she whispered over and over again. "I'm so . . ."

She knew this meeting would come. Deep, deep down inside, Freddie always knew that one day God would right the wrong they'd done. She'd dreamed it asleep and awake. She'd waited for it and maybe even hoped for it. But she hadn't hoped for it in years, and now, she was unprepared for it.

Freddie stared wildly at that woman, seeing glimpses of that baby's eyes in her grown face.

"Freddie?" The woman's voice shook. She stalked Freddie toward her bedroom, but in an instant, Freddie disappeared into her room and slammed the door shut behind her.

Tasha heard the unmistakable sound of it locking.

"Tasha?" She heard Felicia calling from downstairs. Felicia hurried up the stairs. "Did you find it?"

Before she turned around, Tasha dried her eyes. "Yeah. I found it."

Felicia started heading back down the stairs. "Come on. It's almost time to eat."

She followed Felicia as far as the kitchen, and then without saying good-bye, Tasha hurried toward the front door and left.

Fanning the Flames

46

❧

Renetta's father had worked nights, sometimes. He was work-ing that night and the three of them had all huddled together in that basement waiting as one of them started to give birth.

One of the girls had insisted on calling paramedics or rushing off to the hospital, but there was no time for that. Before any of them could make sense of what was happen-ing, the child had started to crown.

Phyllis remembered a conversation the three of them had had months before that night.

"How can you keep something like this a secret from everybody?"

The pregnant girl shrugged. "Stay in my room a lot. Stay out of the house. Stay late after school, or go to the library, or spend the night with my friends."

"You don't look pregnant. Not real pregnant."

"I think you should tell."

"No!"

"Then what's going to happen when it's time to have it? What are you going to do then?"

There was no proof that the woman who'd come to her of-fice had been that child, and there was no proof that she wasn't.

Phyllis had been sitting in her office all morning with instructions to her assistant not to disturb her. Thirty years was a long time, and if she had been looking for the three of them, and if she'd managed to find them, then why the hell hadn't she done it five, ten years ago. Why now?

The executive staff meeting droned on like it always did, but this time, Phyllis was without her usual contribution. Jeff gave an overview of his latest business trip, some kind of executive team-building retreat, which in corporate code translated to endless rounds of golf and late-night parties. She wondered if anyone else in the room noticed the exceptionally golden hue to his walnut-colored complexion.

Did he know? she wondered, unable to take her eyes off of him. Had that woman spoken to Jeff about any of this?

An uneasy feeling began to sweep over Phyllis. It couldn't have been a coincidence that Jeff and that woman, Tasha, were dating.

"Phyllis?" The sound of his voice broke through her concentration. "Did you want to add something?"

Had she gotten to know him just to get to Phyllis? "What?" she asked dumbfounded.

"You looked like you had something to say."

"No," she said, quickly. "Nothing."

After the meeting, Phyllis hesitantly followed him back to his office, concerned that if she spoke to him about this whole thing that she'd either reveal too much or that she'd get more than she bargained for. "Jeff?" she asked, from the doorway of his office.

"Hey, Phyllis," he said, sitting down. "You were unusually quiet this morning in staff," he teased. "You feeling alright?"

She smiled weakly at his attempt at a joke. The lie came to her quickly as she stepped into the room. "You know, I think that I might've run into your girlfriend the other day," she said, casually. "But I couldn't remember her name, which was embarrassing."

He leaned back and stared at her quizzically. "My girlfriend?" Jeff asked casually, leaning back in his chair.

Keep it together, Phyllis. "The one I saw with you at the restaurant a few weeks ago?"

There was something about the look on his face she didn't like. Jeff seemed to be searching for something in Phyllis that made her feel uneasy. "So, why are you telling me this?"

His question caught her off guard. Why was he being so defensive? And what the hell was she going to say? "What was her name again?" she tried asking, innocently. But she'd failed miserably. From the look in his eyes, she knew she'd approached this whole thing all wrong.

"Look, Phyllis," he said, leaning forward and resting his elbows on his desk. Jeff spoke in a low voice. "I thought we agreed to put our past behind us."

She looked confused. "What?"

"What happened between us happened one time," he stated emphatically. "It's over, we've agreed to let it go, so . . . let it go."

She couldn't believe what she was hearing. What was he implying? Did that egotistical bastard really believe she was standing here in his office asking him this question because she was jealous? "Jeff, I don't know what you're thinking. . . ." Yes, she did. "But I truly think we have our signals crossed."

"Really?"

"Really."

"Phyllis, I'm not blind. I saw how you looked at me that night in the restaurant when I introduced my friend to you, and I saw how you went out of your way to ignore her."

"I didn't look at you any kind of way," she said defensively. "And as for her, well—"

"You could've cut the tension with a knife," he interrupted. "Look, we're two mature adults." He stood up and walked past her to the door. "Professionals." Jeff stood next to the door with his hands in his pockets and with an expression that indicated this conversation was over. "Let's remember that. Shall we?"

The number was still in her contacts list on her phone. She'd been trying not to think about making this phone call all week. But Phyllis needed to know. Had any of the others been contacted by this woman?

"Renetta?" Phyllis had to leave a message. "Look, we need to talk. Call me when you get this message. It's important."

She turned to gaze out of her window at the view of the mountains in the distance. Fall was in the air. She couldn't actually see it yet, but she felt it, she smelled it. Dread was a horrible emotion to have, but for the last week, it was the only one she could remember feeling. If this was fate's idea of redemption, then it had taken an unmercifully long time to get here. Twenty years ago, maybe she'd have been better prepared to handle this. But too much time had passed and Phyllis had long since moved beyond taking responsibility for what happened that night. Justice this late in the game was absolutely brutal.

47

"Did she tell you her name?" Renetta asked. The three women agreed to meet at Phyllis's house in Centennial.

Freddie shook her head.

"Tasha," Phyllis said, clearing her throat. She'd thought about telling them that she'd been told her name and introduced to her at a restaurant by her boss, who happened to have been dating the woman, but then thought better of it. That conversation wouldn't do anything but open up another, totally different can of worms that she wasn't in the mood to explain.

"What did she look like?"

Freddie looked at Phyllis, who hadn't really looked at anybody since they'd all sat down.

It felt strange sitting here and talking to the two of them about this after all these years. Phyllis had gone out of her way to avoid Renetta and Freddie not long after it had happened.

Phyllis decided to respond. "Short hair. Pretty. Medium brown skin."

"She was taller than me," Freddie chimed in. "Five-five, maybe."

"Did she look like her mother?" Renetta asked, starting to choke up.

Both women glanced around the room at each other.

"To me she did. Sort of," Phyllis said sheepishly.

"I knew this would happen," Freddie muttered, miserably. "I always knew that one day we'd have to deal with this."

Phyllis rubbed the tension from her temples. "Freddie, please," she said, irritably.

Freddie glared at her. "Please what? Please don't state the obvious? This was bound to happen, Phyllis, and we've been foolish to think it never would," she said angrily.

"Freddie," Renetta said, trying to keep the peace in this room.

"Phyllis, you turned your back on all of this almost from the moment she was born," Freddie said bitterly. "Like you had no part in it!"

"Like you didn't do the same thing?" Phyllis shot back. "I might've walked away from that child that night, Freddie, but so did you! And you too, Renetta!"

"But you're the one who never even wanted to talk about it," Freddie argued. "I tried talking to you when . . ."

"We all shut down, Freddie," Renetta stepped in and said.

"I didn't!" Freddie glared at Renetta.

"Oh, right, Freddie," Phyllis said, sarcastically. "You were the righteous one. The only one among the three of us with a conscience. The prayed-up one!" Phyllis rolled her eyes. "What the fuck ever!"

"We needed to talk! I needed to talk!" Freddie argued.

"What woman in her right mind wouldn't need to talk about something like that?"

"Yeah, well, that's where you messed up," Phyllis said, angrily. "Thinking that any of us was in our right mind after the stunt we'd just pulled!"

Renetta looked heartbroken. "It wasn't a stunt, Phyllis," she admonished softly.

Phyllis sank back into the sofa. "You know what I meant," she muttered. Phyllis stared back and forth between the two women. "What we did was wrong. We all know that. But we were young and the situation was bigger than all three of us put together."

"We weren't that young," Freddie reasoned. "We were selfish, and that selfishness overrode any rational thoughts we could've had."

"I had plans for my life!" Phyllis said defensively.

"Yeah?" Freddie said, with disgust. "You made sure you got on with your precious life too, didn't you?"

"Oh, like you didn't!" Phyllis frowned. "Like you didn't go right ahead and marry Don. Like you didn't have your own babies and move on with your life? Who did you tell, Freddie?" Phyllis challenged. "Does Don know? Maybe we should call him up now and ask him if he knows about what happened that night? Huh? How surprised would he be to find out that his wife . . ."

"Stop it!" Renetta finally shouted. "Arguing isn't doing any one of us a bit of good. None of us is any more or less guilty than the other," she reasoned.

"That's not true, Renetta," Phyllis said softly. "The one who had that little girl"—she swallowed—"she's the guiltiest one of all. I think it's time we all agreed on that."

None of them said a word for several minutes.

"You've just said what we've always felt, Phyllis," Renetta responded, "but could never admit out loud."

"I agree," Freddie added, with tears in her eyes.

"All these years we've all taken responsibility for the decision made by one of us," Renetta continued. "And we've all lived with the guilt like all three of us were the mother."

"We were best friends," Freddie said, passionately. "We were closer than best friends. Back then, it was just understood that it really was all for one and one for all, no matter what."

"Yeah," Phyllis sighed. "And look at where that kind of thinking got us, Freddie. One of us should've stepped up and said something," Phyllis said earnestly. "One of us should've said no, it's not going to go down this way, I don't care how scared you are."

"Blind devotion to that friendship is what got us here," Renetta explained. "It's what got her here, too."

"If she found Phyllis and me, Renetta, she'll find you too."

Renetta nodded. "I know."

"What should we do?" Freddie asked.

Phyllis sighed. "Move to Cabo."

Renetta smiled. Freddie didn't.

"When I see her again"—Freddie's voice shook—"I'm telling her the truth."

"She deserves it," Renetta added solemnly.

Both of them looked at Phyllis. "I'm not going to lie. I don't know what I'll do if I see her again. Part of me hopes I won't have to."

"Maybe you won't have to," Renetta said. "If I'm next on her list, then maybe I can do it."

"Maybe we should all get together," Freddie said quickly. "See if she'll be willing to sit down with all of us so that we can all explain what happened."

"We're not the Three Musketeers anymore, Freddie," Phyllis told her.

"Of course we're not, but we each had a part in this. And I think that we each need to be there to explain our role."

Phyllis turned to Renetta. "When you see her, you can take the liberty of telling her my part for me."

"Phyllis!" Freddie exclaimed.

"Are you sure?" Renetta asked Phyllis.

"She scares me, Renetta," Phyllis admitted, uncharacteristically apprehensive. "What happened to that baby all those years ago and the fact that we could've sunk so low scares me." She shrugged. "I honestly don't believe I can face that woman again."

Renetta nodded. Freddie stared at Phyllis like she'd just admitted that she was a martian.

48

Phil Morrison's expression was friendly but concerned. He'd called Freddie into his office five minutes after she'd arrived at the courthouse and had her close the door behind her. A pale, balding man with a severe comb-over, Phil was a warm, cordial man who looked like he was desperately in need of a sunny beach somewhere, but duty called, and every single day for the last thirty-five years, he'd answered.

"I don't know if I've told you lately," he leaned back in his chair behind his desk, with one leg crossed over the other, his fingers laced across his dated aqua green button-down shirt, "but it is truly a pleasure having you on my team, Freddie," he said sincerely. But Freddie knew him well enough to anticipate a "but" coming on the end of that compliment. "Your dedication and professionalism have always set you apart from so many others that I've worked with, and well"—he smiled graciously—"I just wanted you to know that."

"Thank you, Phil."

"Which is why I'm so perplexed about your recent absences from Judge Wagner's court." He stared at her quizzically.

She knew it was only a matter of time before the issue made its way to Phil. "Well, I didn't leave the judge unattended," Freddie explained. "I've just been extremely busy with other things," she explained, sounding unnaturally cavalier.

"Such as?" he challenged, quickly.

Freddie was caught off guard that he'd asked for specifics. "Such as training the two new clerks that appeared out of nowhere," she smiled. "I had no idea they were coming, Phil," she said, attempting to put her heavy workload off on them.

He sat there waiting for her to continue.

"I have also been working on the reorg project you assigned to me last month." Freddie paused.

Morrison didn't say a word.

"And then there are my doctor's appointments," she lied. "My back." Freddie reached behind her for affect. "It's been giving me problems and my doctor suggested physical therapy . . . for awhile. Didn't I tell you that?" she asked, smiling.

He smiled politely. "I don't recall."

"Yeah, well it's been . . . tough. Giving me lots and lots of . . . problems."

"Under normal circumstances, Freddie all of that would be well and good," Phil said warmly. "However, Judge Wagner has indicated specifically that he would like *you* to be his clerk, and for whatever reason, he has expressed disappointment over the fact that he's not happy with the clerk you've assigned. He's asked me to relay his concerns to you and to possibly see if there's a particular reason you are avoiding his courtroom. Perhaps there are some issues you'd like to discuss with me? In the strictest confidence, of course."

"I have no problems with the judge, Phil," she explained. Freddie rubbed her palms together in her lap, noticing for the first time that she was sweating profusely. Her problems were so much larger than Judge Wagner. They were more important than her job and, in some ways, even her marriage.

"Well, going forward, I would suggest that you try to schedule your appointments around Judge Wagner's docket, and try to be a little more accommodating," Phil smiled, but it wasn't necessarily friendly. It was his I'm-the-boss-and-Judge-Wagner-is-the-boss-and-you-will-bend-over-backward-and-touch-your-goddamn-toes-if-he-asks-you-to-or-else smile.

"Sure, Phil." Freddie stood up to leave. "Of course. Is there anything else?"

The whole situation really was quite silly. For the last week she'd made it a point to avoid Judge Wagner, and having access to his court schedule had been helpful. Occasionally, she'd see him in the cafeteria or pass him in the hallways, but they hadn't exchanged more than a casual glance between each other the whole time since their first official introduction in his office.

"Mrs. Palmer."

She stopped dead in her tracks at her office door and cringed at the sight of Judge Wagner waiting for her.

"I was hoping to catch up with you before you started your day," he said, sounding nothing like the sheepish, undeserving man she'd met a month ago. "I believe that there are some things we need to clarify between us if we're going to be working together." He cleared his throat. "Perhaps I have overstepped my authority, and I'd like it if you and I could discuss the matter and clear the air so that we can both move forward in our collaboration."

Freddie remained cool and stepped inside the doorway. "Of course," she replied, knowing full well that she didn't really have much choice in the matter.

"May I see you in my chambers please, in say, half an hour?"

Freddie agreed and stepped casually aside to let him leave.

Promptly at nine-thirty, Freddie stepped inside the judge's chambers and closed the door behind her. He motioned for her to sit down, and then the judge clasped his hands together on his desk.

"Needless to say, this situation is awkward for the both of us."

"Yes, Judge Wagner. It has been," she replied weakly.

"I must admit," he continued stoically, "I let my curiosity get the best of me, Mrs. Palmer. I had heard about relationships like the one you and I—"

"I wouldn't call it a relationship, Judge," she said defensively.

"Our . . . encounter, then . . ." he explained cautiously. "Like some impulsive and irresponsible teenager, I found myself experimenting," he admitted. "A friend had taken me to . . . that place, and I found it to be amusing and strangely fascinating. I became caught up in the extremes to which people could go in their role-playing, and no one was more surprised than me by how taken I was by all of this."

She nodded, understanding exactly where this man was coming from, because she had felt the same way. "You're not the only one," she said, relieved. "I'm guilty of getting caught up in it, too. It was the fantasy and the fact that everything happening around me was so far removed from anything I'd ever experienced in my life. Walking through those doors, I suddenly had permission to be anyone I wanted to be to the tenth power, and, yes, Judge Wagner, it was very interesting, to say the least."

He surprised her and laughed. "Yes, I know what you mean." Gradually, he seemed to relax and to become more comfortable with her than he'd ever been. And all of a sudden, to Freddie's relief, they were just two people who'd shared an experience together that never really meant anything at all.

"Being a criminal-court judge, I make decisions every day that affect people's lives in dramatic ways. I hold the power in my courtroom to give a man a second chance at his life or to snatch years from him, just like that." He snapped his fingers. "Hell! I can even choose to take his life, because even that is in my power to do!"

Freddie never had a chance to get too comfortable with the ease she'd started to feel with the man. She listened as he spoke, and she watched a strange transformation come over him. There was something in his eyes that made her shift uncomfortably in her seat, something menacing, even wicked.

"I am a powerful, powerful man, Mrs. Palmer," he said again, his steely gaze unnerving and unwavering. "I know powerful people who have the same authority I have, if not more, capable of affecting change in the lives of every human being in this city on a whim."

Freddie nervously cleared her throat. "Yes, Judge Wagner. I understand," she said coolly.

"Having power like that, Mrs. Palmer, is hard work. It can be overwhelming and exhausting, and sometimes," he said, leaning forward, "I just need to let it all go. I need to throw my hands up in the air and say 'Fuck it!' "

She jumped.

"I want to turn it over to somebody else, because having this level of responsibility can be absolutely draining and even unbearable over time, and then . . . I found you."

Freddie looked shocked. "I beg your pardon?"

"The night you walked into the Reformatory, I knew the instant I laid eyes on you that you were the one." His face lit up.

"The one what?" she blurted out.

"You were—are—exactly what I need." He grinned.

Freddie bolted to her feet. "No! What the— No!"

"Yes! I threw myself at your feet hoping that you would

take it upon yourself and claim me, Mrs. Palmer—Mistress Fionna. And you did!"

"That is not what happened, and you know it!" she said, gritting her teeth. "I was just messing around, Judge Wagner! It was bullshit! It was dumb! But I never, ever meant any of it!"

He slowly got to his feet behind his desk. Judge Wagner's eyes glazed over as if he were in some kind of hypnotic trance. "You freed me, Mistress Blue. You liberated this slave from his enormous and overwhelming duty, and I am yours." The man laughed hysterically and stretched out his arms, looking like a giant letter T.

Freddie wanted to run out of that room screaming, jump into her car, speed away and never look back. "Judge Wagner," she said, struggling to remain calm. This fool had lost his mind, and if she wasn't careful, there was no telling what he might do. "Look, I know you might be surprised by this, but I am a happily married woman."

"I'm a happily married man!"

"Then why are you doing this?" she asked, panicking.

"Why are you?" he shot back.

"I told you, I wasn't serious!"

Seconds later he began unbuttoning his shirt. He flung it open and stood tall, proud, and bare-chested as Freddie let out a pitiful and painful groan.

"I've hardly taken them off since that night," he said triumphantly. "And I won't take them off for good until you tell me to."

The man's tiny brown nipples had become red and engorged with blood, tortuously pinched in the nipple clamps she'd placed on them weeks ago.

"Take them off!" she demanded. They looked infected. Goodness gracious! He was probably going to need surgery or at least antibiotics.

Obediently and immediately, he removed them, circled his massive desk, and then fell prostrate at her feet!

"Have I offended you, Mistress?" he asked, fretfully. "Then punish me, Mistress Fionna Blue. Punish me however you see fit."

Freddie was shocked and slowly backed up toward the door.

The judge happened to look up just in time. "I beg you," he said menancingly. "Don't leave me, Mistress."

"Enough!" she said in an angry hushed tone. "You have lost your damn mind, man, and I'm not having anything to do with it! Do you hear me?"

"Yes, Mistress."

"And stop calling me that!"

"Yes, Mi— ma'am."

"Are you crazy?" She begged the question desperately. "Does this really make sense to you? You have no business acting like this." Freddie found herself suddenly standing over him, admonishing him like a child. "If anybody found out about this you and I would be on the front page of the *Denver Post* and blasted all over the evening news, and I don't know about you, but I have no interest in being tabloid gossip, and I *know* for a fact that you have more to lose than I do, *Judge* Wagner!"

"Yes, ma'am. I certainly do."

Finally, she was starting to get through to this fool. Maybe now he could see reason. "Get up," she commanded.

Joseph quickly hurried to his feet, averting his eyes from hers. He stood at attention like a soldier.

"Now," she said, taking a deep breath. "I am going to assign you a new clerk. You will accept the staffing change, and you will not complain to my boss. Is that clear?"

He swallowed nervously before responding. "Yes, Mistress."

"Good."

"And no," he quickly added.

"No? What the hell do you mean 'no'?"

"I mean, I'd prefer not to have another clerk, ma'am. I prefer you."

"Oh, it's not about what you prefer." She stood close to him. "You don't have a choice, Judge Wagner. I am not going to subject myself to this kind of stress just because you *prefer* something. My job is on the line here, and I'm not going to let you or anybody else put my career in jeopardy just because you *prefer* something."

"I beg your pardon, ma'am," he said nervously, and then glanced daringly at her. "But I think your job is already on the line." And there it was: the threat, underlying and subtle but definitive.

"Excuse me?" she asked, annoyed.

"I know I've disappointed you, Mistress," he said, desperately. Joseph squeezed his eyes shut in shame. "I know you aren't happy with me, but I need you." This time he stared deeply into Freddie's eyes. "I need you more than you know, Mistress, and I will do what I have to do to keep from losing you."

She slowly started to back away again, awed and shaken

by what was unfolding here in this room today. Never in her life would she have ever suspected she'd be put in this situation. But never in her life did she ever believe she could have done anything that would have led to this.

"I love my job," she said quietly. "But not so much that I can't walk away. You don't have to threaten to get me fired." Freddie glared angrily at him. "I quit."

She turned to leave, but before she could, he came back with the ultimate betrayal. "Do you love your husband?"

Freddie froze with her hand on the doorknob. Her heart sank down into her shoes.

"Don?" The judge dared to utter her husband's name. "Do you think Don would be so understanding, Mistress, because I know for a fact that my wife wouldn't be."

She turned angrily on her heels. "We never had sex!" she said, gritting her teeth. "I have never cheated on my husband."

The judge's expression melted into something pitiful. "Of course you have," he said, his voice trembling. "We have both been unfaithful, Mistress. And I know, like you know, that they would never understand what it is we have done together. If you don't believe me, then we can call both of our spouses together and tell them about our relationship."

"We don't have a relationship," she insisted.

"That's exactly what we have," he responded softly. "And that's how your husband and my wife will see it. I promise you that."

She and Don's marriage had survived a whole lot of things in the thirty years they'd been together. Maybe it could even survive this. But as good a man as Don Palmer was, he was, after all, only human, and staring at Joe Wagner with his opened shirt and red, inflamed nipples, courtesy of Freddie "Mistress Fionna Blue" Palmer, she knew that dear, sweet Don did not deserve this kind of humiliation.

The trek back to her office was a long one. Freddie was numb. Wagner had certainly put it all in perspective. What had been harmless fun to her would equate to the ultimate betrayal to Don. It was all too much. The boring life she used to complain so much about had become a chaotic mess that threatened to upset the balance of everything she held dear.

She slumped back into her office, longing for the mundane, robotic routine that she used to have. Freddie desperately needed that life back, but the stage for disaster had been set, and Freddie felt helpless to do anything about it. She knew one thing, though. That sonofabitch Wagner wasn't going to pull her puppet strings much longer. If getting away from him meant leaving her job, then she was gone.

But before she let that sonofabitch say one word about this to her husband, Freddie would take her chances and beat him to the punch. And then, right after he recovered from that, if he recovered, she'd tell him about Tasha. Freddie sighed, feeling utterly and completely spent, and feeling like she could really use a nice, stiff shot of tequila.

49

It had been weeks since she had last spoken to Abby. Phyllis couldn't help but be worried about her, but she wasn't about to call Marcus to ask if he'd heard from her and if she was alright. Of course, he'd have called if something bad had happened. But that didn't stop her from needing to speak to her kid. Abby claimed to need Phyllis right now more than ever, but what she didn't know, and what Phyllis didn't even realize until this moment, was how much she needed Abby in *her* life now, more than ever.

"Hey, sweetheart," she said warmly over the phone. "How are you feeling?"

"Hi, Mom," Abby answered. "I'm good."

"And the baby?" Of course she wasn't the monster Abby might've thought she was. Hell, Phyllis wasn't even the monster she herself sometimes thought she was. She was just vain, that's all.

"He's fine, too."

"What are you now, about four months along?"

"Almost five."

"Oh. Good. That's good, baby. I hadn't heard from you in a while. I called a couple of times. Did you get my messages?"

"I did. I meant to call you back, but I got busy." *The little liar,* Phyllis thought affectionately.

"I just wanted to make sure you and the baby were doing okay," she said sweetly.

"Like I said, the baby and I are fine."

Suddenly, Phyllis was at a loss for words, and Abby wasn't helping the conversation any. But the last thing she wanted was for that call to end. Talking to Abby rooted her and reminded her of the best things in her life. Even when the two of them weren't seeing eye to eye, there was no breaking the bond she felt with Abby.

Say something, Phyllis, she scolded herself. *Anything. Just don't let her hang up yet.*

"How's your father—and his wife?" *Shit! Why'd she have to say that?*

"They're fine."

Were they really? Curiosity got the best of her and Phyllis had to ask: "He and Sharon getting along alright?"

Abby hesitated before finally responding. "I suppose. Why?"

"No reason, Abby," she said quickly.

"Come on, Mom," Abby chided. "This is me you're talking to, and I know you better than anybody. Of course there's a reason."

Phyllis detected a distinctive smugness in her daughter. "No reason that's any of your business, little girl. So how's that?"

"Like I don't already know that you've still got the hots for the man."

"What?" Phyllis said, caught totally off guard.

"Please," Abby laughed. "I see the way you look at him when he's around, how you get that glazed over, dreamy look in your eyes when I bring up his name in conversation."

"Abby, you're being ridiculous."

Abby laughed. "No, Mom. You're being ridiculous. Dad's

a good catch. If you'd been paying attention all those years ago you'd have realized that then, instead of now, when he's married to someone else."

"Do you enjoy hurting my feelings?"

"I'm just telling you what you already know, what I knew when I was twelve, what my friends knew, and what their moms knew."

Abby's friends all learned pretty quickly that they could count on Mr. Neville for a ride home or to practice. They knew that they were always welcome at the house, even when they weren't getting along with their own parents. Marcus was a mediator, the voice of reason, the one who encouraged, laughed at their jokes, knew all the lyrics to their rap songs, and even made up a few jokes of his own to make them laugh. But when they needed it most, Marcus was also that father figure that some of them didn't have. He had a way of disciplining children without raising his hand or his voice.

Abby was astute enough to know how lucky she was to have him, but Phyllis knew of another little girl who might not have had it so good. Phyllis had worked her whole life avoiding feeling guilty. She'd been lying to herself however, and guilt was all she did feel.

"I had an idea that I wanted to run past you, Abby."

"Really? What is it?"

"I, uh . . . well, I think that the closer you get to having the baby . . . it might be a good idea if you came up here and stayed with me. You know? So, I can keep an eye on you and . . . help with him . . . after he's born."

Abby didn't answer right away. Phyllis felt her heart start to break with her daughter's extended silence.

"Sounds like guilt talk to me, Mom," Abby said dryly.

"I'm trying, Abby. Why can't you give me credit for trying?"

"Because you're my mother," Abby cried out. "The bar is raised for you by virtue of that fact alone, Phyllis. I'm almost a mother too, but I'm already learning that it's not all about me."

Abby sighed, exasperated and irritable. "Seems like lately that's all it's about Abby."

Oh Lord! She didn't mean to say that, at least not out loud. Phyllis wanted to reach through the phone and snatch those words back before they ever reached Colorado Springs, but it was too late.

"Well, I am your daughter."

"I didn't mean that," Phyllis retorted quickly.

"Of course you did. And believe it or not, I understand it."

"I really didn't mean it, Abby."

"I've spent my whole life studying you, Phyllis," Abby explained calmly. "I learned at an early age what I needed to do to get you to pay attention to me."

"You act as if I was the worst mother in the world," Phyllis blurted out.

"Not the worst, Mom. Just the most preoccupied."

"What about the time we did spend together?" Phyllis argued. "Why can't you focus on that as much as you harp on the times I wasn't there?"

"The time we spent together was interrupted by phone calls, or they were cut short because you had to go out of town unexpectedly. Or what about all those times you dragged me into the office and sat me down at your desk to color or draw while you ran off to some meeting called at the last minute? Or when you'd forget that you promised me we'd spend the day together, only to call and cancel at the last minute because you'd forgotten that you'd had a client flying into town and you felt more obligated to entertain them than me?"

Phyllis's frustration had finally caught up with her and was about to spill out all over the phone and into Abby's ear. Her life wasn't the clean and neat little package it had once been, designed by her down to the nth degree. And Abby was sitting there on the other end of that phone, twenty-seven years old, still holding grudges? Hell! It could've just as easily have been her left in that hospital emergency room.

"Fine, Abby," she said, annoyed. "You want to blame me for all the ills in our relationship. Fine. I'm tired of arguing. I'm tired of trying to justify myself, and I'm tired of trying to fix something that you obviously don't want to see fixed, because if it was, then your spoiled little ass would have nothing else to complain about!"

"Spoiled? I'm spoiled?"

"Did it ever occur to you how good you had it growing up? Did it ever occur to you that you had two parents who loved you and who wanted nothing but the best for you, even if one of them happened to have been me, and even if I happened to have had a little thing called a life of my own going on? I have always loved you, Abby! I have always wanted you to be happy!"

"Most of the time we spent together, Mom," Abby continued, "only happened because I guilted you into it. I whined, complained, cried . . . because that's what it took for you to even remember you had a daughter. At least, that's how it felt to me."

Phyllis tried to swallow the lump swelling in her throat.

"And you're still whining and crying and playing on my guilt. You're not a child anymore, Abby. You had it damn good growing up, believe me; it could've been a whole lot worse."

"And it could've been a whole lot better," she said smartly.

"I know of children who didn't have either parent, Abby," she admitted. "I know of one child in particular who didn't have it half as good as you did." It was pure speculation, but Phyllis doubted she was far off the mark. "Even if I let you down, you still had your father!" Phyllis discovered she was suddenly crying. "Which is more than I can say for . . ."

Abby waited for her to finish, then probed further. "Than who?"

Phyllis thought about telling her. Through the years, when she was at her most vulnerable, she'd thought about telling a lot of people but could never bring herself to do it. Abby already had given her a negative rating in the caring human being department. Telling her this would only make it worse.

"Look, I know I've let you down more times than you could probably count, but, uh . . . I did my best, kiddo," she whispered. "I really did."

Abby sighed. "I know, Mom. Now that I'm about to have a child of my own, I just hope I do much, much better."

50

❦

"Hey, lady." Avery sat on the side of Renetta's bed dressed and ready to go. He leaned down and kissed the side of her face.

"Mmmmmm," she moaned, smiling. "Leaving so soon? What's the matter? I'm not treating you good enough?"

He laughed. "Oh, you're treating me damn good. I just have to start tailing this dude today to see what he's up to, and he ought to be leaving the house in about an hour."

"A detective's work is never done," she teased.

"Thank goodness." He leaned down and kissed her again. "Or I'd have to find another line of work."

"I'll call you," she promised seductively.

"I'll be waiting."

Renetta watched him leave and realized that, lately, she seemed to miss him when he wasn't around. What had started out as something casual and easy for her to dismiss was beginning to feel like something else, and she wasn't all that sure she was comfortable with it. After Vincent, Renetta had worked hard to remain aloof and detached. Over the years, she'd gotten good at it. So good, in fact, that it was now second nature, but Avery was getting to her. Renetta wasn't in love or anything like that, just like he wasn't in love with her. She just enjoyed his company. That's all. She'd even gotten to the point where she was starting to prefer it over her convenient and obedient boy-toys. She turned over and stretched, then caught a whiff of his cologne still on the pillow next to her. Relationships were bad, she'd always told herself. But maybe, just maybe, she could find a happy medium with Avery and he could be her boyfriend, but only when she was in the mood for one.

He noticed her reflection in his car window just before he was climbing inside. Avery turned in time to see Tasha stomping toward him. "Oh, shit," he muttered under his breath. It didn't take a detective to know that the woman was livid.

"What the hell are you doing, Avery?" She stopped in front of him, looking like she was ready to throw a few blows.

He needed to be cool. "Tasha." He tried smiling. "How've you been?"

"Cut the shit, man!" She was pissed. "What the fuck are you doing here?"

"Keep your voice down, Tasha," he said as reasonably as he could. "The neighbors around here are . . ."

Tasha looked like she had just crawled out of bed. She had on a long knit sweater over her pajamas and was still wearing her silk scarf tied around her head. "I don't give a damn about the goddamn neighbors!" She twisted her face in disbelief. "What? You think this shit is funny? You think this is cool?"

As cool as he knew he needed to be, Avery was a grown-ass man, and he wasn't about to let Tasha or anybody else talk to him any way they wanted. "Look, you paid me, Tasha. I provided my services to you, and what I do when our business is finished is none of *your* business," he explained calmly.

"I paid you to find the bitch!" She pointed a stiff finger hard in his chest. "Not to *do* her, Avery!"

"Please keep your hands off me," he said stiffly. Avery did not believe in hitting women, but he had nothing against picking one up off the ground and tossing her into the bushes if he had to.

Tasha was so angry she was shaking; even her breathing was strong and erratic. "I can't believe you're doing this."

"I can't believe you haven't confronted her yet," he shot back. "What the hell are you doing parked outside this woman's house this early in the morning, Tasha?"

"Don't worry about what I'm doing!"

"You stalking her? You know who this woman is. You've known for a while now, and she still doesn't know you exist?"

"You know what?" She stepped closer to him and got up in his face. "Don't you worry about what I'm doing. What you're doing is fuckin' unethical, and you know it!"

"How?" he asked, defensively. "How the fuck am I being unethical, Tasha? I don't owe you a damn thing, and you need to take your little ass home and handle your business, baby girl. This is getting ridiculous."

"Ridiculous! How can you say—"

"Avery?"

He looked over Tasha's shoulder and right into Renetta's eyes.

"You forgot your watch."

The expression on her face told him that she'd heard too much, and Avery was left speechless.

Renetta's gaze locked on the other woman's. Nobody had to tell her who the woman was. Subtle resemblances to her mother were evident. She approached her slowly, staring at her as if she were something Renetta had dreamed up. Dear God, she was beautiful.

The girl looked like a wild animal backed into a corner. With each step Renetta took toward her, she took a step backward; her eyes glazed over with tears and perhaps fear.

"Tasha? That's your name?" she asked tenderly.

Tasha backed up until Avery's car stopped her. She didn't answer Renetta. She opened her mouth to say something but couldn't.

Renetta's memory flashed back to that night in April 1979, to that small and fragile infant squirming in her hands, wrapped in a striped bath towel. "I'm Renetta," she said softly. "But then"—she glanced at Avery—"you know that already."

Renetta wanted so badly to reach out to her and to pull this confused young woman into her arms and hold her tight, to tell her how sorry she was until her throat ached from saying it.

"We have a lot to talk about, Tasha." She swallowed. "There's so much that I need to tell you. So much that I owe you."

She was close enough now to see the depths of the pain in the woman's eyes, and it broke her heart so much more than she'd ever believed it could. Tears formed in Renetta's own eyes, and she made the mistake of reaching out to Tasha.

"I'm so sorry, baby," she whispered.

Tasha's hand seemed to come from nowhere and landed burning against the side of Renetta's face.

"Tasha!" Avery protested, and started to grab her.

Renetta raised her hand to stop him. She looked at Tasha, who stood there glaring at her.

Tasha's lips quivered. "I am *so* not your fuckin' baby," she said through clenched teeth.

With that, she turned quickly, ran back to her car, and drove away.

Renetta watched her leave and then walked slowly back to her house without saying a word to Avery.

51

Tasha was losing her mind. She hurried inside her apartment and slammed the door shut behind her, then collapsed crying on the living room floor. She had no idea what she was doing anymore. A curiosity had turned into an obsession. She'd become so consumed with who these women were and the lives they led now, that she'd lost focus of what all of this had been about in the beginning.

"I just want to find my mother, Mr. Stallings. I just want to know why she left me."

Tasha hadn't been trying to get to the bottom of who her mother was. She had been looking for ways to torture them, to make each of them pay for what they'd done to her, and, in the process, she was torturing herself too, making a bigger mess of things than they already were.

She spent the whole day inside her apartment curled up in bed, drifting in and out of restless sleep. Miss Lucy's sweet face appeared in most of them, smiling, warm, reassuring.

"You are my good girl, Tasha," she would say in her thick accent. "My good and sweet girl."

"Don't send me away, Miss Lucy. I'll be good. I promise."

A crashing sound, twenty years old, shattered her thoughts, and made her jump.

"You broke it!" The shrill sound of her voice still pierced Tasha down to the core. "My grandmother gave this to my mother." Miss Lucy's hands shook as she gathered the tiny porcelain fragments from the carpet. "My mother gave it to me."

Tasha was ten, and she'd broken Miss Lucy's porcelain figurine of English roses in a tiny basket. Michael, another boy in the house, had run passed her and pushed her into the table that it was sitting on, but Miss Lucy didn't care about that. All she saw was Tasha, her good girl, standing next to that end table, with the shattered glass at her feet, looking guilty as sin itself.

"I'm sorry, Miss Lucy," she wanted to say. But the words never came.

"Go into your space, Tasha," the old woman said, her voice shaking as much as her hands. "Go into your space and wait for me. Don't come out until I say so."

Tasha's space was a small room at the back of the house. There was one small window in that room, an old mattress on the floor, and a small crib in one corner of the room. She sat on that dirty mattress, waiting with dread for Miss Lucy to come into that room. Tasha hardly moved, except to lie down to sleep. She even wet her pants waiting on Miss Lucy to arrive. Two and a half days later, the door to that room finally opened and Miss Lucy came in and stood over Tasha.

"I am not mad anymore, Tasha," she said warmly. "But

I am disappointed, and I have called social services and told them how disappointed in you I am."

Her worst fear was of being sent away. Miss Lucy had told her so many horrible things about what happened to other children who didn't have as nice a place to stay as Tasha did.

"Some of the children are beaten terribly, beaten so badly that they are maimed for life. Some are left out in the streets with no food or warm beds to sleep in. They have no coats or shoes, and bad men take them and do terrible things.

"They asked me if I wanted them to come and pick you up to take you away," she continued solemnly.

Tasha felt sick to her stomach as she waited to hear what the woman's answer had been to social services.

"I told them that I would forgive you and let you stay. But this is the last time I will forgive you, Tasha. The next time, I won't be so kind, and I will send you away. Is that understood?"

Tasha nodded quickly and in appreciation.

Miss Lucy turned to leave and stopped in the doorway. "Go upstairs and take a bath. Put on clean clothes. Dinner will be ready soon."

Tasha wanted to be the one to tell Jeff, and she wanted to make sure she told him before Phyllis did, *if* Phyllis did. Jeff hadn't offered any insight into Phyllis the way Tasha had hoped. She'd tried to get him to open up about the woman, but all he'd wanted to do was to get Tasha to open up about herself. It was time to end this.

"Jeff? Hi, it's Tasha."

"Hey. How you doing?"

"Not so good. Listen. Do you think you could stop by after work?"

"Sure," he said, concerned. "Do you need me to bring you anything?"

"No. We just need to talk."

Tasha came dangerously close to feeling sorry for him. But the damage was done, and eventually, he'd get over his hurt feelings and move on.

He looked as sick to his stomach as she thought he would, especially when she told him the part about Phyllis Neville.

"So . . . you planned . . . this between you and me?"

"Yeah, I planned it," she said coolly.

He tried not to look hurt, but she knew that he was, and if he expected her to care he'd only end up disappointed. "Damn, Tasha. So, you used me to get closer to Phyllis?"

"I did what I had to do," she responded indifferently.

"No," Jeff said, shaking his head. "You didn't have to do this."

Some things were second nature to Tasha, like dismissing people and cutting her ties. Even if she'd wanted to care for Jeff, or anybody for that matter, she could never bring herself to do it.

"I wanted to get to Phyllis," she explained.

He looked at her. "You could've gotten to her without using me."

She stared at him. "You fucked her, didn't you?"

Jeff didn't bother answering.

"Imagine how she'll feel, especially if it turns out that she is my mother, when she finds out that you fucked me too."

52

⚛️

Freddie sat huddled over her desk in her office, her hand cupped over the mouthpiece of her phone, trying desperately to get Bianca to understand the severity of what was going on at her job.

"He's a fuckin' lunatic!" she said, clenching her jaws. "I have told him time and time again to leave me alone. I've warned him that he's on the verge of a sexual harassment lawsuit, and that if the media were to find out what a federal court judge was forcing me to do in his chambers in the middle of the day at the expense of our tax dollars, they'd have a field day with him and his career would be over in the blink of an eye."

"And?" Bianca asked.

Freddie was ready to pull out her hair. "And he's not listening! He calls me into his chambers almost every day, Bianca, crawling around on all fours, following me around his desk, begging me to do things to him."

"Like what?"

Freddie rolled her eyes. "Like what do you think?"

"Spanking?"

"Yes."

"Humiliation?"

"Tons."

"Sex?"

"No," she said quickly. "That's where I draw the line."

"It might come to that, Freddie," she explained.

"I will walk right out of that door if he even suggests it, and I'll tell these people they can take this damn job and shove it before it comes to that, Bianca!"

"I had a bad feeling about him the first time we saw him," she admitted.

Freddie was shocked. "Well, if you had a bad feeling about him, why didn't you say something?"

"You seemed like you were having a good time," she said matter-of-factly. "And besides, how was I to know you were going to end up working with the man?"

"Well, what kind of bad feeling did you have?"

"He just seemed a little pushy for a submissive, that's all. It was almost as if he were the dominant one manipulating you, instead of it being the other way around."

"You should've warned me!" Freddie was livid. "You knew I was clueless."

"Look, Freddie, I'm sorry you're in this mess, but maybe you should follow through with your threat and bring him up on sexual harassment charges. Call your own bluff."

"I can't!"

"Why not? He is harassing you, and that is illegal."

"Because . . ."

"Because what?"

"Don doesn't know."

"Well, tell him."

"I tried."

"Freddie, come on. He's your husband, I mean, what's the worst that can happen?"

By this time, Freddie's imagination had carried her through all sorts of scenarios of what could happen. Don could go ballistic, jump in his car, rush into the courthouse, find Judge Wagner's chambers, beat the shit out of him, and then end up in prison. Don could rant, rave, and yell at her, pack all of his things, move out of the house, and file for divorce. Don could look at her as if she were crazy, call her crazy, treat her as if she were crazy, tell his whole family she was crazy, and file for divorce.

"I should've told him a long time ago," she finally admitted.

"It's not too late, sweetie. He loves you, and I don't think you've done anything that was all that wrong."

Freddie pursed her lips together and tried not to cry. "I practically cheated on him, Bianca."

Bianca laughed. "What? Please. You did no such thing. You played dress up and pretend with some guy you hardly knew, but I wouldn't call that cheating."

"That's because you're way more liberal and open-minded than Don and I are."

"So what are you going to do, then? Continue to be a pawn in this man's game? Quit your job? He's going to continue manipulating you as long as you let him, Freddie, and right now he's using Don as leverage. Take away his leverage, and he's got nothing left. It really is that simple."

He saw her before she saw him. "Mrs. Palmer," Judge Wagner called out to her as he made his way toward his chambers. "My chambers, please," he said. "Fifteen minutes?"

"I'm on my way to a meeting, Judge." She said it hoping it would be enough, knowing that it wouldn't be.

"Fifteen minutes," he reiterated, and then followed it quickly and submissively. "Please?"

Freddie shuffled back to her small office and collapsed exhausted into her chair. This whole situation had gotten out of hand a long time ago, and she was just about at the end of her rope. She rubbed her temples, willing her headache away. Freddie had done some dumb things in her life, but this beat the cake by a mile.

"I don't know what's going on with you," Don had told her that morning before he left for work. "But when I get home, we need to get to the bottom of it, and I don't want to hear nothing about hormones. You hear?"

"Don, baby"—she imagined the conversation in her head—*"I'm a dominatrix."*

Of course he'd look confused. *"A what?"*

"Well, I've only pretended to be a dominatrix, actually. But I really didn't mean it, I mean, I was just messing around, and, oh, by the way, how does fried chicken sound for dinner?"

Freddie slowly opened her eyes. Don was a good man, but could he possibly be that good? Good enough to forgive her for this one little transgression? All she could do was hope.

The judge sat smugly behind his desk, until he looked up and saw Freddie closing the door behind her. Then he hurried over to where she stood, ripped off his robe, and stood with his bare chest exposed in front of her, donning those ridiculous nipple clamps connected by a silver chain, hanging in a half-moon just above his diaphragm. "I beg you, Mistress Fionna Blue," he said breathlessly, closing his eyes and throwing back his head. "Make it tighter."

His dumb ass called her all in the way in here for this? All of a sudden, Freddie was furious, and she gripped that chain in her palm and pulled so hard it forced him down to his knees. He groaned low and deep and then stared up at her with an astonished and anguished look on his face.

"Is this tight enough?" she said, gritting her teeth and leaning over him.

An agonizing sound came from deep inside him. Freddie knew that some things hurt too badly to scream, and from the terrible shade of red rising in his small nipples, this had to be one of them. "I am sick and tired of playing this sick little game with you, Joe!"

His mouth was open, but no sound came out. His eyes bulged painfully, and his hands trembled uncontrollably as he held them surrendered in the air.

"I'm not going to let this continue. I'm going to tell my husband everything," she threatened. "And then I'm going to bring you up on charges. Is that understood?"

He nodded slowly.

"You're going to keep your ass out of my marriage, Joe," she said, tugging tighter. "I couldn't give a damn about this job, when it's all said and done, but you will not fuck with me and my man! Nod your head, Joe!" she commanded. "Let me know you understand what I'm talking about, or I swear, I'll pull those little berries right off your damn chest and flush them down the toilet. You'd better hurry up and nod, dammit!"

He obediently did as he was told.

Freddie finally released the chain moments before it appeared the man was about to pass out. She stepped back and glared down at him gasping for air and doubled over, rubbing his throbbing little nipples.

"You remember what I said, Judge Wagner. I'm not the

only one in this room who's got a lot to lose. And I'm not just talking about nipples, either."

Joe Wagner watched her disappear from his office and casually shut the door behind her. The agony surging through his chest throbbed so deliciously that his erection nearly burst through his trousers. He smiled.

53

"Phyllis." She recognized his voice immediately. Phyllis turned over and looked at the clock on the nightstand next to her bed. It was after eleven and she'd been sound asleep. "Abby's been in a car accident," Marcus explained.

"Is . . . is she alright?" She sat up. Her heart immediately began to race.

"She's unconscious. We're at Memorial. Get here as quickly as you can."

The hour drive to Colorado Springs was the longest hour of her life. Phyllis had hurried and managed to pack a few things so that she wouldn't have to worry about having what she needed after she got there.

She'd called Marcus again when she passed through Castle Rock on I-25. "Marcus," she asked, frantically. "How is she? Has she regained consciousness?"

He sighed wearily. "Not yet. They haven't told me much of anything since they took her into the emergency room."

"Do you even know what happened?"

"No. Just that she was rear-ended. They think . . . they think she might lose the baby, Phyllis."

Dread washed over her. Phyllis hung up praying that Abby would be alright and praying that she didn't lose this baby. It would destroy her if she she did. Her thoughts immediately drifted back to the last conversation she'd had with her daughter and to the awful things she'd said to her. Phyllis hated herself more than Abby ever could.

A little more than an hour after getting the phone call, Phyllis found Marcus and his wife, Sharon, in the emergency room of Memorial Hospital. "How is she?" she asked, panicked.

Both Marcus and Sharon stood up when they saw her. "I don't know," he said, trying to remain calm.

"What do you mean you don't know, Marcus?" *How could he not know? He'd been here an hour.* "Marcus," she said desperately. "We need to find out something. Somebody's got to tell us what's going on."

"I'm sure they're doing the best they can, Phyllis," Sharon added, but Phyllis ignored her.

"I'm going to go ask a nurse. Somebody's got to tell me how my baby is—"

"Stay here," he told her. "You stay here and I'll find someone who can give us an update."

She sat down next to Sharon. The two of them couldn't have been waiting more than a few minutes before Marcus came back, but it felt like they'd been waiting an eternity.

The nurse he'd brought back with him sat down between Phyllis and Sharon. "Are you her mother?" she asked Sharon.

"*I* am!" Phyllis blurted out.

The woman turned to her. "I'm sorry. We've got Abby stabilized."

"Is she conscious?" Marcus hurried and asked.

"She's been in and out of consciousness, but other than a concussion there is no sign of any serious head injury and the doctor believes that she should regain consciousness soon."

"The baby?" Phyllis muttered, low, surprised at herself that she'd even thought enough about it to ask. "Is the baby alright?"

The woman's expression turned grim. "I'm afraid she lost the baby."

A little while later, Abby was resting comfortably in recovery. Sharon had gone home to get some rest, but Marcus and Phyllis decided to stay. From the window behind the nurses station, she could see the sun starting to rise.

"Where you staying?" he finally asked.

Phyllis shrugged. "I hadn't thought about it. I don't know."

He sighed. The two of them were exhausted, but neither of them wanted to leave. "We're not going to be any good for her when she wakes up, and we're beat," he said wearily. "Maybe we should both go and try to get some sleep."

Phyllis rubbed the tired from her eyes. "You go ahead. One of us needs to be here in case she wakes up." She turned to him and smiled. "I'll call you when she does."

"There's a hotel a few blocks from here. As gorgeous as I normally think you are, right now you look like hell."

Despite her worries, Phyllis managed to laugh. "Thanks, Marcus. I think."

He reached over and took her hand in his and then

surprised her and raised it to his lips and kissed it. "She's going to be fine, momma," he said, lovingly.

She returned the favor, and kissed his hand. "I believe you, daddy."

He stood up to go and so did Phyllis. Marcus pulled her into his arms and squeezed her tight. Phyllis wished he'd never let go. She tilted back her head, closed her eyes, and believed with all of her heart that he would kiss her. Marcus didn't let her down.

"I still love you," she whispered, opening her eyes. "I never stopped."

He smiled. "I know, sugah. I always kind of hoped you wouldn't." He let her go. "Call me as soon as she opens her eyes."

She nodded.

Marcus turned to leave—and stopped dead in his tracks.

"I decided that I needed to be here with you," Sharon said with tears glistening in her eyes. She looked past him and glared at Phyllis.

He dropped his head and walked over to Sharon and took hold of her hand. Without looking back, the two of them left without saying a word.

"Mom?" Abby was heavily sedated but finally conscious.

Phyllis had called Marcus as soon as the doctor told her that Abby was awake. Abby's face was bruised and swollen almost beyond recognition. But for Abby's sake, Phyllis was careful not to overreact.

"Hey, baby," she said, moving to her bedside. Phyllis tried not to cry, but the tears came anyway—tears of joy that her daughter was okay, and tears of sadness because she knew how hard losing this baby would be for Abby. "You're okay, Abby." She smoothed Abby's hair away from her face. "Your father and I are so happy you're okay, sweetie."

Tears streamed down the sides of Abby's face. "I lost the baby," she said softly.

Phyllis nodded and kissed Abby's cheek. "I know, Abby. I'm so sorry. I am so, so sorry," she sobbed. "You go ahead and cry, Abby. It's okay to cry."

Abby needed her mother, and Phyllis would be there for her.

54

"Nice office."

Avery looked up from his desk and saw Renetta standing in the doorway. He stood up, at a loss for words, but dammit if he didn't need to say something.

"Hello, Renetta," she said mockingly in a deep voice.

Her sarcasm caught him off guard. "Hey, Renetta." He hadn't seen her in almost a week. Avery had called, but of course, she hadn't returned any of his calls. "Sit down."

Renetta had closed the door on any opportunity he'd had with her. He could see it in her eyes, and he couldn't blame her.

"When were you going to tell me, Avery?"

Avery was amazed at how cool this lady was, even in the midst of turmoil. She sat across from him, legs crossed, every hair in place, makeup flawless, looking good in those jeans and teasing the mess out of him in that tight white T-shirt, hugging breasts the envy of any woman twenty years younger than she was.

"Probably never," he admitted, smiling.

Renetta wasn't amused. "So how did it go down? She came in and asked you to find her mother, and then you decided to get your rocks off with me just for kicks?"

"No. She asked me to find three girls." Avery got up, went over to his file cabinet, and then came back and placed a file down on his desk in front of Renetta.

She flipped through it, stopping at a copy of the old newspaper clipping.

"That was the starting point."

She looked at him. "You got this from Tasha?"

He nodded. "Yep. She got it from her foster mother."

She leaned back and studied him. "How'd you find us, Avery? No one else could identify those girls. How'd you do it?"

Her question gave him cause for hesitation, and he wondered if he should be insulted or not. Avery took his pen and pointed to the ring on one of the girl's hands. "That ring, a whole bunch of yearbooks, and three girls who had to have been absolutely inseparable."

"It was that easy?"

"It wasn't *that* easy, Renetta. But with a little patience, it wasn't impossible."

"No," she said, coolly. "Doesn't sound like it."

Avery stirred nervously under the pressure of her gaze.

"Look, I apologize for putting you in this position, Renetta," he said sincerely. "It wasn't supposed to turn out like this."

She stared surprised at him. "So, how was it supposed to turn out?"

He didn't know what to say.

"That girl is going to get the answers she's looking for, Avery. How did you expect to explain your role in this to me when she did? To her? Or didn't you think you had done anything that needed to be explained?"

He shrugged. "I did my job, Renetta. She asked me to find you and I did. I can't help that I liked what I found."

"I really was just starting to like you," she said coolly.

"Yeah," he responded regrettably.

"I came here today to tell you two things. One, I don't ever want to see or hear from you again."

Avery fought tooth and nail to maintain what was left of his dignity. "And two?"

"Where do I find Tasha?"

Avery wrote down the information and handed it to her.

"Her name is Tasha Darden," Renetta told Freddie over the phone on her drive home. "I have her address and phone number."

"How'd you manage to find out all of that?"

"A friend," was all Renetta would say. "We need to go ahead and confront this, Freddie. We need to find her and talk to her and tell her the truth, once and for all."

Freddie was quiet at first, but then responded. "I agree. Are you going to call her first?"

"I don't think so. When I saw her, she looked pretty shaken up. Besides, she'd probably hang up on me."

"What about Phyllis?" Freddie asked. "Is she coming?"

"I left her a message. I don't know if she'll come or not, Freddie, but it doesn't matter. Someone has to tell this girl what happened. Someone's got to tell her the truth, and it's going to have to be us."

Freddie sighed. "I need to tell my husband."

"Yeah, you do."

Renetta felt sorry for Freddie. Of course Don wouldn't take it well, and that could mean a whole lot of things for her marriage, for her entire family, for that matter. Fortunately for Renetta the only person she ever told was lying mute in a nursing home a hundred miles away. And whatever damage telling him could do had been done to her a thousand times over.

55

It was late, but Freddie was still at the courthouse, sitting in her office, dreading the conversation she planned to have with her husband that night.

Freddie's phone on her desk rang, and the caller ID displayed Don's name and cell phone number. "Hello?" she answered hesitantly.

"Hey, baby." He was in his car. "What time are you leaving?"

Freddie rubbed the stress from her eyes. "Soon. I'm on my way out. Are you heading home?"

"I was, but I kinda had me a taste for some jerk chicken. What about you? You want to meet me at Welton Street Café? I'll buy you ice cream afterward?"

Freddie didn't have an appetite, and the thought of eating just made her nauseous. "Sure," she said, apprehensively. "I can meet you there. Half an hour?"

"Sounds good." Don hung up.

It was a five-minute drive to the restaurant, so Freddie decided to kill some time and started cleaning off her desk. All kinds of shit was about to hit the proverbial fan in her world. Telling Don about Tasha was the first order of business and would undoubtedly shake the very foundation of her marriage. Don was a loving, forgiving, and tolerant man, but she doubted seriously that he could forgive her this.

The thought of seeing Tasha again was overwhelming. Leaving that child behind had been the biggest, most sorrowful regret of Freddie's whole life, but seeing her again, especially now after so many years, was more than painful. Freddie mentally retraced her steps through time, when she wished she could've turned back the clock to that moment and made a different decision. She'd actually faced her biggest fear and had raised children, good children, but knowing that only deepened the guilt she felt for Tasha Darden. Raising children was hard, especially for a young woman. It was especially difficult for a single mother with little more than a high school education, but it wouldn't have been impossible. That child had been cheated.

To top it off, Freddie was going to have to tell her husband that she'd lost her job. Telling Don the truth, that she'd actually resigned, on top of everything else, just seemed like a cruel thing to do to that man. By itself, Don's knowing about Freddie's role-playing might be forgivable, eventually, but with everything else, it would all be too much, and she just couldn't bring herself to put him through all that.

"I got fired, Don," she planned to tell him. "I've been making too many mistakes at work, and well, they all caught up with me, and my boss let me go."

A small part of her couldn't help but wonder, however, if she really should've considered leaving this place a long time ago. It seemed like Freddie had spent almost as much time in this office looking for that elusive secret to her happiness as she did working in it. For most of her life, no matter where she was at the moment, Freddie always seemed to be wishing she were someplace else. But through the years, she'd managed to slip and fall perfectly into marriage, motherhood, and a government job, all of which she loved, and at the same time, all of which left her longing for more. Leaving here was an opportunity to start over someplace new, to do something different.

"You're still here?" Judge Wagner asked, standing in the doorway of her small office, glaring at her.

She loathed him, and she looked at him as if she loathed him, too. "I was just getting ready to leave."

He stepped inside and closed the door behind him.

For a moment, she panicked: the two of them alone in her office, in a building that was empty except for the security guard in the main lobby.

He stood rigid in front of the door. "I hoped I could see you one last time before leaving for the day."

Freddie stood up and folded her arms. "Like I said," she stated sternly, "I'm on my way out."

Judge Wagner couldn't take his eyes off of Freddie. He dropped down to his knees, gazing admirably at her, caught up in the fantasy playing out in his mind. He needed her, and he needed her to take their relationship to the next level, just this once. He longed to touch her, to kiss her, to feel the sensation of her intimately. How many times had he closed his eyes and seen the images flashing behind them, of Fionna Blue straddling him, her full breasts ballooning and spilling out over the top of her corset, nipples taunting him.

"What are you doing?" she asked, shocked.

He began unbuttoning his shirt. "I'm offering myself to you," he said dreamily. It was the stuff bad movies were made of and she half expected him to burst out laughing. The look in his eyes warned her that he was actually serious.

Without thinking, Freddie picked up the stapler on the corner of her desk and gripped it in her fist. She needed to get out of there, now. This man had lost his damned mind, and Freddie was terrified of what he might be capable of.

"I want you so badly," he said, breathless, "that I ache for you, Mistress."

The judge spread open his shirt, exposing a corset bound tightly around his midsection. "Just this once," he pleaded, "and I swear I'll leave you alone. Just once. Let me touch—let me touch you, Mistress. Let me—please!"

There were two ways out of that room—over the top of her desk or through him. Freddie swung her hand, holding the stapler between them. "Stay away from me!" she yelled, missing him by inches.

He grinned. "There's the Blue I know and love. Command me again, Mistress!"

She raised her foot and kicked at him. "If you don't get away from me, I'll—"

"You'll what?" Judge Wagner quickly turned his back to her and fell down on all fours, thrusting his behind to Freddie. "You'll punish me?" he said and laughed.

Freddie was on the verge of tears. This whole scene was like something out of a bad dream. She'd fight him if she had to, and the crazier he acted, the more she concluded that it would actually come down to that.

"What the fuck is going on?" Don looked confused at that crazy man down on his hands and knees at his wife's feet, and even more confused when the judge suddenly bolted to his feet and stood gawking back at the man before he realized what he must've looked like.

Wagner closed his shirt and turned a strange purple color. "I, uh . . ." he stammered, glancing back and forth between Freddie and Don, who, once he overcame the initial shock, got angry. "What the hell you doing to my wife, man?" He rushed Wagner.

But Freddie jumped in between them. "Don! No!"

Don put his hands around her, lifted her off the ground, and sat her down out of the way. He was just about to pounce on the man again, but Freddie was too quick.

"What the fuck?" he shouted, spraying spit in the man's face.

"Don! Stop it!" Freddie shouted.

Freddie wasn't as concerned with saving Wagner from a beat down as she was about saving her husband from the ramifications of giving a federal, well-connected judge the beat-down.

He finally looked down at her. "What's going on, Freddie?"

"Calm down and I'll explain!"

"No, you explain now, and I'll think about calming down!" he argued.

"Tell him, Freddie," Wagner urged.

Don stared at him and pointed. "You shut the fuck up!"

"Don, please." Tears started to fill her eyes.

This was her moment of truth. Freddie had used every excuse in the book for not coming clean about all of this. Now she was backed into a corner and had no choice.

"Let him leave," she said, trying to calm her husband, "and we can talk."

The judge almost made it out of the door unscathed, but Don managed to sucker punch him one good time on the side of the head before he did.

"Bitch!" Don called after him.

It took several minutes for her husband to calm down enough to sit down. The whole time, Freddie half expected security to come rushing in like the guys from *Cops*, guns blazing, wrestling him to the ground and handcuffing him for hitting a government official. But they never came. He listened intently as she told him the story of her and Wagner, going all the way back to the beginning when they met at the Reformatory. Listening to herself talk, Freddie could hardly believe it herself. It sounded like a story someone would make up or something she'd seen on a sitcom. And the whole time she spoke, Freddie began to wonder: What in the world had happened to her good sense to make her behave that way?

After she finished, she waited for him to say something, but Don never said a word. He quietly stood up, turned, and walked out of her office, without even saying good-bye.

56

❧

"I can stay, sweetheart," Phyllis pleaded with Abby in her apartment. "I want to stay."

She'd been staying with her daughter for the last several days, since she'd been released from the hospital. The swelling in her face was starting to go down, and Abby was still stiff and sore from the impact of the crash, but thankfully, other than losing the baby, she had no major injuries.

Abby squeezed her mother's hand. "I know, Mom. And I'm glad you've been here, but I really need some time to myself," she said solemnly. "Dad and Sharon are a phone call away if I need anything," she tried reassuring Phyllis.

"I don't care. You haven't been out of the hospital that long, and . . ."

"Mom. I need to process what's happened," she said tearfully. "I mean, I really need to process it on my own and alone, and I need you to understand that."

Phyllis looked away, dejected.

Abby slid closer to her mother on the sofa and kissed her cheek. "I love you. And I'm sorry for all the terrible things that I ever said to you."

Phyllis waved her hand dismissively in the air. "None of it matters, and besides, I probably deserved it."

"Not all of it," Abby confessed.

Phyllis shrugged. "Okay. You're right," she said, smirking.

"I really wanted this baby, Mom. I wanted him more than anything."

"I know, Abby. Believe me, even though I didn't always come across as the most supportive mother in the world, I know what having this baby meant to you."

"Then you should also know that I need to find peace about losing him, and I can't do that with you buzzing around like a bumblebee in my apartment." She tried to smile. "I need time alone."

"But I want you to be alright, baby."

"Eventually." She swallowed. "I think I will be. It won't happen overnight, though. I have to get there, Mom. Right now, I need to kind of mourn him. You know what I mean?"

Phyllis's eyes watered, and she nodded. "I know exactly what you mean."

Phyllis's house seemed bigger and felt lonelier than it had before she'd left. She ran a hot bath as soon as she arrived, poured herself a glass of wine, and soaked in the tub for what seemed like hours. She'd left Abby a message as soon as she'd gotten home.

"I'm home, baby. Please, if you need anything, call me."

Until Abby had lost that child, Phyllis hadn't realized how

much she had actually been looking forward to him being here. The resentment she'd had at first for that baby had more to do with her than him. Phyllis was forty-eight, which wasn't old, but it was old enough. She'd been afraid that having a grandchild would suddenly turn her into a senior citizen. But that baby would've been more than welcome in her life, and he would've been loved, and Nana (not Grandma) would've most certainly spoiled him rotten. She sobbed quietly at *her* loss too.

After putting on her nightgown, Phyllis climbed with her exhausted body into her bed, sighed deeply, and nestled down into her Egyptian cotton sheets, satisfied as she eased into the comforts of its familiar surroundings. Sleeping on Abby's sofa bed had wreaked havoc on her spine, making her own bed feel as comfortable as sleeping on a cloud.

Phyllis picked up her cell phone on the nightstand and finally decided to check her voice mail. In the week she'd been gone, Phyllis hadn't checked e-mails or voice mails and had actually appreciated the peace and quiet of being totally detached from work and the rest of the world.

"Phyllis." She shuddered at the sound of Renetta's voice. "The woman's name is Tasha Darden. I have her address and I think we should all get together and meet with her as soon as possible. Freddie's already agreed to come. I was thinking we could meet at her place on Sunday. Three o'clock. Call me." Renetta had spouted off an address before hanging up.

Phyllis felt sadness as she recalled Tasha's face. *She had her mother's mouth. Maybe even her smile.* But Phyllis couldn't recall ever seeing her smile. For years, Phyllis had prided herself on the control she'd had over her own life. She'd never been one to waver when it came time to making a decision. She'd never been one to look back and lament over her mistakes or torture herself about things she could've done differently. You learn from your mistakes, and then you move on. You make a decision, and then you move on. Tasha Darden was the exception to Phyllis's way of thinking. Come hell or high water, that child—woman—would have her retribution, and deservedly so.

"Hello, Phyllis. Jeff Lang. I was calling to see how your daughter is doing? Did she get the flowers we sent? We're just concerned. That's all."

She dialed his office number without even thinking about it. "Jeff, it's Phyllis."

"Phyllis."

"Is this a bad time?"

"No. I'm between meetings right now. How is Abby?"

"She's . . . doing about as well as can be expected, I suppose."

"Are you still in the Springs?"

"I'm home. I should be back in the office in a few days. I just need some rest."

"No. I understand. Take all the time you need. We, uh . . . we miss you around here."

"I'll probably get online tomorrow. I know I must have a million e-mails in my in-box."

"Yeah," he replied. "Look, I think you should know that I spoke to Tasha not too long ago."

Phyllis didn't have the energy to talk to Jeff about Tasha. The last time she tried, he treated her as if she were a fool, a jealous fool whose only desire in life was him.

"She told me everything, Phyllis."

"Everything? What's everything?" Of course, she knew, but she couldn't believe that she'd tell him the truth.

"She told me that you might be her mother," he said, reluctantly. "She planned getting to know me so that she could get closer to you." Jeff sounded like his pride had been crushed, and it served him right, as far as Phyllis was concerned.

It was just another blow to the mess that had quickly become her life. Phyllis had been intimate with the man, which had been bad enough, but now he knew this too? If it was Tasha Darden's plan to get back at Phyllis, Renetta, and Freddie to ruin their lives as payback for ruining hers, then she was doing a hell of a job.

"You didn't have to tell me that," she responded dismally.

"Yes I did. And I have to apologize for how I acted when—"

"You know, Jeff," she interrupted him. "I'm really not up for talking about this right now. I'm going to go."

She hung up before he could say another word. A bold, thick knot twisted in her stomach. Phyllis pulled the covers over her head and prayed silently for God to make her disappear.

57

❧

The three women sat and stared at each other without saying a word. The longer Freddie and Renetta looked at Tasha, the more refined her features seemed to become. The longer they stared, the more they each picked her apart and discovered the resemblance to her birth mother.

She hadn't expected them to show up at her door. Tasha had almost fainted when she saw Freddie and Renetta standing there. Phyllis, of course, wasn't in the mix. For some reason, Tasha wasn't surprised by her absence.

Tasha's heart raced. This was the moment she'd been waiting for all her life, and now that it was finally here, she wasn't sure what to do with it. "So, which one of you is it?" she asked bluntly. The expression on her face was unmistakably resentful. The expression on each of theirs was a mixture of sadness and pity.

Renetta spoke first. "We'd like to tell you what happened the night you were born, Tasha."

She glared at Renetta. "I don't give a damn about the night I was born. I just want to know which one of you is the woman who had me."

"It would help," Freddie chimed in nervously, "if you'd just let us tell you everything."

"Why?" Tasha glowered. "You think telling me everything is going to make it alright? You think that by telling me everything, I'll understand what you were going through back then, and forgive you?" She shot a look at Renetta. "Or you? I don't care what happened," she said coolly. "All I want is the answer to one question: Which one of you is she?"

She looked at each of them and waited for someone to confess. Freddie was shaking in her Payless shoes, but Renetta raised her chin defiantly. "You'll get your answer, but only after you listen to what we have to say. Otherwise . . ."

Tasha raised her eyebrows. "You're threatening me, Renetta? You're giving me ultimatums?"

"Just listen, Tasha," Freddie said calmly. "Please."

Renetta started. "The three of us were best friends back then," she started slowly. "We were inseparable and loyal to a fault to each other. When one of us was in trouble, we all were. When one of us had a problem, we all shared it."

"Did you all share being pregnant too?" Tasha said sarcastically.

"Yes," Freddie said, surprising her. She looked at Renetta, who smiled. "When one of us was afraid we were all afraid. Your mother was young, Tasha, barely eighteen, and she didn't know what to do."

"She wasn't that damn young!" Tasha said, impatiently. "Why does everyone keep trying to use her age as an excuse for what she did? Legally, she was a grown woman. Plenty of women, every day, younger than eighteen have babies, and take care of them. The bitch just didn't want me. Why don't you just accept that? I have."

Tasha stared intently at Freddie, searching her eyes for the confession that she was her mother. "Why didn't she go to her parents, Freddie? A school counselor, nurse, a teacher?"

"That would've made sense," Renetta added. "She kept her pregnancy a secret from everyone except us."

"How can you keep being pregnant a secret for nine months?" she asked with disbelief.

"You do whatever it takes," Freddie explained. "Teenagers are amazing creatures, Tasha." Freddie forced a smile. "And if parents aren't paying attention, close attention, teenagers can get away with just about anything."

"I take it I wasn't born in a hospital."

"You were born in the basement of my house," Renetta told her.

Tasha stared at both of them, astonished. "And the three of you delivered me?"

They both nodded.

"Oh, come on!" she shouted. "Give me a damn break! Are you serious? How the hell did any of you know how to deliver a baby?"

"We let the baby take the lead." Renetta shrugged. "Labor started quickly. You crowned quickly, and by the time we figured out what was happening, all that was left to do was push."

"I don't believe this," Tasha said with tears in her eyes. "That's the dumbest thing I've ever heard, Renetta."

"We never claimed to have been very bright, Tasha. It was the dumbest thing any of us ever did. When we saw you it scared the hell out of us. Until that moment, I don't think it was real to any of us that there really was a baby."

"So the three of you decided to ditch me in a hospital like trash." Tasha's voice trailed off.

Freddie responded warmly. "We were wrong, Tasha. We made a terrible mistake with you, exercised awful judgment, and have all regretted it ever since."

"Really, Freddie?" she asked smugly. "Did you regret it enough to look for me?"

Neither Freddie nor Renetta responded.

"I guess not."

"I don't think any of us had the courage," Renetta admitted. "We felt guilty and ashamed."

Tasha rolled her eyes. "Like I give a damn how guilty you felt. Imagine how I felt, Renetta."

"You don't need to give a damn about anything, sweetheart," Renetta said. "You can spend the rest of your life knowing that you had a fool for a mother, and her two friends, who were just as foolish. You can hate us, if that's what you want to do, and never forgive us for what we've done. But we want you to know the truth, the whole truth, Tasha, because we owe you at least that much."

"It doesn't help me to know this, Renetta." Tasha shook her head. "It's too late."

"As long as there's breath in the body, it's never too late, Tasha," Freddie said firmly. "Hate us if that's what you need to do. But you were a blessing back then, Tasha, and you are a blessing now. We squandered that blessing before." She looked at Renetta. "We won't make the same mistake now."

"She's right," Renetta added.

"I have turned my back on you long enough." Freddie stared at her. "I won't keep doing it. I can't, baby. And I don't care what it costs me. I will be here. I will be here for you. Now, you can do what you want with that, but I'm not going anywhere," she said defiantly.

Tasha stared at her like she was crazy.

"Freddie's not your mother, Tasha," Renetta said, to everyone's surprise. Renetta's gaze rested on her friend, and Renetta felt more appreciation for that woman than she'd ever felt in her life for anyone.

Tasha looked into Renetta's eyes, but before she could ask the question, a knock on the door stopped her.

Tasha hesitated, waiting for Renetta to tell her what she'd been waiting her whole life to hear.

Renetta smiled. "That's probably Phyllis."

Tasha reluctantly got up to answer the door.

"Tasha," Phyllis said, looking into her eyes. "Can I come in?"

Freddie and Renetta stood up, walked over to Phyllis, and hugged her.

"Does she know?" Phyllis asked them.

"Not yet, sweetie," Renetta smiled.

Phyllis put down her handbag and walked over to Tasha.

Tasha fought to catch her breath. "You?"

Phyllis nodded. "I am so sorry, Tasha," she sobbed. "I am so very sorry."

58

Being at home was hard now. Freddie had quit her job at the courthouse and had started working part-time at the Tattered Cover Bookstore in lower downtown. Working part-time meant being home more. The hard part was that Don was home a whole lot less.

"I'm working late tonight, Freddie. I'll catch a bite to eat on my way home, so don't bother keeping anything warm."

She'd put a lot on him all at once, and Don's sulking was his way of trying to make sense on his own of everything she'd told him. He hadn't left her, though. She'd been the one to bring up divorce, but Don's reaction surprised her.

"Is that what you want?" he asked gruffly.

"No, Don. I don't want that. I want you to know how sorry I am, and I want us to get through this. But I don't want a divorce."

"Alright," was all he'd say on the matter. But it wasn't alright. And things between them wouldn't be alright for quite some time. Their marriage had been dealt some serious blows almost overnight, and if it could last through this tumultuous time, then it could withstand anything.

"Have you heard from Tasha?" Renetta asked one day when she called.

Freddie sighed. "No. But I don't expect that we will anytime soon, if ever. Have you spoken to Phyllis?"

"Briefly, a few days ago. She was in Colorado Springs visiting her daughter."

"How is Abby?"

"Better."

"I've been living with the guilt of all of this for so long, I don't know what to do with myself now that it's out in the open," Freddie admitted. "So, what do we do now?"

"We do what we've always done, Freddie. We go on with our lives. If she wants to have anything to do with us, she'll reach out to us, and this time we'll be there. Other than that, what else can we do?"

Renetta was right. They'd done all they could. What happened next was up to Tasha.

"You know it's rude not to return a phone call." Bianca showed up at the checkout counter smiling at Freddie, whom she hadn't seen in months.

Freddie rolled her eyes. "Hanging out with you got me into all kinds of trouble."

"Well, that's why I called. I wanted to apologize for getting you into trouble."

"Apology accepted," Freddie said dryly.

"And to see if you're still writing?" she asked, hopeful.

"I'm retired."

Bianca said, "You're too young to retire, Freddie. And besides, how are you going to retire when you were just getting started?"

"Writing is what got me into all that mess, Bianca."

"No, it wasn't writing. It was me, and S and M. Writing had nothing to do with either of those things."

"But you said . . ."

"I said whatever I had to to get you to come out with me," she pouted. "I was wrong, and I know that. So, new rule: Never ask your married friend to wear latex or don a whip, unless she brings her husband along."

"That's a very good rule."

"I don't think you should give up writing, though, Freddie," she said sincerely. "I know how much you loved doing it. And I really do think you've got potential. I wouldn't say it if I didn't mean it."

Freddie curled her lip at the corner, as if to say, *Yeah, right.*

"I mean it. In fact, I showed those first few chapters of yours to my agent, and she thought they were incredible. And, if you're interested, she'd like to see more."

Freddie stared, disbelieving. "Get outta here."

"Really. She loved it. And I think that you need to focus on finishing what you started. Let her read it. If she likes it, she'll sign you and then try and sell your book to publishers."

"And if she doesn't?"

Bianca shrugged. "Then, you finished it. And maybe another agent will like it. You're good, Freddie. Really. Please just think about it. You never know. Something seriously brilliant could happen."

Freddie hadn't stopped writing. She worked on her book from time to time, usually before going to bed. Until now, however, she hadn't given much thought to writing professionally.

She stared at Bianca. "Seriously brilliant, huh?"

Bianca nodded. "Yeah. Wouldn't that blow your mind?"

Freddie nodded too. "It would."

59

Phyllis hadn't seen or heard from Tasha since that day in her apartment a few months ago when she admitted to being her mother. She'd called her several times and left messages, but Tasha had never returned any of them. "Tasha. It's Phyllis. Call me when you're ready."

Coming to terms with what she'd done had never been easy for Phyllis. Most of the time, she'd just gone out of her way to forget it had ever happened, because it seemed like the only thing she could do. Looking back now, however, it was easy to see that she'd never forgotten, and every relationship in her life from that night on had somehow been tainted by the night she'd handed that child over to Renetta and turned her back on her.

Abby had accused Phyllis of not really being there for her

when she was growing up, and she'd been right. Physically she'd been there for her, as much as her time would allow, but emotionally she'd been almost as detached from Abby as she'd been with Tasha. Because how could she bring herself to love Abby when she hadn't been there for her sister? In her mind, she'd tried, but in her soul, there had never been any peace.

"We need to talk." She'd called Marcus one morning.

"No. We need to stay away from each other," he insisted. "I've got to focus on my marriage, Phyllis. What happened between us shouldn't have happened at all."

"I'm not talking about that, Marcus."

"Then we don't need to be talking, period. Let me work through my problems on my end. You need to move forward on your end."

Phyllis didn't push the issue, more for her than for him. The truth was, she wasn't ready to tell him yet. She didn't know how. Eventually Abby would need to know too, but not before she told Marcus. Unless . . . unless Tasha disappeared and left without ever wanting to see her again. Phyllis was ashamed of herself for the thought, but at the same time, she savored it. Tasha had come into their lives wanting to know who her mother was; well, now she knew. And maybe that was enough. She'd lived thirty years without Phyllis in her life. A small part of Phyllis couldn't help but quietly hope Tasha could move on to the next thirty without her.

"Phyllis." Her assistant stood in the doorway of her office. "Carl Johnson is here for your two o'clock."

"Send him in."

Phyllis's meeting wrapped up an hour later, and she relished the fact that she'd just picked up a new client for Skyland Advertising.

Phyllis was busy jotting down notes when her phone rang. "Phyllis Neville," she answered.

"It's me. Tasha."

Phyllis put down her pen and prepared herself for the unexpected. In the back of her mind she'd braced herself for the day that Tasha did decide to call. But the two were strangers to each other and there was no way to tell where this relationship would end up. If things could be alright between them, that would be fine. If Tasha could forgive her, that would be fine. But instinct told her that there would be nothing fine about this relationship, now or ever.

"Yes, Tasha?" she responded, clearing her throat.

"Can we have lunch, sometime?" she asked apprehensively. "I have so many questions. And so many things to say."

Phyllis took a deep breath. "Yes. Of course."

"Oh, and just so you know, I'm not seeing Jeff anymore."

Phyllis felt uneasy. "It's none of my business, Tasha."

"Well, I just thought that since the two of you—"

"No." Phyllis couldn't bring herself to think about what had transpired between her and Jeff, and she was appalled by it. "Nothing is going on between us."

Tasha didn't respond right away. "But something did. Not that I care."

"When do you want to meet?" she asked. Phyllis felt so lost with this woman.

"Soon, Phyllis. We have a lot to discuss."

"Whatever you want to talk about is fine. Whatever I can

do to be . . . How about this weekend? You can come to my house and I'll make us lunch?"

"That would be fine."

"Noon?"

"Yes."

There was no easy remedy for what might lie ahead. No quick fixes or happy endings. Tasha's search for her mother didn't end with Phyllis's confession. It had just begun.

60

Renetta had driven an hour to Pueblo to see him. Vincent would be surprised to see her, because she only ever visited him on his birthday and Christmas. Renetta stood at the end of his bed, staring down at him hooked to that machine that breathed for him. Vincent's eyes locked onto hers, and if he could've plucked them out of his head and beat her upside the head with them, she knew he would've.

He looked so old and so frail. Not at all like the foaming-at-the-mouth beast he'd once been. After his stroke, Renetta shed layers of skin the way she'd shed her husband. The pounds came off, and she came out the other side looking absolutely happy and radiant, and nothing like the woman he'd married.

She'd learned about yohimbine from a Web site. And

really, Renetta's intentions back then had been to help her husband with his problem, because in helping him, she was helping herself. Impotence was a bitch for Vincent, and it was even worse for her because she bore the brunt of his frustration. Yohimbine was an aphrodisiac, used by many to enhance sexual performance, and an impotent man's dream come true. After researching it more thoroughly, she almost decided not to give it to him. Vincent had high blood pressure. Not bad enough, as far as she was concerned, but smoking and drinking the way he did only added to the problems of his piss-poor health, and yohimbine could've been lethal for a man like him. Or it could give him the hard-on of his life. She prayed for the latter—and got something else, even better.

"Your husband is alive, Mrs. Jones," the doctor had said. "But I'm afraid he isn't breathing on his own, and he's paralyzed from the neck down. He'll need around-the-clock care."

"Life without the possibility of parole," she'd whispered in his ear after the doctor left. "And I'm the fuckin' warden."

His gaze followed her as she walked over to the side of the bed. Renetta sat down and pulled her chair close to him.

"Hi, honey," she said sweetly.

Vincent batted his eyes, which she'd learned over the years pretty much equated to the words *Fuck you*.

She should've just left him. The opportunity had been there numerous times, but Renetta had stayed on and taken her punishment like a champ. Eventually, leaving Vincent wasn't an option, because she'd been too angry to leave.

"Surprise," she said, softly. "Look, I know I'm here early. Your birthday isn't for another three months, but I came because I wanted to see you one last time before I set you free, Vincent."

He blinked and desperately wanted to turn his head to face her, but he couldn't.

"I've had a revelation in recent weeks, and I realize now that we've punished each other long enough, babe. Holding on to grudges is hard work, exhausting work, and I don't know about you, but I need a break."

He couldn't hide the confusion in his eyes. Vincent was a tortured soul, and in this moment she almost felt sorry for him.

"Don't you worry, Vincent. No. No one is going to turn off that machine. That's your machine, and you need it. Don't ever think I'd do something like that to you. That would be cruel."

She pressed her hand gently against his forehead and then kissed his cheek. Vincent blinked frantically.

"I'm going away. I'm going to leave you to the peace and quiet of your life, honey, and I think it's time that I got on with mine too. I've filed for divorce, finally. But I'm still going to make sure you're taken care of, for as long as you need me to, Vincent. However, I won't be visiting like I have been. No. No. Don't thank me," she chuckled. "It's the least I can do, for all the shit you've done for me."

Renetta gathered her purse to leave. She pressed a comforting hand on his shoulder and smiled one last time. "Be good. Oh, and stay out of trouble." Tears filled her eyes. "Lord knows, we've had more than our fair share."